Kmoz

USA TODAY BESTSELLING AUTHOR

DALE MAYER

Nabbed in the Nasturtiums

Lovely Lethal Gardens 14

NABBED IN THE NASTURTIUMS: LOVELY LETHAL GARDENS, BOOK 14
Dale Mayer
Valley Publishing

ISBN-13: 978-1-773363-68-4
Print Edition

Books in This Series:

Arsenic in the Azaleas, Book 1

Bones in the Begonias, Book 2

Corpse in the Carnations, Book 3

Daggers in the Dahlias, Book 4

Evidence in the Echinacea, Book 5

Footprints in the Ferns, Book 6

Gun in the Gardenias, Book 7

Handcuffs in the Heather, Book 8

Ice Pick in the Ivy, Book 9

Jewels in the Juniper, Book 10

Killer in the Kiwis, Book 11

Lifeless in the Lilies, Book 12

Murder in the Marigolds, Book 13

Nabbed in the Nasturtiums, Book 14

Offed in the Orchids, Book 15

Lovely Lethal Gardens, Books 1–2

Lovely Lethal Gardens, Books 3–4

Lovely Lethal Gardens, Books 5–6

Lovely Lethal Gardens, Books 7–8

Lovely Lethal Gardens, Books 9–10

About This Book

A new cozy mystery series from *USA Today* best-selling author Dale Mayer. Follow gardener and amateur sleuth Doreen Montgomery—and her amusing and mostly lovable cat, dog, and parrot—as they catch murderers and solve crimes in lovely Kelowna, British Columbia.

Riches to rags … Chaos might be slowing … Only a new murder occurs … Sending her off the trail again …

It's been a tough few weeks since Robin and Mathew, Doreen's ex-lawyer and her ex-husband, slid back into her life.

Okay, so maybe Robin isn't here any longer to cause torment, but Mathew is. And he's not planning to leave Doreen alone anytime soon, although thankfully he's gone back home for a while. Trying to recuperate looks doubtful for Doreen, when a local gardener is kidnapped, while picking nasturtiums for dinner.

The case heats up when the missing man's niece appears on Doreen's doorstep, looking for help, including asking Doreen to accompany her to the police station.

Not at all sure what's going on, but willing to help someone in need—particularly after having been a suspect herself—Doreen tags along, looking to do her good deed for the day.

But no good deed goes unpunished, and, when Mathew calls, Doreen gets more than she bargained for, including all the usual suspects: love, jealousy, and … greed. It takes everything from her feathered and furred critter team to keep her safe, as she digs to the bottom of yet another crazy case …

Sign up to be notified of all Dale's releases here!

http://smarturl.it/dmnewsletter

Prologue

Several Days Later …

DOREEN WAS STILL babying herself, several days later, just sitting at home, doing a jigsaw puzzle that Richie had loaned her from the abundant supply they had at Rosemoor. Doreen had it spread out on the kitchen table, and it provided a mindless enjoyable fun that didn't require abstract thinking. She wanted to get bored for a change and just relax. She had puttered around in the garden, made a sandwich, worked on the puzzle, then puttered in the garden some more. And that was about the extent of her days.

When she heard a car door slam and footsteps, she smiled as Mugs raced to the front door, his tail wagging. When the front door opened, she peered around the corner and said, "Hey, Mack."

He walked in with groceries and said, "You up for some dinner?"

"If I don't have to do a single thing about it, absolutely."

He walked in, then frowned at her. "You're still feeling down?"

"It's not so much about feeling *down*," she said. "I'm just tired."

"Good," he said, "a few more days of relaxation will be good for you."

"If you say so," she said, with a smile. "I was thinking that it would be about time to pick up something else of interest, but so far nothing has really appealed."

"Again, good," he said. "Maybe you'll stay out of trouble for a change."

She laughed. "There isn't anything for me to get into trouble with," she said. "You've got everybody already locked up."

"Yes, that is quite true," he said.

She said, "I was thinking about looking at the Bob Small cases, but nothing jumped out at me for now. I didn't find anything that sparked my interest. I need to look into the Solomon files but not just yet."

He looked at her in surprise. "That's a pretty big serial killer case involving Bob Small," he said. "It won't be a case of a single crime."

"No, but he never was caught, was he? He was only a suspect."

"And we don't know that he is to blame for any of them."

"One of the cases was in Vernon. A young woman, a model, who was found in an orchard. It was originally thought he was to blame, but they caught the killer. So they solved that one, didn't they?"

He nodded. "Yeah, they did. So it's not a case for you."

She stretched, rolled her neck, and said, "Surely something interesting is happening around town, isn't there?"

"I thought you just said you would take a few more days off?"

"I did, and I will," she said, "but, as you know, we just

finished up with the *Murder in the Marigolds* case." He stopped, stared at her, and she chuckled and said, "Well, the name fits."

"So, what's next then?" he asked in exasperation.

"I don't know," she said. "It could be all kinds of things."

At that, Mack's phone buzzed. He looked down and frowned. "I will need a rain check on dinner."

"Why is that?"

"We have a kidnapping," he said, immediately racing to the front door.

"What? What kind of a kidnapping?"

"A gardener," he said, looking at her. "A gardener was kidnapped while working in his garden."

"Wait," she said. "Do you know what kind of flowers he had?"

He frowned, shaking his head, and said, "What difference does it make?"

She shrugged. "Maybe nothing."

He looked down at the text message on his phone. "Nasturtium. He was picking nasturtium flowers for a salad."

"Oh, one of those kinds of gardens," she said, clapping her hands in delight. "Nasturtiums are lovely to eat."

He stared at her. "I'm gone."

And, with that, she felt all her fatigue falling away. She stepped out in the front yard and said, "Call me when you know more."

"Like heck I will," he said. "Go back to your puzzle."

"Nope," she said. "I'd rather work on yours." And, with that, she gave him a huge fat grin and waved him off. She hoped the smile on her face brightened his mood, since he'd been worried about her, and clearly she was much happier now.

Turning to the animals, she said, "Look at that. We have a new case to work on. It's not a cold case, but it's a case. *Nabbed in the Nasturtiums.*"

Chapter 1

Saturday Morning …

DOREEN WORKED HARD, trying to stay on top of the news, but found no mention of the gardener nabbed in the nasturtium bed. It tickled her fancy to label it that, even though she didn't know much about the poor man or his family. Or woman?

What wasn't funny was Mack's attitude in keeping Doreen out of the loop, no matter who the victim. Mack could save her so much time researching on the internet. As an afterthought, Doreen wondered if that was not his whole intent, keeping her home, tied to her computer. No matter. After her research, she always headed outside anyway.

She stopped to think about the gender of the gardener again. Nobody ever said that the kidnap victim was a male or a female. And did *kidnapped* mean the same thing as *nabbed*? She wasn't so sure. Maybe the gardener had been stealing something, and somebody had nabbed him in the act? She didn't know what that meant either. Either way, she was looking for any kind of news coverage, but so far it was mighty slim. But it got her thinking about other cases in town that might remain unsolved.

What if somebody had been caught doing something, but, when they were taken in for questioning, maybe they disappeared? Or maybe somebody was supposed to get caught but never showed up to commit a crime that the police had a tip on? Or maybe somebody was kidnapped and was never found again? All these scenarios kept running through her head, and, of course, that just brought her back to the stack of newspaper clippings about the Bob Small case.

Finally she gave up pretending to be disinterested, rose, pulled out the basket, and sorted the articles. Nan had said her friend had collected all these clippings, and that woman had clearly had a serious passion for it. Doreen didn't know exactly what it was that had brought Nan's friend to the point of following Small so much, but a quick text to Nan would hopefully get some answers. Nan immediately called her instead. As soon as she answered, Doreen said, "It was just a question, Nan."

"Why?" she asked, sounding absolutely thrilled. "Are you on another case?"

"I'm just thinking about studying this basketful of newspaper clippings that you had here from your friend."

"Oh my," she said, "that will take you quite a while to sort out. Are you sure you're up to it?" she asked, her tone worried. "It's a lot."

"I'm fine. I'm recovering nicely."

"Maybe you are," she said, "but you've been under a lot of strain lately, and I don't want you to overdo it."

"Wow," Doreen said into her phone. "Are you sure you haven't been talking to Mack?"

"No, is he worried about you too?" Nan asked, sounding even more thrilled.

"Of course he is," she muttered. "He always worries

about me. Even when there's no need to."

"Of course he does. He cares, and anybody who cares worries," she said. "So you really should do what you can to not cause them to worry."

At that, Doreen snorted. "In that case, I might as well crawl into a glass room and stay there."

That tickled Nan, as she burst out laughing with joy. "Oh, I do like to hear your train of thought these days. You do think differently than everybody else."

Doreen stared down at the phone. "I don't think I do," she said. "It seems pretty normal to me."

"What's normal for you is not normal for everyone else."

"Are you sure?"

"How many people do you think are out there, tracking down these cold cases?"

"I'm intrigued every time I hear about these crimes, past or present. Most recently it's because of the kidnapping that happened last night. I named the case *Nabbed in the Nasturtiums*, but, if he was *kidnapped*, then he wasn't necessarily *nabbed*."

"It would be, I mean, if he was trying to evade somebody."

"*Hmm*," Doreen said, as she thought about it. "I guess that would work too."

"Regardless," Nan said, "you haven't even told me about the case."

"I've been trying to find some news coverage all morning," she said, "but it seems like Mack has managed to squeeze out the press."

"So tell me," Nan said, her voice and tone elevated. "You always have such interesting tidbits before anyone else does."

"I don't really know anything, and you know I don't like

to be kept out of the loop."

"You might not like it, but Mack sure wants to keep you out of it. He's only thinking of your safety, dear."

"That may be," Doreen said in a grumpy voice. "Doesn't mean I have to like it."

"Besides, that Bob Small stuff," Nan said, with a sad note, "it tore apart a lot of people. Especially my girlfriend."

"Mack says he was involved in a lot of investigations that may have involved Bob Small," she muttered.

"More than a lot. *A lot* is a euphemism. In this case I think we're talking like fifty or sixty cases," Nan said quietly. "That's an awful lot of families who were torn apart."

"But nobody was ever charged?" Doreen asked in horror.

"That's because the man died."

"I don't think he did," Doreen said, frowning, looking at what she had written down. "I think he went to jail for something completely unrelated."

"It would be ironic if he spent a lifetime in jail for something unrelated to all the killings he was involved in."

"Do we know for sure that he was involved in the killings?" Doreen asked.

"Oh, yes," Nan said.

"You seem awfully adamant."

"My girlfriend was very adamant and committed to making sure that this man paid for his crimes."

"But he didn't."

"No, and she has passed away now," Nan said sadly. "So no justice there."

"Oh, Nan, I'm so sorry. I thought she was living in the Lower Mainland."

"She passed away recently, but I didn't even know. I told you that I would call her a while back. Remember? I didn't get it done, and then, out of the blue one day, I called," she said. "And, when I did, I found out she'd already passed. It broke my heart. I so wish I had at least called earlier, so I could have said goodbye."

"I'm so sorry, Nan," Doreen said. "That is rough."

"It is. Life is full of regrets, and you have to minimize the ones you can."

"I gather she had a personal reason for following this Small guy?"

"Her niece," Nan said. "Her niece died many years ago. The crime was never solved, and she put it down to this Bob Small guy."

"Did she have any proof, evidence, photos, or even a time line? Anything?"

"I don't know," Nan said. "I do know that I'm getting some of her belongings though. You can take a look, when they get here."

"What do you mean?"

"When I called and learned of her death, her granddaughter asked if I wanted her books. And I said yes. She said she had also found some notebooks, some journals in there too, and I said that would be lovely too. I guess they don't quite know what to do with her personal belongings. None of us ever really do. When we die, we leave all this stuff," she said. "It's only important to us while we're alive, and, after we're dead, it's a burden for others to dispose of, as it's not important to anybody anymore."

"I don't know about that," Doreen said. "You had filled your house with antiques, specifically for me to do what I wanted with. I chose to put them up for auction, at some point getting cash instead, which you were perfectly happy with. If you had passed on at any time after that, I would still have been eternally grateful for your stuff."

Nan chuckled. "And how do you feel about the stuff I have with me here?"

"I highly doubt you have very much," Doreen said. And then she hesitated, before adding, "Or do you?"

"It doesn't seem like much, but I'm sure, when you start clearing it out, whenever the time comes," she said, "you'll think it's too much anyway."

"I want you over your things, Nan. But once … but then," she said, "I'll treasure everything you have. And please let's not talk about your demise anymore," she said. "I was having a good day, and I really don't want to start crying."

"Oh dear," she said. "If it makes you feel any better, go ahead and look into this Bob Small thing. I'll let you know when Hinja's boxes get here and if there's anything of interest."

"Okay, will do," she said. "Oh, Nan, what was her niece's name?"

"Annalise. Annalise Bergmont," she said. "A really lovely girl."

"Do you remember what happened?"

"She was coming home from ballet practice—I think it was—some sort of dance anyway. It was early evening. Her class was like at six to seven that night. And she was fifteen years old. Her mom let her go on her own all the time, and she would walk home afterward. One day she just never came home."

"Was her body ever found?"

"No, it sure wasn't. Nothing."

"Oh, gosh, those are the hardest cases," Doreen murmured. "To have no answers, no closure, that's the worst of it all."

"To not have them come home is the worst part," Nan said, "but no answers makes for a lifetime of looking over your shoulder, wondering what you could have done differently and how you could have saved her, when it's way past the time when you could have done anything."

"I think living with the regrets, living with the what-ifs, that makes it very difficult," Doreen admitted. "Maybe it's a good thing I never had any kids."

"No, and it's not too late yet," she said, "if you would give Mack a little more encouragement." And, with that, she laughed and hung up on her.

Doreen stared down at her phone, but it was hard because, all of a sudden, she was beset with ideas and images of having Mack's baby. "What a bad idea," she muttered to herself, shaking her head. "I like the man, but I'm not sure I'm ready to start a family with him." *Best to not go there.* "Besides, I've never been around a little kid in my life."

"Thaddeus is here. Thaddeus is here."

She looked to see Thaddeus strutting at her feet. "I know. I'm not my usual high-energy self, am I? And you guys are all probably wondering what's going on. But still, I might have a new case—or at least something to think about. That'll make me feel better."

She looked around for the rest of her crew of animals, smiled, and asked, "Hey, do you guys want to go for a walk?"

Immediately when Mugs heard the magical word, he jumped up and barked. That got Goliath all excited, who'd been sleeping in a tiny ball on one of the two pot chairs in the living room. If there were such a thing as *tiny*, when it came to a cat of that size. But he came over to join Doreen, hopped up onto the kitchen table, and proceeded to shoot one leg sky-high and clean his butt.

She looked at him and said, "Do you really have to do that on the kitchen table?"

He completely ignored her, but then what else was new? The animals always ignored her. At least when she was telling them off. She got up, grabbed a leash for Mugs, and put it on. She then looked at Goliath and asked, "Should we try this again?"

He gave her a scowl, and she had to laugh at such a disdainful expression. "It would be good if you would learn though," she said, coming toward him, her smile coaxing. But, as soon as he caught sight of the cat harness, he was gone, like a rocket. She groaned. "This isn't helping, Goliath," Doreen cried out. "You can't keep avoiding this forever."

A half cackle came from Thaddeus. She glared at him. "That isn't helping either."

"Maybe not," he said.

She stopped and asked, "What did you just say?"

"Maybe not, maybe not, maybe not."

"Oh, my goodness," she said. "Sometimes I wonder if you do understand what I'm saying."

"Maybe not, maybe not, maybe not."

"And then the rest of the time I know you have absolutely no clue," she said, staring at him, chuckling.

Thaddeus seemed to take offense and glared back at her. She groaned. "You guys will end up making me nuts. You all know that, right?"

He made another weird cackling sound.

She sighed. "Oh, fine, point taken. Let's go before I get any more nuts."

Of course if it would help or not was a matter of opinion. With the animals at her side she walked down to the river path. Thaddeus had taken up a perch on her shoulder and was even now peering around her head, as if trying to see everything all at once.

"It hasn't been *that* long since we've been out here," she muttered. "Stop making me feel bad."

But they weren't exactly ready to let her off the hook, and even Mugs was determined to sniff every little bush. Goliath was quite content to wander around, as long as he could keep just far enough away from her that she couldn't catch him. She'd stuffed the cat harness into her pocket anyway, thinking maybe the opportunity would present itself to try again.

She wasn't even sure when or how it had all gone so badly, but it had definitely taken a turn for the worse somewhere along the line. Most likely she just hadn't been consistent with the training. That was the thing about animals; she was supposed to be so consistent, and she was anything but. Her approach appeared to be lackadaisical when it came to a lot of things in life.

Thankfully she hadn't heard from Mathew in the last four days. She hadn't heard from Mack's brother, Nick, either, but then she knew that he was dealing with the fallout from Robin's death. That had to throw a wrench in his plans. To think that her former divorce lawyer had been murdered was already chaotic, but to think Robin had been murdered by her own ex-husband was even worse. As for Rex, Mathew's henchman and Robin's lover, Doreen wasn't sure if he was being charged with anything or not. After all, he did kidnap Doreen on Mathew's orders.

She'd walked away from that whole incident and would just let the chips fall where they may. Nobody would be too upset at the police whenever investigating the various people involved. Her neighbors were probably more concerned about the neighborhood going to pot with all these extra cases, but at least this latest kidnapping case didn't involve Doreen.

Trouble was that Robin and Mathew and Rex and then Robin's ex-husband, James, had all come here to Kelowna because of Doreen being here. And, for that, she was sorry, yet she didn't really want to think of any of this mess as her responsibility.

Mack would say she wasn't responsible at all, but he was always trying to let her off the hook because he was a nice guy. She wasn't sure anybody else was too willing to do the same, particularly her neighbors. Richard was barely civil most of the time, and now, since Robin had died shortly after being on her front porch, Doreen found a suspiciousness to Richard's sideways looks. She didn't think he really believed that Doreen had done something, but she could never really tell. He would just prefer that she would disappear and stay that way.

Not that it would happen. This was now her home, whether Richard liked it or not. With her menagerie all around her, she headed down past the back of Richard's house, then several others, until she came around the corner, and the animals automatically headed toward Nan's place. But she tugged Mugs in the opposite direction. "Nope, we'll keep going for a while."

Excited at the thought of a longer outing, they all happily headed in the new direction. Doreen smiled. "See? It's good to go someplace else sometimes."

Mugs woofed in delight and dropped his nose to the ground.

They wandered around, appreciating the afternoon sunshine and the chance to stroll around. She really enjoyed walking. A couple grocery stores were up ahead, but she'd have a hard time going in with all the animals.

"I guess we'll do without a few groceries," she muttered. Mugs woofed again, but this one was different, more urgent somehow. She looked at her dog and frowned. "We still have dog food, don't we?" He woofed again, and that made her wonder if they were a little bit on the low side, but she didn't think so. Granted it was a huge bag in the front closet and, while Doreen reached in to scoop up dog food, she didn't look inside the deep bag. However, her routine today had her fingers sweeping through more dog food in the bag to get her scoop filled, so she thought there was plenty for another week. Mugs just didn't want to run out. She looked over at Thaddeus. "We still have bird seed and cat food, so we should be doing okay with all you guys."

At least she hoped so. She needed to start a grocery list. But it was still something foreign to her. The whole process of being responsible for cooking and buying groceries and everything else that she needed for daily life was such a new responsibility. Just like cooking. Mack had shown her several dishes, but some of them she couldn't afford to buy food for, like salmon. She had been stricken with shock the first time she went to buy a piece to cook. Then again, seeing the price of many different items—ones she was accustomed to eating—she'd quietly written them off her menu permanently.

Chapter 2

JUST THINKING ABOUT the change in her circumstances brought her pending divorce from Mathew—and Robin's will—to mind. Before Robin's death and before finding out about Robin's will, Doreen had been reconciled to what the fates had handed to her and had appreciated her freedom from her controlling husband Mathew more than ever. And now, with Robin's will dangled in front of her, … Doreen had to wonder if it was even legit.

Mack wasn't saying anything. Nobody had contacted her about it. Doreen hadn't seen names as to who was the executor on Robin's will, but Doreen wasn't sure she could even trust the executor. Robin's world was full of vipers. It just amazed Doreen how people could be so bad in this world. In her cold-case reviews, she'd seen some crimes that were more accidental or more protective of somebody else they loved, but those motives were not involved when dealing with Mathew, Robin, Rex, and James. Each were all about vindictive greed.

Doreen would never understand. Mathew was the same as he always was. She was seeing that more easily now. Even when he'd come here, he'd demonstrated the same kind of attitude. She didn't understand it, didn't understand him. All she wanted was for him to stay out of her life. Having him show up on her doorstep had been unnerving.

As she walked, her phone rang. She looked at it and frowned, then clicked Talk. "Hello, Nick," she said. "I was wondering if you would even bother with my case now that Robin is gone."

"No such luck," he said, laughing. "Just because Robin is dead doesn't change the fact that she created serious damage while she was alive."

"What does that change though?" she asked, looking around to see if anyone could hear them. "It's not like she's there to punish anymore."

"Nope," he said, "although I understand there might have been some change of heart on her part."

"Supposedly. I don't even know what you've talked to Mack about," she said, "but it still won't change the facts with my ex-husband."

"That's where you're wrong," he said. "I've filed an injunction, regarding several of her cases and the criminal manner in which she acted. Several of those have been paused and put on hold, while another lawyer looks at the outcome of Robin's actions."

"Oh," Doreen said, frowning at all that lawyer stuff. "But what does that actually mean?"

"It means that your separation agreement is no longer valid."

"You said it wasn't valid anyway," she said.

"Well, it was valid in that you signed it, but you were under duress, with fraudulent information being passed on to you as the truth," he said, "but now that's not even a legal issue."

"So?" She let her word draw out, as she tried to understand exactly what Nick was trying to say.

"It means that, at the moment, with no agreement in place of any kind, you're entitled to half of everything as always, including any money he has made since."

"Since what?"

"Since you left."

"Wow. Okay, that'll really piss him off when he finds out."

"That's another reason why I'm calling … to warn you."

"Warn me? Why?" she asked, her heart sinking. *Please not more about Mathew.*

"Because a formal letter has just gone out, saying that I am representing you in your separation."

"Uh-oh," she said, with a heavy sigh. "Does that mean he is on his way back here?"

"I don't know," he said. "Would he likely come in person?"

"I don't know," she said thoughtfully, hoping not. "Maybe he'll be even angrier because Rex failed to pull off kidnapping me."

"Maybe so, but that's not your problem," he said. "If Mathew does contact you, do not respond and do not answer the door. Don't talk to him. As soon as he opens his mouth, you say that you are not allowed to speak to him without your lawyer present."

"Are you my lawyer?"

"I just said I was, didn't I?"

"I don't recall retaining you," she said doubtfully. "Don't we need some sort of agreement?"

Silence came first, and then he chuckled. "That is quite correct. Am I retained as your lawyer?"

"I'd like to say yes, but I don't have any money to pay you," she said cautiously.

"Where are you right now?" Nick asked.

"We're walking to the Eco Center to check out the park. The animals and I are just out for a nice morning walk."

"I'm at the grocery store, not too far away," he said. "I'll meet you at the eco center." And, with that, he hung up.

She frowned into the phone. "What difference does that make, for crying out loud?" she muttered, but she obediently picked up the pace and made her way toward the eco center. The center was filled with lovely parks, covered picnic tables, and barbecue areas, plus a big information center and a gorgeous log house. And all of it was beside a spawning channel. She would never get tired of coming here because she always found something to look at and to enjoy. She hadn't been here more than ten minutes when a large black Mercedes drove up and parked. She watched as Nick got out, a big smile on his face. He raised his hand in greeting.

"You don't live here in town, do you?" she asked.

"Not technically, no," he said. "I'm at the Lower Mainland. But I am looking at buying a condo up here. I'm here often enough." She looked at him in surprise, and he shrugged. "I've been thinking it might be nice to come and visit family a little more often."

"I certainly agree with that," she said, studying him. "Your mother would be overjoyed to have you here more. You all seem pretty close, and I'm surprised you've been working down in Vancouver as it is."

"Maybe," he said, "but that's where a good share of the work happens."

She laughed. "Oh, I think we have plenty to keep the lawyers here busy too."

He grinned. "Hey, you're giving me an opportunity to go up against a badass," he said. "By the way, do you happen to have any change?"

She stared, yet instinctively dug into her pockets, but they were empty. Then she pulled her purse in front of her to check. "Are there parking fees here?" she asked, looking around. She opened her purse, found a few coins, and triumphantly handed them over.

"Ah, so now," he said, gently taking the change and putting it in his pocket, "you have officially retained your lawyer."

She watched as his empty hand came out of his pocket, and asked, "Is that legal?"

"Absolutely legal," he said, "and it's now binding."

She tilted her head, studying him. "Is that why you drove here?"

"Precisely," he said, "and now you are fully covered."

"Okay, if you think that's a good idea."

"I think it's the best idea," he said cheerfully. "Now remember. No talking to him anymore."

"That might be a little hard. He'll think it's bizarre if I'm not talking to him the next time. He was just here, and I was friendly with him."

"You won't be friendly anymore," Nick said sternly.

She winced. "You don't understand," she said. "That's not really a viable option."

"Why is that?" he asked.

"Because, when I went out to dinner with him, I seemed to fall right back into this pattern of the obedient wife."

"And you were an obedient wife," he said, "which will make the difference when it comes to your settlement."

She stared around her in confusion. "Wow," she said,

"this flips things and will take a bit to get used to."

"You have a lot to adjust to," he said, "and that's okay. I know Mathew was a controlling man, who abused you physically and verbally. But you are away from him now. You have Mack and me and Nan and others in this community to help you. You can do this."

"Maybe," she said cautiously, "but what about Rex?"

"What about Rex?" Nick asked, raising his eyebrows. "Have you heard from him again?"

"No," she said. "I haven't talked to him for days, not since he crammed me in the trunk of that car."

"Good," he said. "Remember. No talking to anybody associated with your husband without your lawyer present."

"What about Mack?"

Nick rolled his eyes. "Mack knows to call me." He walked back to his Mercedes and said, "Now go enjoy the rest of your day."

She watched him get into his car and drive onto Springfield Road toward the Mission District. She looked at Mugs. "Okay, so they're very different people, Nick and Mack, but both are very caring." At least they seemed to care about her.

She still couldn't believe that Nick drove over just for a few coins. If that's all he would charge her, she should be laughing at that. She frowned. She hadn't asked about fees. She quickly texted Nick. **I forgot to ask about your fees for handling the divorce.**

His response was immediate. **You just paid it.**

She stared at her phone in delight, then sent him a thank-you note and a heart emoji. She sat down on one of the park benches and searched Google on this topic for a few minutes and soon realized that the small transaction seemed to be all that was required. Nick was now her representative, and, according to him, she didn't have to pay more. That was just amazing. She bounced to her feet, laughing, now too energized to sit still.

As she walked, several people lifted their hands, and she greeted them, sometimes not even knowing who they were. She remembered the odd friendly face, and she came to a stop, when she recognized one of the scuba divers from a couple months ago. She thought his name was Warren. Or maybe Brandon.

He lifted a hand in greeting and called out, "Do you want a hot dog?"

She stopped, stared, and said, "I'd love one."

He motioned toward some public group event happening. "You should join in the fun."

"What's going on?"

"Oh, it's just a meeting for naturalists around town," he said. "We're all water nuts, bird nuts, you know." He gave her a lopsided grin. "We're just plain nuts."

"Hey, I like nuts," she said, "and you seem a whole lot more natural to me than a lot of so-called normal folk are."

He burst out laughing at that, then pointed at the barbecue pit area, heaped high with hot dog buns and hot dogs.

"Wow," she said, "this is a great spread."

"When I saw you walking there, with all the animals earlier, I wanted to call you over. But then I saw you with someone and didn't want to interrupt."

"Yeah," she said, "that was Nick, Mack's brother."

He looked at her. "The lawyer?"

And she laughed. "I keep forgetting how small the town is. Of course you know who Nick is."

"I know of Nick anyway. I grew up with the two brothers," he said. "Don't forget that Millicent has been around this area for decades and decades."

She grinned. "I look after Millicent's garden right now too."

"Is that right? You do keep busy, don't you?"

"Hi, Brandon," called out a passerby.

He waved to them and picked up a particularly beautiful-looking hot dog, nicely golden and sizzling on all sides, put it in a bun for her, saying, "Mustard, ketchup, relish, and anything else you want is over there. When you're done with that one, come back for another."

She hesitated. "Are we supposed to pay for these?" She mentally calculated how much money she had on hand, and it wasn't much, but, if the hot dog were only a couple dollars, she would be okay.

He shook his head. "Nope, this is free for everybody today. We paid for it out of our bottle-drive fund that we keep going for get-togethers like this. It's just a social happy hour," he said, "without the booze."

"Thanks." She grinned, as she walked along to the condiment area and loaded up on mustard, ketchup, and relish. "That is really lovely. Thank you."

"It doesn't happen often," he said, "but you're welcome to join us anytime. I don't know how much luck you've had meeting people in the area. I imagine it could be hard."

She nodded. "It can be." She looked at the full condiment selection that included onions and tomatoes. "Wow," she said, "I don't think I've ever had any of these things on a hot dog before."

"Then you have to try it," he said. "Honestly you should."

"Okay." She was agreeable but a little hesitant on the onions. But she put a few on her hot dog and added tomato too. Then wrapping it up in a napkin, she said, "I'll make such a huge mess with this."

He pointed off to the side, toward a big covered area with lots of tables. "We'll all be gathering over there soon."

"What about you?" she asked. "Will you eat?"

"I will," he muttered, as he put out a fire on one of the pits. "Just not for a few minutes yet. A huge line up will happen here pretty fast. Grab a chair there, if you want to stay and visit."

She did, indeed, want to stay for a visit. Mugs was eyeing the hot dog in her hand with great interest, but, as she went to pick up the hot dog and put it closer to her mouth, Thaddeus popped out from under her hair and stole a piece of tomato.

"Thaddeus is here. Thaddeus is here," he crowed.

Brandon jumped. "Good Lord Almighty," he said. "I saw the dog, thought I saw the cat, but I completely forgot about the bird." He stared in amazement, as Thaddeus disappeared under the fall of her hair. "He is so big, you'd think it wasn't even possible for him to hide, but it's amazing how well he blends in."

She smiled, picked up a piece of tomato, and held it up. "And how much he steals," she grumbled, as he reached out and took the tomato gently from her fingers.

"So how do you stop Mugs from getting all upset?"

"I'll save him a piece of the hot dog," she confessed. And, with several napkins to help her, she managed to start at one end of the big hot dog and make her way down to the end, saving the last bite for Mugs. And she was pleasantly full by the time she was done. "That was delicious."

"Good," Brandon said, with a big smile. He pointed off in the other direction. "Here comes the first group, back from their walk."

She looked over to see at least thirty people coming toward him. "Wow," she said, "I got in just before them."

"You did, indeed," he said. "You don't eat nearly enough. You're always so skinny. Here. Have a second one." With that, he plunked a second one right down in front of her, then turned to face the crowd.

She was full, but, at the same time, it was hard for her not to indulge. She quickly put just mustard and ketchup on this one. She retook her seat and, as the crowd swelled around her, decided it was more prudent to back away, since she had the animals. She pulled back farther and farther, until she was on the edge of the crowd.

There she polished off her hot dog, again giving the last bite to Mugs, and thought about her life, always on the edge of crowds. Even when she was still with her husband, they were either surrounded by people, or she was mingling, but she was never really part of it. She was always working the crowd, always sitting on the outside of real friends.

But she had to remind herself, as she tossed her napkins into the garbage can, that she had been invited here out of kindness. And that made her feel good. She saw Brandon lifting his head and looking around the crowd, as if scanning for her, but he didn't look in her direction. Such a din was around her that she didn't want to yell to get Brandon's attention, which would just draw the crowd's attention to her as well, so she quietly backed away with the animals. She rounded up her animals and said, "Come on, guys. Let's go home."

And happily the four of them headed off.

Chapter 3

Sunday Morning …

THE PHONE WOKE Doreen the next morning. Rubbing the sleep from her eyes, she reached for her cell and said, "Good morning, Mack."

"Nick told me," he said, without preamble.

"That's nice. I'm glad he told you. Let me in on the secret. What did he tell you?" she said, yawning. "You do realize I haven't had coffee yet."

"It's not that early," he said.

She looked at her phone and said, "It's not that late either."

"It's almost eight," he said. "Normally you're up and about. Otherwise I wouldn't have called so early."

"Not a problem," she said, as she staggered upright and headed to look out the window.

"Still, I could have waited," he said. "I'm sorry."

"I'm up now," she said crossly. "So what difference does it make that Nick told you something, and just what was it that he told you?"

"That you've retained him as your lawyer."

"Something about all of Robin's client cases being null

and void and the investigation of her ex-husband's parents murder and the fact that she was murdered. Besides, he was handling it all anyway. This just made it official."

"Well, that her crimes play into it to a degree, but it was largely the investigation into her fraudulent scams as an attorney that caused it," he said.

"The end result is that I don't have a valid separation agreement anymore, and Nick sent a letter to my ex. Explaining that and introduced himself as my attorney."

At that, Mack whistled.

"And told me that I'm not allowed to talk to him without my lawyer present," she muttered, as she pushed the hair from her face. "And, in order for me to have a lawyer present, I figured I had to have one. Legitimately, you know?"

"He told me that he charged you one dollar to retain him for his services."

"Is that how much he got?" It's not like she'd counted the change she'd handed over. "Yeah, well, did he tell you the part about tricking me into it? I thought he needed change for parking or something."

Laughing, Mack said, "No, he didn't mention that part."

"Yeah, I thought he lived in the Lower Mainland though," she said. "What good will that do if Mathew is around here?"

"Lawyers can work with clients all over the world. I wouldn't mind if my brother moved back home again," he said. "But he does very well down there."

"He could do very well if he went into big business," she said. "The kind of work he does won't pay his rent. A one-dollar retainer, really?"

Mack burst out laughing. "He's just trying to help you

out. I told you before that he does a certain amount of pro bono work every year."

"Is that to salve his conscience for triple charging other clients?"

"No, I just think he knows that some people aren't getting a fair shake, and he wanted to help out."

"It's appreciated," she admitted. "I'm hoping that Mathew ignores me. Especially after getting Nick's letter."

"I hope so, but I doubt it. Which is another reason I'm calling."

"Why is that?"

"After I spoke to Nick, I checked the airlines."

With her heart sinking, she said, "And?"

"He's coming in on the noon flight. So be warned." And, with that, Mack hung up.

Swearing gently to herself, she headed into the shower, turned on the hot water and stepped under it. By the time she was dressed and downstairs, she was craving coffee, just a few minutes away, and the animals all needed food too, plus access to the backyard. She propped open the back door for them.

To think that Mathew was on his way back here—and undoubtedly angry—meant that she would see him today. She should have asked Mack if he'd contacted Nick with the news. She sent him a quick text, as she waited for the grinder to stop. By the time the coffee was dripping, he'd answered in the affirmative.

"That's good at least," she said. Determined to have something to think about that wasn't related to her ex, to her former divorce lawyer, or to Mack's brother, she grabbed the Bob Small stuff, sorting out the cases by year. She couldn't even be sure that this was all the cases which could be related to Bob Small. When she had them all laid out, she had over fifty clippings, but some of the articles covered the same missing person's incident, so were duplicates in a sense.

Trying to get her head wrapped around what she had organized, she typed a summary by date on her laptop and sorted the scans she'd previously done to go with it. It took all morning, but it was a great way of keeping her occupied, so she didn't worry about the noon flight.

She knew as soon as Mathew landed because he was now calling her. Completely forgetting the warnings, she answered the call. "Hello, Mathew," she said cheerfully, as she opened the fridge to find anything to eat. The hot dogs from the day before were rumbling through her stomach as a distant but happy memory, and she wanted more.

"I'm fine," he said, his tone brisk. "But I gather we have a lawyer issue."

"Not sure about a lawyer issue," she said. "My former lawyer screwed me over and took over my bed in your house," she said, "and now she is dead."

"Yes, and of course now the agreement between us is null and void."

"That figures," she said nonchalantly. "It always was, wasn't it? She was defrauding me back then too."

"We'll do something about it, I guess. I brought a copy for you to sign again," he said.

At that, she stiffened. "The same document?"

"Of course," he said. "I'm just about out of the airport. I've got a rental," he said. Such disdain was in his voice, as he added, "It's just a car."

"Ah, not one of your luxury models, huh?" she said. "I can't sign it right now anyway."

"Why not? You signed it before. You can sign it again."

"Is it that simple?" she asked. "I mean, my former lawyer screwed me over with that document, so obviously I'll need my new lawyer to take a look this time."

"You can't afford a lawyer, can you?" he said, this time his tone overridden by mockery.

She stiffened at the insult, as she stared out the window. "I do have a lawyer this time," she said. "Of course I had one before, for all the good that did me."

"Lawyers are thieves," he said. "Robin should have proven that to you."

"Maybe so," she muttered, "but, at the same time, this one is quite different."

"I doubt it," he said, "they're after one thing, and that's money."

"I haven't had too much experience with lawyers, but the last one was after more than just money," she muttered.

"Exactly," he said. "Robin screwed us both over, so let's not involve any lawyers this time," he said, his tone turning persuasive.

"But Robin didn't screw you out of anything, did she?" Doreen asked in confusion. "Or is there something you're not telling me?"

"She stole some information from me," he said, "and that I find unforgivable."

"Ah," she said, "well, she did appear to be one who took advantage of situations."

"You're not kidding," he said. "Something was definitely wrong with that woman."

"Since she is dead now, let's not speak unkindly of the dead."

"I'll speak unkindly of anybody I want," he said. "Just because she got herself killed doesn't make her an angel.

That woman was a capital B."

"I'm not arguing there," she said. "But my new lawyer has made it very clear that I'm not signing anything. In fact, I'm not supposed to even talk to you without him here. So …" And she let her voice trail off. She reached up and pinched the bridge of her nose. "I really don't want to deal with any more just now," she said. "I've had a headache all morning."

"All the more reason to get this solved another way," he said briskly. "I'll be there in twenty minutes." And, with that, he hung up the phone.

She stared at her phone and groaned. "Now what am I supposed to do?" she muttered. She quickly sent Mack a text.

Mathew will be here in twenty minutes.

Instead of responding, he called her. "You're not allowed to see him."

"What do you want me to do?" she cried out. "He already called me. He's bringing the exact same document and expects me to sign it."

"Nonsense," he said. "I'm calling Nick."

"What good will that do?" she wailed, but Mack was already gone. And, of course, nobody responded again. She groaned and put on more coffee, as if she needed more. But some things just called for coffee. It was either that or open up a bottle of wine and start guzzling. And that wasn't a habit she wanted to get into, no matter how tempting it might be.

She kept walking back and forth between the front and back doors, staring all the while. Mugs was pacing along with her, and so was Goliath. Thaddeus, on the other hand, was perched on his roost in the living room and completely ignoring her, snoozing. She had both front and back doors locked because she had that sneaking sense that Mathew would enter without knocking, and that was the last thing she wanted.

On the other hand, he was the kind who would sneak in somehow, and she wouldn't even see it coming. Then he'd act like it was totally normal. She had no idea how she was supposed to get out of this, and she didn't think telling him that the lawyer said she couldn't sign anything would be good enough to get rid of him. Would he go so far as to hurt her? That she didn't know. And it's not what she wanted to think about, but it was all too possible that he would do it now, if she put up any kind of argument.

Almost simultaneously she watched three vehicles fly up the cul-de-sac and park. Mack got here first, and he pulled into the driveway. Her ex and his little rental car pulled around and parked out front. Finally Nick parked curbside.

Hopping out, Mathew took one look at Mack and glared. "What are you doing here?"

"What are you doing here?" Mack asked, as if he didn't know.

"I came to see my wife," Mathew said stiffly.

"Look at that," Mack said, a big grin on his face. "So did I."

"Oh dear," Doreen said to herself. "This won't be good. On the other hand, with Mack obviously quite capable of handling Mathew, it could be great fun." She stepped out onto the front porch and glared at the two of them. Mathew looked at her and said, "Really? A cop?"

She shrugged. "Really? Why not?" she said. "I mean, it's not like you weren't sleeping with my former divorce lawyer."

"I didn't know that she was a criminal," he growled.

"Oh, please, that's a lie," she said. "Tell me another one." She waved him away with her hand, as she watched Nick get out of the third vehicle.

"And who is this?" Mathew asked, as he turned to look at Nick.

"My new attorney," she said. "I told you that I won't sign anything without him reviewing the document first."

Mathew stiffened. "I flew all the way up here," he said, "so we could do this without the lawyers."

"Well then, you should have spoken to me before you did that," she said, trying for a commonsense easygoing attitude. But that had never worked before, so it was unlikely to work now.

He shook his head. "If you'll be difficult," he said, "I'm not leaving the document."

"That's fine," Nick said. "We'll write up a document for you to sign then."

"What kind of document?" he asked stiffly, looking at Nick suspiciously.

Nick pulled a business card from his wallet, handed it over, and said, "If you don't want to deal with your lawyer, that's fine," he said, "we can deal between the two of us."

"For what?"

"The divorce settlement of course," Nick said, his eyes opening wide. "I mean, that is what you're here about, isn't it?"

Her ex slowly nodded, but he was stiffening, and his body language showed that he wanted to be anywhere but here.

"That's what he said," she called out from the front step.

Mathew turned and looked at her and asked, "Why are you doing this?"

"Doing what?" she asked in innocence.

"The document is null and void, so we just sign another, that's all." He raised the brown envelope in his hand. "This is the one that you need to sign again," he said. "It's simple. You just sign it, and we're all good to go."

"If my lawyer at the time was a criminal, and she is the one who wrote that document," she said, "why would I sign it again? Obviously we need a new one," she said. "And, in order to get a new one, I had to get a new lawyer."

"No," he said, "you didn't have to get a new lawyer. As a matter of fact, we don't need to get a new lawyer."

"*We*? Is that you and your whole team of lawyers?" she asked. "So you're protected. It's just me who isn't."

"Of course you're protected," he said, with an eye roll and that genial look. "I've looked after you for all these years," he said. "I won't screw you around now."

"And yet there was that other document," Nick said. "You know? The one where Robin screwed Doreen over?"

"Yes, but," Mathew said, raising a finger, "Doreen signed the paperwork, so I just assumed she had agreed to it."

"Doreen agreed to it because her lawyer told her to sign it, saying it was the best agreement Robin could get Doreen, and that you didn't owe her anything," Nick said, rocking back on his heels, with a delightful tone of voice.

Doreen couldn't even quite place the tenor of his voice, but just something about it fascinated her. She looked over at Mack to see him glaring at her. She opened her eyes wide, threw out her hands, and raised her voice. "What?"

Mack just shook his head, then took several steps forward toward her.

Mathew asked, "What's the matter? Are they hurting

you?"

"Of course they're not hurting me," she said, staring at Mathew in confusion. "Does it look like he's hurting me?"

"You yelled at him."

"I yell at him all the time," she said, with a shoulder shrug. "It makes no difference."

Chapter 4

MACK BURST OUT laughing. Even Nick laughed like a crazy man.

Mathew looked at her in surprise. "You never yell."

"I wasn't allowed to yell," she said. "You made very sure of that."

"It's not like that's a bad thing," he said. "In our world, yelling is hardly a sign of control."

"But you know something?" she said. "It's awfully freeing."

He shook his head and said, "I don't even understand you anymore."

Nick said, "May I have the agreement? I'll go over it, and then we'll do up a counteragreement."

With Nick standing there, his hand held out, and Mathew holding the envelope, looking stupid, he had no choice but to slowly hand it over. "Fine. But she signed this once, so there's no reason she can't sign it again."

"I'll be the judge of that," Nick said. Then he looked over at Doreen. "Mack is taking you out for lunch, isn't he?"

Her eyebrows raised, but she managed to keep a straight face as she nodded. "I think that was the plan, yes." She glanced at Mack, who was glaring at his brother in outrage, while she just grinned. "Unless you have something better to do."

Immediately Mack shook his head. "No, I don't have anything better to do," he said. "Are we going with the animals or without?"

"It depends if we're doing takeout and hitting the beach," she said, with a big smile, "or if you're planning on taking me to a fancy restaurant."

"Why would you take those animals anywhere?" Mathew said in disgust. "I mean, the dog maybe, but not in a restaurant. Not anywhere except in the house. He has become an undisciplined mutt."

"I think he was always undisciplined," she said, "but you weren't around him enough to ever know."

"Good," he said. "At least you knew enough to keep him out of my sight most of the time." With that, he shook his head and said, "Well, here I was planning on taking you out for lunch."

"Sorry," she said, "if you would have called earlier, then I could have told you."

"I see how it is. So much for us getting back together again."

"Considering you were only looking to see if I had the information Robin stole from you," she said, "I didn't take that talk very seriously. Not that it interested me in the slightest. Did you ever contact the cops about Robin stealing from you?" Then there were the USB sticks Mack had yet to update her on. She needed to quiz him on that. "I'm sure Mack here could help you out with that."

"Nope," Mathew said, walking around his car. "That hick-town cop is the last person I want to talk to."

"I have great connections down in Vancouver, if you want them," Mack said, studying him. "If Robin did you wrong, it's a good time for it all to come out in the open. They're doing quite an investigation into all her criminal activities as it is."

"Why do they even care?" Mathew asked, staring at him in horror over the roof of the car. "She's dead."

"She defrauded a lot of people," he said. "And she helped murder her ex-husband's parents."

Mathew shuddered. "I didn't know anything about that," he said. "My God, I'm lucky to be alive."

"In many ways, yes," Mack said. "We don't know how many other people she may have been involved with. But we have her ex-husband in custody now, so the investigation is widening."

"You stay out of my business," Mathew told Mack. "I might have been done wrong by her, but I'm sure as heck not going after a dead person."

"Maybe not," Mack said, "but her estate needs to be cleaned up."

Doreen's husband stilled, looked at Mack, and asked, "Do we know who inherits everything?"

Mack immediately shook his head. "I don't know," he said. "I haven't talked to whoever is handling her estate."

Mathew nodded slowly. "I would think that would be her ex-husband."

"But he's in jail, so that's not likely."

"She had a colleague. I think her name was Lisa," Mathew muttered, half under his breath.

"I'll call and see who is handling that. Do you know her last name?" Mack asked, pulling out a notebook.

"Lisa Phellpis," he said and even spelled it out.

Mack looked at that name, with a frown. "She was at the same law firm?"

"Yep. Stratford and Sons."

"Both women, both attorneys," Doreen said, with a sarcastic tone.

At that, her soon-to-be-ex-husband looked at her. "Men rule the world. Remember that. I've certainly told you often enough."

"No argument there," she said, "but apparently Robin was determined to get a chunk for herself."

Not for the first time, Doreen felt a twinge of sadness for Robin and for the life she'd led, wondering why she had such a need to cheat, lie, and steal in order to get what she wanted in life. "There are other ways to get through in life, without targeting others."

"Whatever," Mathew said. "I'll talk to Lisa when I get to the airport, see what I can find out."

"What difference does it make to you?" she asked him curiously. "The two of you broke up months ago. You said so yourself."

He glanced at her, with a one-armed shrug. "Yeah, but you never know," he muttered. "She might have been sweet on me enough to have changed her will in my favor."

"She was still in cahoots with her ex-husband," she said, staring at Mathew. "Why would you think that a short-term affair with you would cause her to do something like that? Besides, I thought she was sleeping with Rex. Maybe she left everything to him."

Hearing that, her husband hopped back out of the vehicle and glared at her over the roof. "What did you just say?"

And she realized she shouldn't have opened her mouth. "How do you know she didn't have a relationship with somebody else in your world?" she asked curiously. "I mean, that was the name of the game for Robin."

"And I told you before that there's nobody else! She wouldn't dare."

"Okay," she said, "you knew her far better than I did."

He nodded. "You're damn right I did." And he hopped back into his rented vehicle and took off.

She looked over at Mack, wincing. "I'm so sorry. I should never have mentioned Rex to him."

"Well," he said, staring, as Mathew's vehicle took off, "you are a gal who likes to shake the tiger's tail."

Nick walked closer and said, "But that tiger might just bite."

"Oh, he definitely bites," she said softly. "I felt the sting of his teeth more than once."

"Did he ever hurt you physically?" Mack asked.

"A few times," she said, her hand going up to her cheek in remembrance. "I admit to feeling fairly vulnerable after that."

"It's all a pattern of power and abuse," he said. "They do whatever they have to do that keeps you in line and that ensures you don't argue with them. At some point in time, telling you off, keeping you locked up, or taking away your favorite things aren't enough, and it becomes physical."

"I was a fast learner," she said. "Too fast apparently because I fell in line without any argument."

"But you were also trained to do that," he said, "from the very beginning of your marriage, I presume, so don't worry about it. Besides, like he said, you never used to yell. And now you yell all the time."

"Only at you," she said, glaring at Mack. "And usually only because you won't let me help or let me get involved in your cases."

Nick started to laugh. "I really enjoy seeing the two of you together," he said. "It makes my heart smile." And, with that, he lifted a hand and said, "I'll get back to you about these documents."

"Yeah," she said. "Please don't think badly of me, when you see what I signed."

He looked at her, his voice gentle, and said, "Don't worry. I've seen a lot in my life. Including victims." He smiled and opened his car door and jumped in.

She shoved her hands into her pockets and rocked on her heels, as she watched Nick drive away. Then she looked back at Mack. "You don't have to take me out for lunch. I know he put you on the spot."

Mack shook his head and said, "It brings up a good point."

"What's that?"

"I have yet to take you out for a meal."

"So what?" she said. "You've fed me countless times here at home. Besides, I kind of like eating here."

"I liked your idea of picking up something and going to the beach with the animals," he said. "How about it?"

She looked at him in delight. "Really?"

"Absolutely," he said, "but only if we call it something different."

"What do we call it then?" she asked in confusion.

He looked at her and said, "A date."

Chapter 5

MACK'S WORDS KEPT going over and over in her head, as they drove in Mack's truck to a special little restaurant that Doreen had never heard of before.

"They do all kinds of stuff here, but they cater more to the commercial district," he said. "It's called Street Food, and I've already ordered ahead. We'll pick it up, and then we'll find a nice little spot on the river, where we can sit there and enjoy it."

"Suits me," she said.

They drove into this tiny parking lot out in front of a very small building, and he disappeared inside and came back out with two large bags of food. He plunked them on her lap, and Mugs immediately hopped up, his paws on her knees, sniffing the bags.

"Better keep the animals out of those bags," Mack warned, "or I'll turn around and take them back home."

She stared at the bags and said, "Honestly, Mack. How many meals did you buy?"

He laughed. "Just enough for lunch."

"It looks like at least enough for lunch and dinner," she said, and her stomach growled.

He looked over at her. "Did you eat breakfast?"

She shook her head. "No, you kind of upset me with the news that Mathew was on his way," she said. "I've only had coffee this morning."

He sighed. "Sorry. I wanted to warn you and to give you some time before he showed up. But I didn't mean to upset you that much." He took a turn and pulled out onto one of the main roads, crossed the highway, and headed toward the river.

"Where are we going?"

"If you go up this way," he said, "we follow the river for a bit. Quite a few pullouts are here, where we can find a spot along the river to eat. Mugs won't have to be on a leash, and Goliath can sit there and enjoy it with us."

Sure enough, Mack came to a small pullout, and he pulled in, turned off the engine, and said, "Get ready to hop out on that side."

He came around, opened the door, took the bags from her, and she awkwardly got out with all the animals. And then he said, "Now we'll head down here to the corner. It's really a popular area in the summertime, with people swimming here, but some spots off to the side are really very nice and are quite private."

He led her through some of the underbrush—disturbing the birds, groundhogs, and squirrels alike—and then came out to a spot where the sun dappled onto the river, making her cry out in joy.

"This is beautiful," she said, looking up at the cliff on the other side of the river. "I've never been here before."

"Good," he said. "Like I said, it's a popular swimming hole and can get kind of crazy here. But right now, it's nice and quiet." He motioned to a couple logs off on the side. "We don't have picnic blankets, but we could sit on some logs here." She immediately walked over, plunked her butt down, Mugs at her heels, then unhooked him from his leash and said, "Go for it."

Once Mugs was free, he wandered over to the creek, and, where it was shallow, he waded around in just enough water to cover his big clunky paws, to have a drink, and to wander back and forth in curiosity, while Goliath hopped up on one of the big rocks beside them and stretched out in the sun. Thaddeus, never to be outdone, walked from her shoulder to the closest branch right there beside her, then followed it until it dropped to the ground, where he casually hopped off. The branch swung right back up, barely missing her.

Mack shook his head. "Having the animals around is always such an adventure."

She grinned. "But it's a great one." She looked at the bags. "So, while we sort out the food," she said, "you can tell me more about *Nabbed in the Nasturtiums.*"

"No, ma'am. No talk about cases. Lunch and enjoying the scenery, that's it."

"That's hardly fair. All I wanted to know was—"

Mack gave her a look, which told her that he was completely serious. "This is a date. Remember? No cases, no discussion."

She glared at him. "Then when?"

"Coffee at your place, when we head back," he said, with a fat grin. "Now, no more shop." He gently stroked her uninjured shoulder. "We're here to enjoy ourselves. Let's focus on that instead." He gazed at her steadily, looking for some agreement.

It's not what she wanted, but this time with him was special. The rest could wait.

At least for a little while.

Chapter 6

A LITTLE WHILE turned out to be hours later, as Doreen was outside, enjoying a cup of coffee on the deck, and Mack joined her.

"That was wonderful today," she said. "Thank you." She waited a bit. "So tell me about *Nabbed in the Nasturtiums.*"

He looked at her with a shake of his head, then a weary resignation crossed his face. "*Kidnapped* is not the same as *nabbed.*"

"I guess it depends," she said.

"Depends on what?" he asked in exasperation.

She looked up, grinned, and said, "Depends on who nabbed him." She watched his reaction, but he just sighed loudly.

"That doesn't work."

"Sure, it does," she said. "If he was trying to evade somebody, and he got *Nabbed in the Nasturtiums*, it means he got caught there."

"Sure, but why kidnap him?"

"There could be lots of reasons," she said, waving a hand eerily about. "What if he was being blackmailed? What if he had kidnapped somebody else? What if he owed someone money? What if—" She shrugged. "You get my drift."

"Sure," he said, "but how likely is that?"

"In our world," she said, "after the things that I've seen in the last few months? Very likely."

His frown deepened, and then he shrugged. "Okay, I'll give you that. We have seen some pretty crazy things in these last few months."

"Beyond pretty crazy," she said, with a nod. "There have been some really seriously problematic areas of society."

"But everybody had a reason," he reminded her, with a grin.

"And that's what I'm saying," she said. "Everybody has a reason. We just don't know what the reason is, and, until we do, I like *Nabbed in the Nasturtiums.*"

"The name of the case is hardly worth arguing about," he said in exasperation. "That's the least of our problems."

"Least of *your* problems," she said, with a bright cheerful smile. "Me, I'm not even allowed on the case."

"Right," he agreed, "exactly. So why are we arguing about this?" He glared at her, and she just gave him an impudent smile right back. He shook his head again. "You make me crazy. You know that, right?"

"No, you make me crazy," she said.

"So we can agree that we're going crazy together," he said, with a sneaky grin. "It's just that yours is more visible than mine."

She gasped at that. "That's not fair."

He gave her a smug look. "Crazy is as crazy does."

She stared at him. "What does that even mean?"

He frowned. "I'm not exactly sure," he said, "but it sounds good."

"Only because it's a jab at me," she said. "Now tell me

about the case."

"I can't tell you about the case," he said. "You're not a cop. Remember?"

"I'm helping you. Remember?"

"It's my case. Remember that? And you're not allowed to help me." This time his tone deepened in a way that said he was done arguing.

She groaned and said, "Fine. I'll just dig into all these Bob Small cases. I did get a start, but, man, that's a lot of cases."

"We don't have any proof of what he's been involved in."

"No, I get that. But one of Nan's friends had a niece who went missing, and she was pretty sure Bob Small did it."

"And?" he said.

"She ended up dying, without getting justice for her niece."

"So you can't help her," he said. "As sad as it is, sometimes that happens. We can't help everyone."

"I know," she said, "but now I'm stuck on it."

"That was Annalise, Annalise Bergmont, if I remember correctly. She was supposed to come home from a dance class or something, wasn't she?"

"Yeah," Doreen said. "She was supposed to be on her way home from ballet class but didn't make it."

"See? Something so open-ended like that?" Mack added, "It could have been anybody."

"True, so maybe I need to solve it from that point of view, not even try to pigeonhole it into one of the possible Bob Small cases, just to see exactly what did happen."

"And how will you do that?" he asked. "It was down in the Lower Mainland."

"That is quite true. She was in Vancouver," she said, frowning. "I guess I can't get a copy of the files out of Vancouver, can I?"

"Nope," he said, with a wry note of satisfaction.

She glared at him. "You could help."

"Nope," he said. "The whole idea is for you to find a hobby that doesn't get you hurt all the time."

"If this woman has been dead for a long time, who'll hurt me?"

"Whoever killed her," he said, staring at her.

"Besides them."

"There is no *besides them*," he said, groaning. "You and I both know you put yourself into these crazy cases, and you're the one who ends up getting attacked."

"You could just help me *not* get attacked," she said. "Besides, I'm a long way from this one, so surely it would be less dangerous."

He studied her for a moment, his fingers drumming the deck railing, and she realized he was thinking about it.

"I'm becoming a great amateur detective," she said, "and that's a huge hobby. I'm also helping people, you know? Finding closure and all. I mean, I'm doing all kinds of stuff, and it's good for me, and it's good for them. Why is it not good for you?"

"Don't start spinning this around and blaming me," he muttered on a groan.

"I would if I could," she said, "but somehow you always turn it back around against me."

"I'm not *against* you," he said. "I'm trying to keep you safe."

She smiled. "And I really do appreciate that. Honestly." He rolled his eyes at her, and she chuckled. "Okay, I know I don't always appear to be thankful, and I probably haven't even said *thank you* for all kinds of things in the past that I should have," she admitted. "Apparently I'm not very good at saying *thank you* at all." After a few moments of silence, she frowned, looked at him, and said, "Now you're making me feel terrible."

He raised both hands in frustration. "I'm not making you do anything," he said. "You're the one doing it all."

"See? There you go, making me feel bad again."

He closed his eyes, pinched the bridge of his nose, and said, "Okay, this crazy conversation has gone on long enough."

"So does that mean you'll help me out then?"

"No," he roared. He hopped to his feet.

"Uh-oh. You're not leaving, are you?" she asked.

"I should." He looked at his watch and said, "Yet I guess we need food again, if you're hungry."

"We sure do, and, yes, I am," she said, with a big smile. "What did you bring?"

"Basics," he said. "I just brought over some veggies. You probably don't have any meat, do you?"

"I've got some." She hopped up to look in the fridge and the freezer, while he unloaded the bags that he'd brought. "I've got some ground beef, but there's not very much of it." She held up the small package she found. "I got it on sale. I also have a couple chicken breasts in the freezer."

"How about a chicken stir-fry then?" he asked. "I even grabbed some chow mein noodles, without even realizing that's where we were heading."

She looked at the noodles. "I don't think I've ever had those."

"They're crunchy," he said. "You make up your stir-fry

and toss them in afterward."

"And you eat them crunchy and uncooked?"

"They're technically cooked already," he said, "and you can eat them soft or hard."

She shrugged. "You're the master." He snagged the chicken breasts, put them in the microwave to defrost, as she watched. Frowning, she said, "I thought defrosting meat in the microwave wasn't a good idea?"

"Sometimes you have to. In this case I'm not really defrosting it, not fully. I'm just defrosting them enough so I can slice them." When they were done, he took them to the cutting board with a big knife and sliced them thinly.

"Now what?"

"Now get a bowl and some soy sauce and start to marinate all of these in it." He gave her a bunch of other spices to add in, including something called five-spice powder.

She shook her head. "Why not do the individual spices?"

"Why not just conveniently put them all together as one?" he countered.

"You're the chef," she muttered. She followed his instructions, ending up with dark-looking chicken slices. Then he brought out the wok, tossed in some oil, and had her wash a mound of veggies. "That's a lot of food."

"I'm starving," he snapped. "Nothing like being around you to make me hungry."

"Oh," she said. "I don't want to be responsible for you gaining weight." He stopped and stared at her. She shrugged. "Not that you are."

"Are you saying I'm fat?"

Her lips twitched.

He glared at her. "Don't look away. Are you saying I'm fat?"

She shook her head slowly. "Never," she said, but something was in her tone.

He turned, looked at her, crossed his arms over his chest, and said, "Are you calling me fat? Don't evade the question. Yes or no?"

She shook her head, tried to control herself, but, against her best efforts, her lips twitched. Again. And she started to snicker. Then, giving up the fight, she laughed and laughed and laughed. By the time she had control of herself, she was sitting on the kitchen floor, wiping the tears from her face.

Mack glared at her, but thankfully he had a grin on his face. "I gather you're not calling me fat."

"I wouldn't dare," she said, laughing. "And, besides, you are not fat at all. You know that."

"Of course not," he said. "I work out. I eat healthy, and I'm fit. You're the one who's so skinny."

"So why'd you get so upset at me?"

"Just to piss you off," he said, "but it had an even better reaction. You look really good when you're laughing."

"I don't think I've done enough of it," she said. "Honestly it doesn't seem like I've had a whole lot to laugh at."

"There is now," he said.

She snickered. "Yeah, you."

He gave her a mock look of outrage and said, "You're pretty cheeky tonight."

"Yeah, I'm getting dinner soon," she said.

"You mean, you're *hoping* to get dinner soon," he muttered.

She made her way back over to his side, so she could watch, as he waited for the oil in the electric wok to be hot. Then he threw in most of the veggies, all the meat, and all of the onions. "It doesn't look like there's a whole lot to making this."

"There isn't," he said. "I should be having you make it."

"Maybe," she said, "next time."

He said, "You should practice. It's not hard. You just get the oil hot, throw in your veggies and meat, toss them and stir them. If you want them cooked a little bit longer, add a bit of water, throw on a lid, and, when that steam comes out of the side, wait three minutes, and the veggies are perfect."

He put the lid on and watched, while she counted. As soon as the three minutes were up, he lifted the lid, and she cried out in amazement. "They're perfect." He nodded, stirred it all up, made a well in the center and added a little bit of a cornstarch mixture. "So that'll thicken it?" she asked, watching.

He nodded and said, "See that bubbling up in the center?" She watched tiny bubbles appear, and he said, "Now you stir it. The cornstarch won't thicken unless it's bubbling. But now look." And, sure enough, the cornstarch was well and truly thickened. "It's all good to go."

"Do you want rice with it?"

"Nope," he said. "That's why we have the noodles."

He grabbed the bag of noodles, brought them over to the wok, and upended half the bag into it. He said, "That's probably about right. We'll try it and see."

"It looks fascinating," she said. "I've never seen those noodles before."

"I like them," he said. "I'm sure other people would choose other kinds of noodles, but this is great for a change."

Since she had never tasted them herself, she wasn't a judge. But, when she sat down and tucked in enthusiastically, she nodded. "Good choice."

"Glad you think so," he said, watching her eat with satisfaction.

When she realized he wasn't eating, she looked up and asked, "What's the matter?"

He chuckled. "Nothing," he said. "It's just very rewarding to cook for you."

"Why?" she asked in astonishment.

"Because you eat everything with such enthusiasm, so it doesn't really matter if it's good or bad."

"But that would imply that it could be terrible and that I'd still eat it," she said, frowning up at him.

"And you would," he said. "You're also very polite."

She wrinkled up her nose at him. "You make me sound terribly boring, but I do have an opinion, you know?"

"Oh, I know," he said. "Trust me. I've heard them many a time."

"Then you can always count on me to be honest about food."

"I'm really glad to hear that. I've wondered, every once in a while, if maybe you were just eating for the sake of eating."

"Meaning, because I'm so hungry?"

He nodded.

"Some things I prefer more when compared to others," she said, "like pasta, but I don't think you've ever cooked me anything I didn't think was delightful."

He searched her face for a long moment and then relaxed. "Good," he said. "So you truly do like everything, don't you?"

She nodded. "Okay, I like food. It wasn't until I ran into a shortage of it that I realized how much and how simple most food truly is."

"It's only complicated if you make it complicated," he

said.

"And I didn't have any prior exposure to realize that," she said. "So your cooking lessons have been quite an eye-opener, and, for that, I thank you."

"You're welcome," he said. "It's been fun, but I need to see you doing more cooking."

"Okay, so I'd like to learn how to do more of these," she said. "How about tomorrow night?"

"That's possible," he said. As he looked around her kitchen, he added, "We probably have enough veggies here to do another stir-fry."

She clapped her hands.

"Perfect." He grinned. "You know that you clap your hands just like Nan does, like a little kid."

Immediately she dropped her hands into her lap and glared at him.

He shrugged. "It's cute."

She sighed. "I don't know about how cute it can be when it's the behavior of an almost eighty-year-old woman."

"I don't think she's quite that old."

"I'm not exactly sure how old she is, and, if I'm honest, I'm not sure she's ever told me—or if she even would."

He laughed at that. "I guess egos are still egos, aren't they?"

"Particularly for her, but she's adorable though."

"Yes, she is," he said, with a big grin. "Don't worry. She is a great friend of mine too."

"I really appreciate that, and I know she gets away with murder sometimes," she said, "but honestly she comes from a good heart."

"Getting away with murder on her gambling, you mean?"

She nodded and winced. "Yeah, it's like she just can't quit."

"That's what addictions are," he said, "and gambling is definitely an addiction."

"Even if you're the one organizing the bets?"

"Absolutely," he muttered. "Think about it. It doesn't really matter who is doing whatever it is. Still, you've got to have your hand into it."

"At least she's not trying to make money off of people anymore."

"Isn't she?" he asked in surprise.

Doreen frowned, shrugged, and said, "I don't think so. I think she's doing it mostly out of fun."

"Just because it's fun for her doesn't mean that it's fun for anybody else, and, if other people aren't as wealthy as she is, then it can be very painful for them to lose that kind of money."

"I don't think they're losing much in the way of money these days. It's become almost like, you know, gambling with chopsticks or toothpicks."

"I'm glad to hear that," he said, "because I know Richie is not as wealthy as Nan."

"Right," she said, "and I guess that would be hard if it was somebody she knew too."

"And we don't always know what people's circumstances are," he reminded her. "Just because a lot of people know about your circumstance doesn't mean everybody does. They all see this house and think that you're lucky enough to own it."

"Which I am," she said.

"Right, but they don't know you're struggling to put food on the table."

She frowned. "No, you're right. Maybe I should have a talk with Nan to make sure she's not fleecing anybody she shouldn't be."

He laughed. "In Nan's world she'd probably say that they're all there to be fleeced."

"You're not wrong there," she muttered. "Still, I don't think she is coldhearted."

"Nope, she sure isn't, and it's all about fun and games. But fun and games can have terrible consequences for some people."

Wanting to change the conversation, she turned her attention back to the food—and Mack's current case. "You still haven't told me much about this gardener."

"Not much to tell," he said, shrugging. Finally he opened up a bit. "He was working in the flower beds and apparently was supposed to return at a certain time with the equipment. When his supervisor realized the gardener hadn't shown up, his boss went down to the site and found no sign of him."

"But how do you know he didn't just drive home then?" she asked.

"Because he's not at home. His vehicle was there. All the equipment that he was supposed to have was there, but still no sign of him was found. Nobody had seen him, and no cameras were around either."

"You sure he didn't just have a heart attack in a ditch?"

"First off, he's younger, only forty-eight. Second, he's more or less healthy, as far as we can tell. So that would be an unlikely occurrence, but still they've been carefully searching and have tried hard to find him."

"So, any ransom note or something like that?"

"No," he said, frowning, looking at his phone, checking

to see if he had any messages. "Nothing at all."

"That's sad," she said, "because, if you have no information, what are you supposed to do?"

"That's where the problem lies," he said. "We have to keep looking and inform the public to keep an eye out. But, at the same time, nothing much we can do. After we've searched everywhere and we can't find him, then what?" he asked, almost with a bit of challenge.

"Any sign of his phone? Any sign of family members having heard from him all day?"

"No, nothing," he said. "It's like he got into another vehicle and drove away."

"Which could have easily happened," she said. "Somebody could have picked him up, like taking him for lunch or something, and never brought him back. I mean, maybe he had a great afternoon somewhere."

"And that could be why he is not answering his phone?"

"Sure, but a lot of people wouldn't, if it came to playing hooky. Chances are, he'll show up tomorrow, apologetic and hoping he still has a job."

"That would be the best-case scenario," Mack said, "but I can't count on it."

"Of course not," she said sympathetically. "Plus, the public is after you to do something."

"Of course," he said. "If it was somebody you knew, you'd be after me too."

"Always," she said, with a nod. "Same as now. I'm looking at this woman who disappeared over twenty-five years ago and wondering what would be left for information to find out who and what. These cases never go away, do they?"

"No, even if we do suspect it's a serial killer, and we can't prove anything, it's not like we close it on the suspicion," he said. "We wait until we have an actual cause. We keep working it until we get it solved."

"Interesting," she murmured. "In which case, you could get me whatever there is on my case, and I could look into it." When he opened his mouth, she cut him off, saying, "Remember. The niece went missing a long way from here, so it's not like I'll get into any trouble from Vancouver."

"As long as I find absolutely no connection to Kelowna," he said. "But, the minute there's one whiff of a connection, I am not helping you."

"That's fine," she said immediately. "I really do mean to be an armchair detective for this one."

He snorted at that. "I wish that would be the case, but you have this bad habit of ending up personally involved in everything."

"Which is why it's so good," she said, beaming, "because I get the benefit of helping somebody."

"You also reap the not-so-nice benefit of getting in trouble and getting hurt all the time."

"That's true," she muttered. "But we can hope that, this time, it won't happen, right?"

Chapter 7

Monday Morning ...

THE NEXT MORNING she woke up to a text message from Mack.

Check your email.

With joy, she hopped up, checked her phone for her email and realized he'd sent her the file on Hinja's missing niece. Doreen raced through her shower, quickly putting on the coffee, and, only then she sat down outside with her notes from the day before and with the file that he'd sent her. The only trouble was, it was too sparse. She groaned when she looked at the few pages in it and then sent him a text message. **Are you sure you didn't forget to send the rest of it?**

Nope, there's no information. Nobody saw anything. Nobody heard anything. She just didn't show up again.

Those cases are the worst.

He sent back a sad emoji. **Yes, for the family especially.**

She sighed. Of course, as a mother, the first thing you would do is wish you'd gone, arranged to pick up your daughter, or sent somebody else to pick her up because that single misstep cost you a lifetime of grief. Doreen shook her head, wondering at that, then sent a message. **No body, Mack?**

No body. So she is considered a missing person, not a dead person.

Exactly. Interesting.

But according to what Hinja had said in her notes about Bob Small, her niece was deceased. Doreen sent Nan a text. **How did Hinja know Annalise was dead? Her body was never found.**

Nan immediately texted back. **The psychic told her.**

Doreen stopped and stared. The corners of her lips kicked up because she knew Mack would not think much of that answer. She wished she could tell him in person, just so she could see his reaction. But she was running out of time, and she wanted to get into this as much as she could. Still, she couldn't wait, so she sent him a quick text. **Asked Nan how her friend knew her niece was deceased and apparently a psychic told her.**

Immediately a series of question marks returned as his response.

She chuckled and set her phone off to one side because, although she hadn't had any experiences with psychics, just the thought of them taking part in this investigation made Doreen smile. She wasn't one to judge. Maybe there was something to this psychic business after all.

Annalise certainly hadn't shown up again, and, according to the police file, she didn't have any credit cards. Back then cell phones weren't the norm, and probably most people couldn't afford one, especially for their teenager. Annalise hadn't been seen or heard from again. As a teen, she didn't have money to pull a disappearing act or the know-how to disappear so completely. Doreen feared Annalise had been kept captive all these years. A concept which made Doreen wince. Absolutely horrible. If it wasn't that, then maybe Annalise was dead.

Looking at these options, Doreen wasn't sure which was worse. If Annalise had disappeared, free and clear on her own, then maybe she was happily living her life somewhere. But she was only fifteen back then. It was pretty hard to imagine anybody that age having the guts, the knowledge, and the resources to disappear like that. Unless she was with an older man … Doreen frowned at that thought. Not wanting to give up or to lose track of some of these theories, she quickly wrote them down. They weren't great, but, as far as she was concerned, death was the most likely end, and that was just plain sad.

But how long ago did she die? Twenty-five years ago, Annalise was fifteen. She'd contacted her mom, as she left home to go to ballet, and, according to the ballet instructor, Annalise had been there for the entire session and had left as she always did afterward. The investigators had checked out the ballet instructor and the other students. Absolutely nobody had seen her beyond when she'd called out goodbye as she left.

They all had assumed Annalise had gotten home on her own, as the rest of them had. But Annalise hadn't contacted anybody since then. And none of the other students knew anything about her or where she'd gone. There had been no talk of a date or if anybody she knew had been acting weird or different. Even the ballet instructor had said in complete bewilderment, "Annalise was a straight-A student at school, and she was a perfect student in class here with us. She was a wonderful young lady. We have no idea what happened to her."

And that just made Doreen suspicious. Because somebody had to know something. According to the police notes, Annalise's girlfriend at the time hadn't had a clue where she'd gone either. The authorities retraced her steps, the path that she had walked all the time, and absolutely nothing had been left behind, like her school backpack or a sweater or anything to suggest that something bad had happened to her. It was as if somebody had just scooped her up and took her away.

Which, as Doreen thought about it, was probably exactly what had happened. Whether Annalise knew the person driving this supposed vehicle or not, the most likely scenario was that she got into a vehicle somehow, somewhere, and was driven away. But this disappearance happened twenty-five years ago. The internet was still a new phenomenon among public users in the 1990s, and the first social media sites were mostly blogging sites which began around 1999. So the social media that we know today was still a long way off back then, more than two decades earlier.

So all this made it really that much harder for Doreen to find out anything. According to the police report, they had checked with the school and her friends, who were the non-troublemaking kind. Annalise wasn't into drugs, booze, or boys.

Frustrated, Doreen sat back, looked up at Thaddeus, perched on the deck railing beside her at her hand-me-down table, and said, "Thaddeus, we don't have much to work with." He immediately walked over and stomped on her notes. She sighed. "That's not helping."

"Thaddeus is here," he said, as he reached down, pecking away at her notes.

"And that's really not helping," she said, snatching the papers out from under him. She quickly typed everything from her rough notes into her laptop and then turned to her basic notes she had typed up regarding the collection of articles regarding Bob Small. But why would somebody assume he was involved in Annalise's disappearance? A trail of some of his cases must have led to him finding Annalise.

Doreen reread her notes that she had already typed up much earlier. One note in there said that the missing girl's family wanted an investigation into Bob Small because he had been seen in Vancouver around the same time Annalise went missing. But that didn't mean that he was guilty. Out of the however-many-million people who lived on the Lower Mainland, not all were the kind you wanted to bring home for Sunday dinner with the family. As was true just about everywhere.

Bob Small might be rolling around, laughing his fool head off at having so many deaths attributed to him here, but that didn't make him guilty. Doreen had just started looking into the girl's disappearance, and, only as she sat here, studying her notes, did another thought come to her. She stared at her phone.

"It's a bad idea," she muttered. But she couldn't stop thinking about it. She had nothing else to really go on, and, if that was a pathway she could follow, then it's the one she needed to. With a sigh of resignation, knowing it would be the wrong thing to do, she texted Nan. **Do you know what psychic Hinja used?**

Nan immediately popped back with a name. **Marjorie.**

"Marjorie?" Doreen said out loud, as if she would know who that was. Seconds later her phone rang. She answered it right away. "Hi, Nan."

"Marjorie used to live here in the home," she said, "but, since her fame and fortune took off, she has her own place now."

"What fame and fortune?" Doreen asked cautiously.

"She has been right about so many things that people now pay her a lot of money to give them insight into cases."

"Ah, interesting," she said.

"She is not a fraud," Nan said. "Honestly I thought she was at the beginning too. She told me one of my lovers was cheating on me way back when. I was so angry at her—when I found out she was right—that I figured somebody must have told her. So I didn't have anything to do with her for years. But, over time, I forgave her for telling me the bad news. You know something? Honestly you should never tell people bad news because they just blame you anyway."

"Whoa, whoa, hang on a minute. What's this got to do with anything?"

"I'm getting there, dear," she said in exasperation. "Listen."

"I'm listening, Nan," Doreen said. "I'm still trying to figure out what this psychic woman told your friend Hinja and why."

"She told her that her niece was dead. That was simple. And this was so many years after she went missing. Everybody could figure that out, and, at the time, I kind of laughed at it and said, *Of course she is.* Obviously I didn't say that to Hinja. I mean, that would have just upset her, and I didn't want to do that."

"No, of course not," she said. "So then what?"

"Then Hinja left it for a while but went back to the psychic a while later and asked for more details. Marjorie said that the girl had been murdered by a serial killer."

"But did she have any proof of that?"

"See? That's the thing about psychics. They don't have proof. They can give you information, but they can't give you a lot of details, and they can't give you anything that is necessarily very helpful. That was always my problem with psychics," she said. "But, I mean, I admit that Marjorie has been correct on a few occasions."

"A few occasions? Like with you?"

"Yes," she said. "I told you about the one, so don't make me bring that up again. It's not very often that I've had men cheat on me, and, when it happens, it's not something I want to hash out again."

"No, of course not," Doreen said, surprised, "and I'm sorry it happened."

"It does happen. But he is dead and gone, and I'm still kicking, so who got the last laugh there?"

Doreen didn't even want to delve into that angle, so she said, "Okay, so back to your friend now."

"Fine," she said, "I didn't want to talk about Bob anyway."

"Bob? Please tell me that it wasn't Bob Small," she cried out.

"Who?"

"You said you didn't want to talk about Bob."

"No, you wanted to change the subject, so I'm not talking about Bob."

"Which Bob?"

After an odd silence, Nan said, "Are you feeling okay, dear?"

Doreen pinched the bridge of her nose. "Please just tell me that the Bob you are *not* talking about is not Bob Small of serial-killer fame."

"Oh my," Nan said, and she started to laugh. "It absolutely is not that horrific Bob Small."

With a heavy sigh of relief, Doreen sat back and muttered, "Whew, well, I'm certainly glad to hear that."

Nan giggled. "I would never go out with a serial killer."

"But it's not like you would know he's a serial killer," she said. "I mean, how would you know, right?"

"Surely I'd know something like that."

"Maybe not," Doreen said. "Nan, with some of these guys, it's pretty hard to tell who is good and who is bad anymore."

"That's because everybody has the ability to be both," Nan said in a definitive voice.

"I think that's quite true," Doreen said thoughtfully.

"It is true," Nan said. "You should listen to me more often."

"I always listen to you," she said affectionately.

"Ah, but not really," Nan said, "otherwise you would have understood this conversation."

At that, Doreen stopped and stared down at her phone. "You could be right there," she said, "because I'm still confused."

"Exactly," Nan said, in a cross tone of voice. "You really should pay more attention, so I don't have to repeat everything."

"I'm sorry, Nan," Doreen said in a small voice. "So please, what can you tell me?"

A moment of silence came, as the older woman regrouped her thoughts. "What I can tell you is this psychic woman said it was a serial killer in Vancouver, but he wasn't always in Vancouver."

"Meaning?"

"He was from here," Nan said in triumph.

"What?" Doreen said. "Are you serious?"

"Of course I'm serious," she said. "I thought I had it written down somewhere. I know when Hinja told me all of this, I wrote a bunch of it down because I didn't believe it, and I would try to disprove it. But I never could."

"You couldn't disprove that this serial killer was from here?"

"He was a long-haul trucker, so he drove a truck all around the province and the States. It's one of the reasons why they figure he's responsible for so many murders and why he kept getting away with it. Nobody was there to stop him. He was all alone. He didn't have any ties to anybody, and nobody was expecting him to show up at any particular time. He didn't have a family, so he had the perfect scenario for a serial killer."

"And you're talking about Bob Small now?"

"Yes, of course," Nan said. And then she sighed. "You really do need to get yourself some vitamins or something so you can keep up, dear."

Doreen raised one eyebrow, but she kept her mouth quiet. "So, what else, Nan?"

"That was the problem. Even though we knew that Bob Small had been through the Okanagan Valley, here in Kelowna and beyond, we didn't have any kind of record as to where he traveled and when."

"But, if he was a trucker, there should be logs of his trips. Do you have any idea of his movements?"

"Hinja had a copy of a logbook from somewhere," she said. "It should be in that basket there that you have."

"I don't think so," she said hesitantly, as she stood and walked to her desk, looking at the stuff still in the basket. "I took out all the newspaper articles and lined them up in a chronological manner to see what I could find. But honestly it's pretty hard to sort anything out. There's just not enough information."

"Well then, let's hope all that stuff is in her personal belongings coming my way."

"Any idea when that'll arrive?"

"Nope, not a clue," she answered cheerfully. "Maybe you should come down here and have some tea or something," she said. "It sounds like you need a break from whatever you're doing."

"Why is that?"

"I don't know, dear, but you do sound a little scattered," she said, her voice gentle. "Maybe all this stuff with Nick and Mack and Robin and Mathew is getting to you."

"It's definitely getting to me," she said, "but it's all at a standstill for the moment."

"I don't think you told me about that," she said. "What do you mean by *at a standstill*?"

Doreen headed back out to her deck, settled at her table again, as she brought Nan up to date on what had happened.

"Wow," Nan said. "You need to come down and have tea. I'll expect you in ten minutes."

And, with that, she hung up.

Chapter 8

DOREEN STARED DOWN at the phone in her hand. "Why is everybody hanging up on me all of a sudden?" she muttered. The fact that she hung up on Mack wasn't the same as everybody else hanging up on her. Besides, Mack was expecting it from her. It was part of their relationship. She frowned at that because, in a way, it was part of their courtship.

If she were honest, that was the right word for it. She was also a little confused as to how she felt about the whole thing. But what she knew for sure was that, if anything happened to Mack, she would be devastated. And she didn't want that to happen. But it did leave her feeling fairly confused about her future. Not to mention her present.

Mack was a main part of her life right now, yet, somehow, she didn't even know how he came to be there. She'd been determined to keep everybody away and to have nothing to do with marriage or men anymore, having lost as much as she had in her first marriage. But here she was, already embroiled in something, and it got to her.

Confused, sad, and worried, she got up, gathered all her things, and returned to the kitchen. Her animals followed, without Doreen urging them to. "Come on, guys. If there is one thing I know, when Nan gives an edict, we follow, so let's go have tea."

Mugs immediately barked, heading for the back door again. She said, "Let's go to the front," but he was at the back door, insisting.

She grabbed his leash, looked over at Goliath and Thaddeus, and asked, "Are you guys coming?"

Thaddeus immediately said, "Coming, coming, coming, coming."

"I'm glad to hear that," she said. "Do you have any idea where we're going though?"

"Going to Nan's, going to Nan's, going to Nan's."

She stopped and stared. "I don't get it," she said. "Sometimes you're the most intelligent bird I've ever seen, like right now, and other times you act like you're not even there."

He gave a harsh cackling laugh that sounded like a *ha-ha-ha* sound and drove her crazy. She stared at him and said, "Again, that almost sounds like you meant that."

"*Ha, ha, ha,*" he said, laughing yet again.

She groaned and said, "Let's go. Maybe I am going crazy. Maybe Nan's right, and I do need to get down there to her place and find some sanity again."

They'd barely been outside for a few moments when she wished she had brought a sweater. She stared at the sky that was suddenly turning dark, then looked at the animals and said, "We'll run for it. Otherwise we'll get soaked."

There hadn't been much rain since she had come to the Okanogan Valley. As she flew down the pathway with the animals in tow, she hit the corner at a half run, while the wind picked up. She saw Nan, sitting on her patio, underneath the little protective balcony, waiting for her. She waved a hand in greeting, as Doreen raced across the lawn and jumped under the shelter of the patio. "You realize I'll have to go home in the rain," she said.

"That's okay," Nan muttered. "A little bit of water won't hurt you."

"Says you," she said, with a smile. "Nan, I need to speak with Marjorie. Do you have her last name or her address?"

Nan frowned. "You know what? I don't have an address and I don't think I ever knew her last name. It's a psychic thing, one name, more mystery."

"Can you ask around here? See if anybody else has more info?"

"Of course." Nan nodded. "I've made tea, dear," she said, pointing to the patio table, already set with plates and silverware. "Now come and sit down. You need to relax. You're sounding very overwrought these days."

"I was feeling very relaxed and calm earlier," she protested.

"You didn't sound that way."

"Yeah? Well, maybe I'm just confused."

"Confused about what?" Then she stopped, turned her eyes wide in delight. "Mack?"

Doreen glared at her grandmother. "I didn't say that."

"No, but you didn't say you're not, so that's a good sign."

Feeling that the world had gone crazy and that everybody was talking in strange languages around her, Doreen decided to ignore Nan. "What I'm trying to figure out," Doreen said, "is when you'll get the information from your friend's estate."

"I won't know until it gets here, will I?" she said. "It would be foolish to even try to anticipate it."

"I get it," she said, "but waiting is hard."

She laughed and laughed. "You have no idea," she said. "Waiting is almost impossible, but you're young, and waiting is harder for you than it is for a lot of people."

"And why is that?" she asked Nan.

"Because you don't have any patience in your life. You don't realize that life is a process, and instead you're all about the end goal."

Doreen stared at her in surprise. "Am I?"

"You are," she said. "You're always trying to solve something or do something or get somewhere."

"That's interesting," she muttered. "I thought I was all about relaxing and doing nothing."

"Apparently not," Nan said, with a light laugh. "Because all I ever see is that you're worried about the tomorrows and not so much focused on enjoying the todays."

"The todays are kind of hard," she said. "Tomorrows always look better."

"And that again is a sign of youth. A sign of somebody who hasn't learned patience."

"And here I thought I was doing so much better."

"You are," Nan said. "I didn't say you weren't. I'm just saying that you still need a little more practice at it."

She groaned and said, "Fine. I'll try to be patient as we wait for this package."

Nan burst out laughing. Just then came a knock on her front door. She looked at Doreen and said, "I'll be right back."

She headed inside, leaving Doreen sitting here on the patio. She reached down and gently patted Mugs and Goliath, who, after an enthusiastic greeting with Nan, had settled right down. "You guys like being this close, don't you?"

Mugs woofed. Goliath just rubbed his head into her hand, looking for cuddles. Thaddeus had taken a perch at the table, his face into the wind, catching just a corner of it as it whipped around the patio. She looked out to see the storm arrive and to see the rain coming down amid a heavy crash of thunder and lightning. "Wow, that came out of nowhere."

Just then Nan walked back onto the patio, and she had a box with her.

"Your mail delivery?" Doreen asked curiously.

Nan nodded. "Apparently you have fortuitous timing because this is from her estate."

Doreen looked at her grandmother in surprise. "Seriously?" Nan nodded but was obviously a little overwhelmed. Doreen realized with a wince that this was still a very emotional time for her. "I'm so sorry you didn't get a chance to speak with your friend again," she said to Nan.

"Me too. It would have been lovely. We were quite close for a very long time. She was devastated over the loss of her niece."

"Of course she was. I'm sorry that she won't be around to hear any answers."

"I firmly believe she'll be up there, watching you," she muttered. "She always believed you would make the right decision someday."

"What's the right decision?" she asked, staring at Nan.

"Leaving Mathew of course. I told her a couple times how I thought you were close, but it never seemed to happen."

Doreen winced, looked at her own plate, which was empty, and asked, "Why did you bring out plates?"

Nan looked at her own plate and said, "Oh my." She hopped up, put the box on her plate on the table, and disappeared inside. When she came back out, she carried a plate of something sliced. Immediately Doreen's stomach grumbled.

"Are you hungry, Doreen?"

"You know me," she said, as she leaned forward to study what Nan brought out. "Zucchini bread?"

"No, this is a banana and zucchini cake," Nan said, with a shrug. "I couldn't decide what to make."

"So you made both?" she asked, laughter in her voice.

"Why not?" she said. "I think I even threw pineapple in there."

"So this is a banana, zucchini, and pineapple bread?"

Nan stared at the bread for a minute and added, "You know what? I might have thrown carrots in too."

Hesitantly Doreen leaned forward to sniff it, then shrugged and said, "It smells good."

"Of course it smells good," she said. "I made it. Just don't ask me what it's called."

"How about Sunday mash-up?" Doreen muttered.

"That'll work, except it's not Sunday, dear." With that, Nan snagged a piece for herself, put it on her plate, and broke up a bit. She held out a little bit to Thaddeus, putting it on the table in front of him, and even he sniffed it, looked at her, and then sniffed it a couple more times.

"Oh, for heaven's sakes," Nan said, "it's perfectly edible," and she popped a bite into her mouth.

Doreen decided to be brave and picked up a slice, put it on her plate, and took a bite. She sat here, thinking about it. "It definitely has a little bit of this and a little bit of that," she said. "But, all around, it's not that bad."

"Of course it's not," Nan said. She pushed off her own plate and looked at Doreen. "It's good, isn't it?"

"It is," she said. "I'm pleasantly surprised."

"You just need to have a little faith."

"Maybe," she said, then nodded toward the box. "Will you open that, or do you need some time?"

Nan sighed. "Probably nothing in it is of any value. It'll just be all kinds of memories that'll bring on the tears, and I don't do tears well."

"So you want to leave it until later?"

"No, there'll be less tears if you're here," she said. She got up and grabbed a knife from the kitchen, then came back and cut the packing tape. As soon as it was open, she flipped up the top of the cardboard box. Meanwhile Doreen removed their plates to make some space. Out came a smaller box, containing a small packet of notebooks and a packet of letters. Nan stared at the letters. "Wow," she said. "I'm not exactly sure what this is all about."

"Could it be love letters?" Doreen asked.

"I don't know about love letters," Nan said. "I don't remember my friend ever being the kind of person to send them, much less to get things like that."

"But we're all a little different when we're younger," Doreen said.

"Very true, very true. I even sent a few love letters in my day," she said, then looked inside the smaller box and said, "That's all of it. A pack of letters and a pack of notebooks."

"Let's take a closer look," Doreen said. "May I?" she asked, and she reached over for the pack of notebooks.

"Absolutely," Nan said. "I don't have a clue what any of this is or why they would send it to me. Is there no personal note?"

In between the notebooks was a note for Nan. Doreen took it out and handed it to her, then unwrapped the binding on the stack of notebooks. They were all small, like six-by-eight. She flicked through the first one and said, "This one sounds like it's from her marriage."

"That's possible," Nan said. "She always kept diaries."

"I've never understood the diary thing myself," Doreen said. "Never understood the appeal."

"I think they do it in order to not forget," Nan said.

"Maybe," Doreen said, then flicked through the next one. "This is about having her children."

"That sounds like her."

"Why would her family think this would be of interest to you though?"

"I have no idea," Nan said. "It's quite possible that her family had no clue what to do with it, and she may have asked them to send everything to me." As Nan flipped open the folded letter addressed to her, she nodded and said, "Oh, yes, here it is in the letter. She told them that whatever they didn't know what to do with that they should send to me. Because I always knew what to do with stuff."

After a moment of silence, Nan laughed, shaking her head. "We used to joke about it. She'd call me up and say, *I don't know what to do with this or that*, and I'd tell her what to do with it."

"That makes a certain amount of sense. So what will you do with all this stuff?" Doreen asked.

"I don't know," Nan said. "Is anything there of any value?"

"Of value, not really, but obviously there are some things of interest."

"Right, and of course *interest* is a very different thing

than *value*," Nan replied.

"Right," Doreen replied. Then she flipped through the third notebook and said, "Did she have two kids?"

"Yes, she did."

"This is on the second one, the pregnancy, and the birth."

"Ha," she said. "Nobody'll want those. Having kids was never my thing. One was enough."

"Maybe she thought you would enjoy experiencing it through her."

"Maybe. You never really know what people think sometimes," she said, shaking her head, as she looked at the notebooks. "Anything of interest there?"

"Maybe, or maybe not," Doreen said, as she got to the last one. "Ah," she said, "this one is on her niece."

"Good. That'll be the one that we want to look at," Nan said.

And, with that, Doreen opened to the first page, winced, and said, "This is the day Annalise went missing."

"Perfect, so that'll have all the information she collected then," Nan said. "I remember her carrying a notebook around." She looked at it, nodded, and said, "You know what? I think that was the one."

"What about those letters?" Doreen asked.

"I'm not exactly sure yet because I'm not sure what they are," she said. "Do you want to go through that journal first?"

"Do you mind if I take it home, so I can match it up with the notes I have at home?"

"No, not at all. That makes sense. I really don't want to know too much about Bob Small's serial-killing life anyway."

With that, Doreen tucked it into her pocket and said,

"Now, what about the letters?"

"I don't know," Nan said, looking at them. "I'm not really sure what to do with somebody's letters, written for only a particular person to see, especially if these are love letters. Seems too personal, too invasive to read them. And I'm her friend. Just think what her children may have thought?"

"May I take a look?" Nan nodded and handed the stack over. "They're all addressed to one person," Doreen said, "and she just calls him B." Doreen winced. "Please tell me that Hinja didn't have a relationship with Bob Small."

"Of course not," Nan said. "Why would she do that?"

"I don't know, but maybe Bob Small found his victims through other people's family and friends."

"Now that would be horrible," Nan said, staring at her. "You mean, have a relationship with Hinja and then steal her niece?"

"It happens all the time," Doreen said quietly. "If he was a trucker, he wouldn't be around much, so I don't know how your friend would have gotten to know him very well."

"She had separated from her husband, not long after the second child was born. She was pretty mixed up for a long time. She did have some pretty wild and terrible relationships," Nan said, staring in horror at the stack of letters in front of her. "I sure hope it's not who you're thinking it is."

"I hope not too. But it would explain why Hinja thinks Bob Small had something to do with Annalise going missing. Maybe something's in here about that."

"Love letters from the dead," Nan said, with a shiver. "That would make for a terrible horror movie."

"Maybe some terrible truths are in here too," Doreen said.

Nan's phone rang. She looked at it and then laughed in delight. "You can take it all home with you," she said. "I don't think I really want to get too close to some of that. I'd like to have a few memories of my friend that aren't tarnished by thinking she was with that guy."

"How about I go through them, and I'll tell you some of what I find?"

"Yes, you do that," she said. "Meanwhile I'm off to play poker."

"Nan," Doreen said in a warning voice.

She looked at her granddaughter. "Ah, don't worry about it," she said. "It'll help take my mind off all that." She pointed at the letters in Doreen's hand. "And you don't want me dwelling on that. It's just very sad. This will make me happy today. So, go off and do your thing, and I'll talk to you tomorrow."

With that, Nan got up and rushed Doreen forward to the patio's edge. It was unlike Nan to be in this much of a hurry to get rid of them, and Doreen said, "Nan, you're worrying me. What's this all about?"

"I'm just feeling upset," she said. "It's been an upsetting day."

"Okay, I'm sorry," she said. "Love you lots." She stepped out into the rain, hating that she would walk home in it. She looked at the animals and said, "Time to run, guys." And they picked up the pace and raced all the way back home again.

Chapter 9

AS SOON AS Doreen got home, she walked in through the back door, only to hear Mack calling out from the front door. She walked through and opened up the front door to find him standing there, a big pizza in his hand. She stared at him in surprise. "Hi. Where'd you get the pizza from?"

"I just ran by and grabbed it," he said. "I can't stay long, but I figured you probably hadn't eaten."

"Depends on if you call *eating* trying Nan's banana-carrot-pineapple-zucchini bread."

He stared at her in horror, but she shrugged. "Nan was a little confused today. She made all that in the same loaf, though honestly it wasn't half bad." He stared at her, as if she had just said something terrible. "I get it," she said. "It's not anything I would normally eat, but it was okay. I did only have one piece though."

"Yeah, I wonder why," he muttered.

She laughed. "Besides, I'm always happy to see food."

"Good," he said. "I know that it's early, but I figured, since I had to go back to my office for a few more hours, this would be a good way to get a bite to eat."

"Perfect," she said, leading the way to the kitchen.

He looked at her and asked, "Did you just come in?"

"Yeah, I came in the back way in the pouring rain," she said, still holding the box she'd gotten from Nan.

"What's all that?"

"Huh," she said. "You won't believe it." She explained, as she got out plates and put on hot coffee.

He asked, "Seriously?"

"Yeah, it looks like it may be love letters and some other stuff," she said, downplaying what was in the box. "I don't know exactly what it is yet—or why anybody would keep a love letter. I understand while you're alive maybe," she said, "but I wouldn't want whoever reading any love letters of mine."

"Your heirs must get rid of it," he said.

"In this case I guess Hinja told them to send everything to Nan."

"That's interesting. I wonder why."

"Apparently Hinja always talked to Nan before doing stuff. So, whenever she had a question about what to do with something, Nan would tell her."

At that, Mack burst out laughing.

"What?" Doreen said.

"It's just bizarre enough to be true," he said, "but why would the family burden Nan with that?"

"Maybe they thought she'd be happy to see it all."

"Maybe," he shrugged and opened up the pizza box. Lifting up two big pieces, he put one on each plate. "There you go," he said. "That's a start."

"And a good start it is," she said enthusiastically, as she immediately took a bite. "I hadn't realized how hungry I was, until I had a piece of that odd bread that Nan made."

"I still can't believe she poured everything into the same recipe."

"I doubt she's the first person to do it," she said. "And I seriously don't know if it was intentional or like an experiment or if she honestly just forgot what she was making."

"In Nan's case it could be any of the above," he said.

"How are things going for you? The case and all?" she asked him.

"What case?" he said smoothly.

She glared at him. "You can't hide forever, you know."

"I can try," he said, with a cheeky grin.

She sighed. "It would be so much easier if you'd just share."

"And it would be so much easier if you'd stay out of that part of my world," he said, wiggling his eyebrows at her.

She really had no answer for that, so she sat in quiet contemplation, enjoying her pizza. "This is really good," she said, with a happy sigh. "You know what? Even though I haven't starved, I worried that maybe I would, when I ended up single. I did have a really rough couple months," she said. "But rather than starving, I think you've taken over the job of feeding me."

"Is that so bad?" he asked.

"Maybe not," she said, "but I do feel guilty about it sometimes."

"No need," he said, "because you'll make me dinner tonight." When his phone buzzed with a text, he glanced at it and added, "At least I hope I can get here."

"Oh, yeah, I'm supposed to cook stir-fry by myself, right?"

"Yep, you sure are," he said. "You are still up for it, right?"

"Absolutely," she said, with a grin. "I'd like to learn how to make that because I really like my veggies."

"Good," he said. He took another piece of pizza, looked at his watch, and groaned. "I can eat this, and I probably won't have time for any more."

She pulled the box closer to her. "That's okay," she said. "I can help you out with that."

He laughed and laughed. She just grinned. "Have you heard from my brother?"

"No. Am I supposed to?" she asked, looking down at the pizza and realizing her stomach was suddenly souring at the thought of more.

"Nope, not necessarily," he said. "I'm just making sure everything is on the up-and-up."

"Me too," she said. "The good news is that, even though I haven't heard from him, I also haven't heard from Mathew."

"You're right. That is the good news. On the other hand," he said, "you definitely have paperwork that needs to be settled."

"What about Robin? Is that all locked up?"

"They're investigating the ex-husband, James, right now," he said, "but that'll be Vancouver's issue, not ours."

"Right, except that he killed her here."

"Yep, but now they are dealing with the older crimes down there. His parents and all."

"He should be made to pay, no matter what."

"He will," he said, "but he doesn't need to be held here, if they have other issues that they need him to deal with down there first. And this case will just add to the pile."

"I guess it doesn't really matter, does it? As long as he goes to trial."

"Absolutely," he said. Mack stood, grabbed a napkin, and wiped his hands and face. "I really would like to stay and have coffee, but—" And his phone buzzed again.

"You're really busy, huh?"

"Always," he said, "since you hit town anyway." Then he laughed and added, "But I'm glad you came."

"Thank you," she said. "That's the nicest thing you've ever said to me."

He looked at her in surprise. "Seriously?"

She shrugged. "Most of the time you're yelling at me."

"But I don't always mean it," he said in a worried tone, and she flashed him a grin.

"I know," she said. "I was just bugging you."

He rolled his eyes, then leaned over, kissed her on the temple, and said, "Now stay safe." And, with that, he was gone.

She reached a hand up to her temple and thought about his words and where they were heading and grinned. If he were still around, she'd have said something to him, but the witty repartee was out of her hands now. At the moment she didn't have a clue what she would have said, and she was still stunned that he'd kissed her. Not that it was a real kiss or anything, but it was hardly something to ignore either. It said a lot about the progression of their relationship.

She sighed and cleaned up the table, surprisingly full after two large pieces of pizza. With enthusiasm and a fully empty table, she got out her laptop and her notes and started in on Hinja's notebook about her niece, Annalise. Even as Doreen read the first page of the notebook, her gaze kept going to the letters. Finally she sighed and said, "Fine, letters first."

She opened the first one, realizing none had envelopes,

and read it. It was a sloppy mess about how Hinja had finally found the true love of her life. It was both tender and endearing. The second was similar; the third one was similar, yet the tone changed over time. In each of the subsequent letters, Hinja worried that her lover wasn't faithful. Complaining about long absences and slow responses on letters. All the letters were address to a Bob—or just to *B* at times. Underlying Doreen's suspicion that Bob Small was Hinja's lover.

But then again, this was *snail mail* versus email, and Doreen didn't think anything happened very fast in the mail back then. By the time she got toward the end of this stack, the letters were very different. Hinja was hurling accusations at Bob and asking if he'd done something to hurt her by hurting her niece. Of course Doreen found no written replies.

That was the odd thing about these letters. There were no replies from Bob; they were all one-sided. And, as Doreen looked at this collection of letters, she realized that somehow Hinja still had these letters. Doreen found no letters written to Hinja from her beloved. So how had Hinja gotten these letters that she'd sent to Bob Small back again? Was there a response anywhere? And if not, why not?

Bob could have marked the envelopes Return to Sender. Is that why Doreen found no envelopes? Why would Hinja have just her letters that she'd sent him? It made no sense and just deepened the mystery. Although Doreen wondered if the poor woman wrote them but never sent them. Like some kind of release, getting closure, without confronting Bob. Even so, after all these years, why would she keep these letters that, if she read and reread them, would just fester all those negative emotions and feelings?

Why?

Chapter 10

THE QUESTIONS WERE piling up, but the answers were not. Frustrated, Doreen set the letters down for the umpteenth time, then looked at her notes and shrugged. "All I have written down," she said aloud to the animals apparently, "is that she had a growing suspicion that her lovely boyfriend, who she thought was the best, may have had something to do with her niece's disappearance. But she offers no proof, and she saved no letters *from* him, no responses at all to confirm or to deny her suspicions. So, of course, none of this is very helpful and doubly frustrating because so little was here."

Putting the letters back into a bundle, Doreen returned them to the box and went back to the notebooks again, that had served as Hinja's journals. Doreen went through every page of the first one, going quickly, but, at the same time, trying to be thorough. But again, it was just about Hinja's personal life way back when. Dropping the first journal back in the box, Doreen went through the second and then the third.

By the time she got to the fourth, which was the one that she knew had the good stuff in it, she had a rhythm to the woman's mind-set. How Hinja thought and how she wrote. Just a simple case of jotting down something before it disappeared from her brain. It would be interesting to ask Nan just what it was that Hinja had died from. It might explain some of her disjointed thoughts. Then again, if somebody were to analyze Doreen's own notes at some point in time, they might look the same. Everybody had a different system that worked for them.

Doreen worked her way through the last journal again and saw that the relationship with Bob had been a huge high for Hinja. She'd fallen in love with this trucker, who traveled all the time. As long as he kept stopping in to see her, when he was back in town, that was enough for her. Apparently they did everything together, when he was here. He stayed with her; they went out for dinners and breakfasts, and, other than that, spent a lot of time in her bedroom.

Doreen thought that was interesting because it was like he came for a roadside stop—like a sailor home on leave—and then left again on a job. Or maybe he didn't? For all Doreen—and obviously Hinja—knew, he had a dozen women like this at various stops across the country. Sometimes he was out trucking for weeks on end.

According to the journal, they kept in touch all the time, or at least as much as they could. He used to phone once a week and more often, if possible. Of course Doreen didn't have copies of their phone bills to see if that could be confirmed. She had no concrete reason to doubt it, and, being so long ago, she had absolutely no way to find that information which would make much difference at this point. Either he had called Hinja or he hadn't. Without his phone records Doreen had no way to check if he'd called anybody else or not.

As Doreen reached the end of the journal, she read about how Hinja found out that sometimes Bob was in town longer than the time he spent with her, and she became suspicious about what he was doing. There was talk about another woman disappearing in a neighboring town a few weeks earlier, and he'd said something odd. Something about her being a pretty little thing. At that, Doreen put down the journal and scrambled for the newspaper clippings in her basket. She pulled out an article, setting it on the table beside her.

Shortly prior to Hinja's niece's disappearance, there had been another young woman, eighteen years old, who had disappeared in a similar manner and in the nearby area. This brunette had curls, the kind that languished all around her shoulders, framing her face and giving her quite an angelic appearance. Again Doreen had absolutely zero information about this particular woman's disappearance, other than what this one article said, and her body had never been found.

"Gone from Abbotsford" was the title of the article, and the journal continued with Hinja's related notes.

> *I didn't want to think about such a thing, but his tone of voice made me wonder. There was just such an admiration, almost a faint lost-love look about his eyes. I asked if he had ever met her, and he shook his head and quickly covered up, saying that he had seen her photo on TV. And, of course, that was quite possible because that's where I had seen it myself. I didn't say anything to him, as I didn't know what to say. I mean, what could I say?*
>
> *It was just such a strange thing, the way he seemed so raptly intent on her features. He even mentioned the*

curls on her shoulders. I did mention at the same time that my niece had a similar hairstyle. He looked quite interested and said that he hadn't realized so many women had curly hair. I told him that a curling iron made even the straightest of hair look like ringlets. He didn't seem to understand what that was, so I showed him mine.

He was quite fascinated at the idea. When I realized that my curling iron had disappeared at the same time as when he headed out on his next trip, I thought something strange was going on. For the longest time I thought maybe I'd just misplaced it, but, after I turned the house upside down, I found absolutely nothing except the irrefutable conclusion that, if my curling iron were nowhere else, it was in his possession. But why the devil would he want a curling iron?

Doreen sat back and wondered the same thing herself. Was it a fetish? Now that he knew he could make curls like that, would he start using the curling iron? But on what? Dolls, dogs, horses, women? She found no mention of Bob requesting that Hinja curl her hair into ringlets like that, but apparently that's where his fascination was.

On that note, Doreen got up and shuffled through the photographs in her basket. Sure enough, almost every woman pictured had curls. Whether they were natural or contrived, all the photos that Doreen had were of women with curls, except for one. She pulled that one up and took a look at it. Just because they had curls at one moment doesn't mean they had curls all the time, especially by the time a photo was taken for the police.

In the write-up on this woman, it said that she had blond curly hair, but, in the picture, she sported a ponytail.

Putting the photo down again, Doreen made mention in her own notes.

> *Serial killer after curly hair. Fascinated with curling iron, not understanding that curls could be created if not naturally inherited.*

She kept reading to see that Hinja's suspicions had continued for a few more weeks. She did see Bob one more time, but his phone calls were less frequent. She got a little worried about it and asked him if he was tired of her. The only response she got was, "No, not at all."

"But I'm not seeing you very much," she replied.

"I just have other things happening right now," he said.

Nothing confirmed that a problem existed, but, for Hinja, nothing else was happening between them, and that was an issue in itself. She didn't know what to say or how to get him back, and then, as time went on, she wondered why she even wanted to. He wasn't even basically attractive. He was huge; he was gaunt and, in many ways, rough around the edges.

Yet she was still attracted to him, and it bothered her a lot because he didn't want her now. So it was much harder for her to separate from him. All in all, the whole thing was very distressing to Hinja. The journal went on and on, with more and more of her complaining about him and about what she was seeing and not seeing.

What was interesting to Doreen was that it had gone from true love to this nasty spiral, where Hinja wrote things like: *What did I ever see in him? Why would I ever want to go out with him? He obviously doesn't care; he obviously doesn't like me.* Then it spiraled into more negative self-loathing for having gone out with him in the first place.

Doreen found that both sad and depressing because Hinja had no reason to have such self-hate over something like that, but that's what Hinja had gone to. But then she mentioned him stopping by again, and she had been so excited to see him, only to find out he was collecting some belongings he had left behind.

Doreen read out loud.

I let him inside to get a few things from the bathroom that he had kept there. It was very depressing to see that this relationship, which I'd held such high hopes for, resulted in the end of it, something so quickly over. When he grabbed his bathroom stuff and a small envelope, I asked him what was in it.

He just looked at it, shrugged, and said, "It's mine."

"Yours?" I asked.

"Yep, mine," he said briskly, as he turned to walk away.

I reached out and snagged the envelope from his hand, and the response was instantaneous. He turned around in a fury and belted me across the face.

Doreen gasped when she read that. She put down the journal and stared out the window. For somebody to turn around with that kind of brutality meant that it was always there, and he'd just kept it hidden.

Reading on, Doreen continued in the journal.

I burst into tears and didn't know what to say. I was so stunned. The envelope had dropped to the ground, and I saw some photos sticking out. Girls, girls with curls. I didn't know who they were or what they meant to Bob, but he quickly snatched them up, glared at me, and said, "Damn good thing that didn't open." Then he turned and walked out.

This time he walked out of my life. But he didn't walk out of my mind. All I could think about was that envelope, wondering if that's why I didn't appeal to him anymore. Because I didn't have curls. I would have gone to the curling iron on a daily basis if I'd realized that's all it took. But it did disturb me because I thought I recognized one of them. I thought that maybe it was the girl from Abbotsford, who had disappeared those few weeks ago.

But how could he have gotten her photo? Except that the newspapers were full of them, only this didn't look like newsprint. I hesitated for a long time, wondering what I was supposed to do with this information, if anything. Then I realized that him hitting me had been more than effective. The bottom line was that I was now terrified to face him or to do anything that could bring that wrath on me again.

I know that it was cowardly and foolish and that I should have gone to the police, but I didn't have anything solid. I didn't have any proof. I didn't have anything.

Doreen read, her voice dropping to a painful whisper. "Oh my," she said to Thaddeus. "It is haunting to even read this. To think that Bob's photos were all just sitting with this poor woman's things."

She sent Nan a quick text, asking if her friend had ever married again. Nan came back with a response quickly.

No, never. She hated men. I always wondered if she was afraid of them. I don't know really. She wouldn't

even go out partying with me. It was very strange.

After reading that, Doreen looked at the journal and said, "No, not really. It's very understandable. That poor woman."

As Doreen read on, she found only a few more pages left, and the next section was about the disappearance of her niece, and the pain and torment she was going through, trying to help her sister find her daughter. Doreen found more and more emotional writing and short phrases.

How could anyone do anything to that beautiful girl? She is so special. Why would anybody want to hurt her?

When Doreen got to the very last page, Hinja finally spoke her mind.

This is the only time I'll put it down, and it's something I'll have to live with. But what if… What if it was Bob? What if he and his collection of curly-haired girls and my mention of my niece are connected? What if… What if… Oh, my God, this thought is absolutely so horrible. What if he took her?

The writing in the journal ended. Blank pages followed after that, but Hinja never wrote any more in it. Did she ever tell the cops? That was the question. Doreen went to the case file, but very little else was there. The authorities interviewed everybody they knew to interview, but Doreen found nothing saying that the aunt had stepped forward with this information. "I wonder if she felt that Bob would come back on her, which he might have, because those photographs and the mention of her niece would have given the police something to go on. That would have given them a suspect.

Or did Hinja go to the cops later, as in much later, and many more girls were gone?" Just then her phone rang.

"So, what are you doing that you're asking these questions?" Nan asked, without any hello.

"I was going through Hinja's journal and her collection of the articles," she said. "The letters just show a woman in love in the beginning, then on through to the breakdown of the relationship," she said. "The journal is a whole lot more interesting, and she did end up suspecting Bob, the man she had a relationship with, of choosing her niece because of her curly hair. Hinja saw an envelope with a series of other photos, but not clearly enough to identify anything but the fact that the women in the photos that she saw had curly hair. Apparently, at some point, Bob also took a curling iron from her place."

After silence on the other end, then Nan whispered, "So that's what bothered her."

"Bothered her how?"

"She was haunted, haunted by it, haunted by him. She wouldn't go out with any other men. She didn't trust any men. The loss of her niece tore her up terribly."

"When you consider it," Doreen said, "I find absolutely no sign that she went to the cops about it."

"I think she did. Much later. Too late though," she said. "That's something that she needed to have done right away."

"Yes, but she didn't," Doreen said. "Did you ever ask her what haunted her?"

"Of course, my dear, over and over again. Finally she told me to just stop and that she wouldn't tell me anything and that the whole thing was her own private hell she'd made for herself and that she had absolutely no absolution from it."

"Ouch," Doreen said. "That's got to be rough. To think that you're responsible for something that you'll pay a penalty for."

"I think that's why she was terrified of death. She never could reconcile the fact that she wouldn't pay for some wrong, but I never understood that this is what she was talking about."

"It is pretty climactic. When you think about it, a tremendous amount of pain had to be associated with losing your niece, and Hinja cared about her a great deal."

"Yes, indeed. Everybody did, really. She was a beautiful girl and one of those very open, caring kinds."

"And that just made it all the worse. It's one thing if you detest somebody, but, if you absolutely love somebody, that makes it all that much harder."

"It was terrible for Hinja back then, made even worse when her sister committed suicide. That just added to the pain."

"Oh, Nan," Doreen said, wincing, "that must have been awful for her. Worse even because then she would carry the guilt for that as well. The thing is, all Hinja needed to do was come forward and talk to the cops. It may or may not have led to something. The thing is, because she didn't do it, we'll never know."

"Exactly," Nan said. "And it is sad, very sad. She used to always say that somebody had fooled her really badly and that he wasn't who she thought he was."

"That fits," Doreen said. "And to feel guilt for inadvertently leading a murderer to somebody you care about, that's a terrible burden."

Chapter 11

Monday Afternoon ...

DOREEN SPENT THE rest of the day, fussing with the bits and pieces that she'd learned, feeling a little guilty that she hadn't told Mack yet that Bob Small may have been from here—or maybe had lived here for a bit. She figured she'd tell him when she could confirm that.

When she checked the clock and realized it was almost time for Mack to arrive, she bolted to her feet and hauled out all the vegetables left by Mack in her fridge, washing them all first. She'd watched as he'd done the prep work for the stir-fry, but, at the same time, she wasn't sure about the sizes. She wanted to make sure that she was well and truly into this before he got here; otherwise it would look like she'd completely ignored it, which she had, but with good reason.

Thankfully she had remembered to take the chicken breasts out of the freezer earlier. She looked at them and realized she would have to slice them. She wrinkled her nose, never having had much exposure to raw meat, especially chicken, and she remembered all the warnings about it. Deciding to focus on the veggies instead, she got a knife and a large bowl and quickly worked away on them. She wasn't sure she was doing it right, but she was willing to bet she would at least get points for trying. Besides, how wrong could it be?

She chopped away and, at some point, realized she had cut the mushrooms too small and the cauliflower too big. She hoped it would be okay. Maybe it just had to do with how long it would take for something to cook. In that case, it could go in a little earlier. It made more sense that way, yet she didn't know how much earlier. The last thing she wanted was soft and soggy vegetables. By the time she heard him come in, she was staring at the chicken breasts, wondering how to get out of touching them.

He walked into the kitchen, greeting Mugs, who was absolutely overjoyed to see him. Mack took one look at her face and asked, "What is that look for?"

She again wrinkled up her nose and said, "The chicken."

"Oh, look at this," he said, with interest, as he walked forward, nodding with approval at the bowl of veggies. "Those look good."

"Yes, they do," she said, "but I have to deal with this." She pointed at the raw chicken with disdain.

"And that's not a problem," he said.

"It's just kind of gross looking," she said.

"That doesn't matter," he said firmly. "If you don't want to touch it, pick it up with paper towel, like this."

He wrapped a paper towel around the end of the fillet, laying it on the cutting board, and said, "You slice from this end."

"Oh," she said, "that makes it easier."

Working awkwardly, his eagle eye over her shoulder, she managed to slice it thin.

"See? You did that really well," he said proudly.

She stared at him. "I did a terrible job," she muttered.

He chuckled. "Come on. Don't be so hard on yourself. I think you did a great job. Remember. This is your first time ever to do this all on your own."

She shrugged and said, "You're such a great cheerleader."

"It's important to be positive in life," he said. "An awful lot of things we can't pick ourselves up from immediately because they knock us for such a loop. So make sure you always give yourself kudos for trying. And, in this case, celebrate your success."

"I forget to do that," she said quietly. "It seems to me that I'm always dealing with somebody laughing at me, or I'm laughing at myself."

"And that's not necessarily wrong. Come on," he said. "It all depends on whether the laughter is nasty or not. If you're mocking yourself, that's not good, but, if you're making light of something because you tried and failed, that's a whole different story."

"But how do you tell the difference?" she said. "My ex was mocking where I live, how I live."

"Do you care about him?"

"No, of course not," she said, frowning at Mack. "Why would you even ask that?"

"If you don't care about him, then why do you care about his opinion?"

That made her jaw drop and then close slowly. "I shouldn't care, should I?" she said slowly. "But it's hard somehow, especially when I hear all the refrains of my history running through my mind."

"Refrains where he was mocking you for being you? That's not good either," he said. "Just remember. You don't have to accept his opinion. He is nobody to you."

She chuckled. "I like the sound of that. But somehow I don't think he would."

"And again, it doesn't matter what he thinks, what he wants, or what he likes because it's none of his business. It's your life, and he's got nothing to do with anything in your world."

"No," she muttered, "that's quite true." She looked up at him. "Have you heard anything from Nick?"

He shrugged and said, "I figured you would hear first."

"I haven't heard anything," she said. "It's just—well, the silence, it's so odd."

"I don't know if he even wrote up a divorce agreement yet, did he?"

"I haven't seen one."

"So then I would presume he doesn't have a finished one to show you yet."

"Is he likely to?"

"Of course, but he has to figure out what assets your husband is trying to hide, so Nick can make sure that you get your fair share of them. Because no way your ex will agree to you getting half of anything that isn't listed. And, if you list some things and not others, you won't get your full compensation."

"Ah," she said, "so it's all about doing your due diligence to find out what he does and doesn't own."

"Something like that," he said, "but it's also hard because you don't want to take too long and give him time to hide things, but you also don't want to go so fast that you miss things and end up shortchanging yourself."

"Right," she said, as she finished slicing the chicken, then put it in the bowl and said, "I forgot what you did with it next."

"Now this is where you get to choose," he said, "depending on what you have for flavoring. We could do soy sauce. We could do lemon and ginger or even orange. We can do all kinds of stuff. It just depends on what flavors you like."

"I like everything so far," she said cautiously, "but I don't have lemon or ginger or oranges."

"In that case, it means we're limited to whatever we have then, right?" He went through her cupboards and said, "How about garlic? Are you up for that?"

"Sure," she said.

He brought out the electric wok, drizzled it with oil, and plugged it in. Then he pulled out the fresh garlic, and they mashed it together, both working on the cloves, as he said, "Now we'll add a little bit of these spices." He pulled spice containers from the cupboard.

She opened one and, following his instruction, sprinkled in spices all across the oil in the wok. "Isn't this kind of a lot?"

"It is," he said, "but sometimes it works. You have to watch the balance, but these are all complementary spices. These are used a lot in Asian cooking."

"Okay," she said. "I'm willing to try anything."

The smells grew in the pan, as they dumped in spices to sauté. She sniffed the air and said, "Wow, that's really potent."

"Is it ugly potent though?" he asked.

She shook her head. "No, it smells delicious."

"Good," he said, "so let's keep working on that then."

And now they dumped in bits of the garlic and then onions and then the meat. By the time the meat was cooked, he was giving her instructions on how to cook the veggies.

"Now look at the chopped ones that you've got there,"

he said. "These are thicker, and they'll take longer. Cauliflower always takes a little bit longer than broccoli. Carrots are the same, depending on how you sliced them. You got these really thin, but the cauliflower is a bit big, so let's do it in order."

And once again she strictly followed his instructions. By the time they were done, she stared at a potful of heavenly glazed smells. "This could grace any five-star restaurant around the world," she said in amazement. "It smells absolutely delicious."

"Sometimes it doesn't always look the best," he said, "depending on the colors of the spices or sauces that you've used. You know? Those various vegetables, if there are too many greens or browns or if you do a ton of cabbage or something, it won't always have that same look. But it's the smell to me—it's all about taste and aroma. The aroma gets your taste buds going, making a promise to your stomach that you really want to keep. Otherwise your stomach will feel like you cheated it this time."

With his help, she split the dinner onto two large plates and realized she'd cooked enough for leftovers. She looked over at him and said, "Do you want the same noodles?"

"Depends on how hungry you are," he said. "We didn't cook any rice, so you might want something a little more substantial with this."

"Right," she said. "We still have the noodles, so we'll just repeat that."

"That works for me," he said, with a smile. They pulled out the noodles and did a repeat of their last dish. They took their plates and drinks outside to the deck, sitting at her hand-me-down table and chairs.

"I really like this," she said, after she'd had several bites.

"The flavors are wonderful."

"Will you remember what you put in there?"

She laughed. "No, I certainly won't," she said. "I'd like to, but I don't think so."

He laughed. "Maybe you won't have to."

"Oh, I think I will," she said, "but I'll call you when it comes to that."

"And you're assuming I'll just remember what we put in," he said, laughing. "What you should do, right after dinner, is write it down."

"Oh, good point," she said. "I never even thought about that."

"Exactly," he said, "and that's the best way."

And that's what she did. By the time she was done, he was still working on a second plateful. So she grabbed a notepad, and, after some discussion, she wrote down the recipe. Satisfied and perfectly happy, she said, "That's the best thing that's happened all day."

He looked over at her, raised an eyebrow, and asked, "What's up?"

She shrugged. "It's just been pretty upsetting, going through Hinja's journals."

He said, "Tell me more." Doreen went on and explained everything she had found. He looked at her and said, "She didn't call the cops?"

She shrugged. "Nan says she did something about it later on, but I can't say that for sure. Nothing in the police file indicated Hinja did anything at the time, and, without telling what she knew, the authorities had no way to really do anything about her niece's disappearance."

"Why do you think that is?" he asked.

"I think it was fear," she said. "I think inside she knew,

and his threat, when he walked out, was something she took to heart. If she had seen those photos from the envelope, he may well have killed her. And, if she had turned him in, he would have come back on her too. He gave her the option to stay alive, and she took it."

"At the cost of her niece?" he asked incredulously.

"The question really is, would coming forward with that information have saved her niece, or was it already too late?"

"What about all the women who came afterward?" he asked. He shook his head and tried to mute the harshness of his tone. "We see it time and time again, and it's hard because you get, like a rape victim, who doesn't want to go through the entire ordeal of coming forward, accusing somebody and going through a trial. But what ends up happening is that the criminal runs free, and often they continue their behavior, so the number of victims just keeps on growing."

"You and I can see both sides of it," she said. "I'm not sure that I could go through a police investigation and trial on something like that either. I'm finding it difficult enough just dealing with my ex, and he never really hit me"—Mack glowered at her on that issue—"Okay, not continually, so I already know that he isn't *that* dangerous."

Mack snorted at that. "Yet he had you kidnapped by his goon Rex. Mathew's dangerous alright. You're still under his thumb, at least mentally, not completely out from under his influence. And that could get you really hurt because you go out to dinner with this guy, who, for all you know, committed murder himself or via another goon."

Doreen shifted uneasily. He wasn't wrong but it was hard to hear.

"So stop talking to him, texting him, answering the door

when he's there. Keep your doors locked. Set the security alarm. Call Nick and me if anything happens." When she remained frozen, he continued, "Doreen, did you hear me?"

"Yes," she said, nodding.

"I mean it, Doreen. Your actions have bad consequences sometimes, and I really hate to scare you, but I'd rather that than having to ID somebody I know in the morgue," he said, his voice softening. "And I understand how difficult it can be to speak up, but it's very frustrating for us when we see a criminal, like this Bob Small, let off because people won't testify against them. And the killers come back to repeat their crimes again and again. So, not only are we dealing with the one victim who has no leads for us, but we deal with more and more victims, plus all their families, all wondering why we haven't done anything to stop him."

"And I guess it's the typical catch-22," she said. "Witnesses don't want to get too involved, and victims don't want to relive the horror of what they've already been through."

"Exactly," he said. "It's not easy for anybody."

"But, at the same time, it's obviously something I need to work on. Because that's something we need to change. If the women felt more protected, then maybe they'd come forward," Doreen said, "but, at times, they feel violated all over again by the process."

He nodded. "Understood," he said. "I do really understand that. And it's hard. But, like you know all too well, you've been in an abusive and controlling marriage. Maybe you could help other women through this scenario." He dipped his chin, as he stared at her. "But … help yourself first."

Chapter 12

IN AN EFFORT to lighten up the conversation because neither of them could do much to solve the ills of the world at the moment, she said, "So fill me in on your *Nabbed in the Nasturtiums* case."

"There is no *Nabbed in the Nasturtiums,*" he said instantly. But the quirk of his lips belied something.

She dug a little deeper. "Come on. I fed you," she said, "and it was a good stir-fry, right?"

He nodded enthusiastically. "It's was a great stir-fry," he said. "Wonderful."

"So then surely you can tell me a little bit about the nasturtium case."

"The gardener was working in the nasturtium bed," he said. "That's hardly a reason to call it that."

"Oh, I don't know," she said. "It seemed like a good name to me. Was he a chef?"

"No, a gardener, and he has worked for the city, assigned to that particular set of gardens, for quite a while. Seven years, in fact."

"Oh, where was he before that?"

He looked over at her, one eyebrow raised, and asked,

"Why?"

"Just wondering." She chuckled. "You just don't want to share anything," she accused him gently.

"I can't share anything," he reminded her.

She nodded, sat back, then looked around her backyard from her position on her new deck and said, "You guys sure did a wonderful job in this garden."

"We did," he said, but he was looking at her, as if waiting for the next question.

She shrugged. "An awful lot is going on," she said. "I'm still trying to figure out what Nick and Mathew are up to and how it'll impact me. Then I started in on this Bob Small business to take my mind away from it all. Now I've gone down a rabbit hole on that," she admitted.

"Not necessarily. It could be a positive rabbit hole."

"That's hard to imagine," she said. "I mean, it's easy to judge Hinja for not going to the police, and, although Nan says Hinja went later, I couldn't find anything in the police file. So I don't know when it might have been."

"Who knows? Maybe they didn't find it credible at that point," he muttered.

"Maybe not."

"Does Hinja mention anybody else in her life at that time? Could it have been anybody else associated with Bob?"

"It's possible, but, according to her, Bob was a loner, and she's the one who mentioned the curly hair."

"Which is a reach at best," he pointed out. "Plus, did Hinja ever say he was Bob Small, or did she just call him Bob all the time?"

"I know. I know," she said, "but he did have those photographs."

"Which she doesn't have, right?"

"No. She doesn't, and I don't know anything about where Bob Small is at this point."

"I'm not sure he's even alive. I thought I heard, at some point, that he was in jail for something different."

"That could explain why the killings stopped."

"Killings can stop for all kinds of reasons," he said. "Incarceration is one of those options, but it could also be that he had his fill. Sometimes serial killers stop from one day to the next. Sometimes they have fulfilled whatever compulsion was driving them, and they just stop."

"Maybe," she said, "but it seems, like you said, thin."

He laughed. "Maybe so, but, at the same time, none of that is enough to go on. Even when all added together."

"And that's probably why Hinja felt the way she did. All she had were her bad feelings and a couple conversations." She paused. "And the photos. And the missing curling iron. And mentioning her niece's curly hair."

"Exactly," he said. "Now, if you found other information or personal belongings of his that gave us more to go on, that would be a different story."

"So, you guys always thought Bob Small had something to do with a lot of these."

"Yes, but we had no proof."

"What about some of this genealogy DNA stuff that's going on?"

"That would be possible," he said, "if we had any funding for it."

"Everything comes down to budget in the end, doesn't it?" she said, staring at him, though not in surprise but almost with an inner resignation.

"Same as you," he said. "You know that you want salmon again, but it's expensive, and you know you can have twenty cans of tuna for the same cost as a good salmon fillet."

"And twenty cans of tuna is twenty meals, versus one, possibly two, from salmon," she said, with a nod. "I get it. The budget money, the manpower, the hours, all have to go to current crimes, versus tracking somebody who may not even be alive anymore."

"Or, if he's in prison, and he's not a danger where he is, that makes a difference too. But an awful lot of cases could be potentially tied to him. But I don't know that there's DNA from very many victims because we don't have very many bodies," he replied.

"Right, so what you really need to find is his body dump."

He nodded. "Did she mention anything like that?"

"Not that I saw," she said, frowning, "and I'm not sure there is anything in the letters beyond the rantings of a betrayed woman."

"In which case," he said, "you have to really weigh that in with her beliefs."

"Yes," she said, with a nod. "But maybe I'll go through them again. There did seem to be a favorite place they used to go."

"Which would be the last place he would use as a body dump," he said. "Is there an address or anything? A location where he lived? Anything?"

"You know what? I'm not sure. I wasn't thinking of things like that at the time, so I'll read it all again." And she needed to rummage around in Solomon's files again. See what he had mentioned in there.

"You do that," he said, "and, if you come up with a location, we'll be more than happy to investigate the place.

Finding a site where he disposed of the bodies would make a huge difference in tying up things regarding all these cases that might involve Bob Small."

"Right, because bodies are the first and foremost source of forensic evidence, aren't they?"

"If there are any, yes," he said. "Just think about it. The cause of death, whether drugs were used, weapons, fibers, hair, DNA, all of that can be gotten from a body."

"I'll read through the letters and that one journal again tonight," she promised.

"You don't have to rush," he said, with a lopsided look her way. "Remember. You're supposed to de-stress, decompress, and relax. That last case took a lot out of you."

"I think a lot of that was just knowing the individuals involved so personally," she murmured. "Knowing it was Mathew and Robin, bringing up all that old hurt and betrayal again."

"With good reason," he said. Then briskly changing the subject, he stood, collected the dishes, and said, "You cooked, so I'll do dishes."

She watched in astonishment as he carried everything inside and started the hot soapy water in the sink. It also wasn't the first time that he'd gotten up and walked away while they were discussing the case involving Mathew. Maybe it made him uncomfortable. Or maybe he was just trying to change the subject to stop her from focusing on it. She rose, collected their cups, and walked back in. "Will you want a cup of coffee when you're done there?"

He looked at her, smiled, and said, "No, not tonight, thanks. I'll head back to the office."

"Really? You're sure putting in a lot of overtime."

"I am," he said, "but, right now, we're kind of overwhelmed with cases." And he wiggled his eyebrows at her.

She smiled. "I guess I really should slow down, shouldn't I?"

"Not on our account," he said. "We're all about the victims and the families. If you come up with something else, just let me know." He pulled the plug on the soapy water, dried his hands, and said, "You did a great job with dinner tonight. Don't ever doubt yourself."

And, with that, he bent down, picked up Goliath, and gave him a great big hug, while Goliath acted like a sack of flour in his arms. But Goliath's heavy diesel engine kicked in, making them both laugh, as the purring began in earnest. Mack bent to cuddle Mugs for a moment and then walked over to the table to Thaddeus and trailed his finger gently over the bird's cheek and back. "Have a good evening, Thaddeus."

Thaddeus stood up, flapped his wings, and said, "Mack, Mack, Mack."

Mack laughed. "Yep, that's me," he said. "I'm here, but I'm leaving now."

"Goodbye, Mack. Goodbye, Mack. Goodbye, Mack."

She walked over, shaking her head. "He learns the darndest things."

"Yep, but he's been a huge savior on many occasions," Mack said, "so we'll forgive him."

"True enough," she said, laughing.

Everybody trooped to the front door, as she watched Mack get into the front seat of his truck and drove away. Feeling a little lost and forlorn, she headed back to the kitchen, put on the teakettle, grabbed the last journal and her notepad, and headed outside. When the teakettle whistled, she went and made a cup of tea and went back to her reading. She started at the beginning, but this time reading a little more intently, looking for more specific information and details. She found bits and pieces, such as this note.

He called from Abbotsford.

And then another one, where he'd called from Abbotsford again. She wished she had some time line log of his travels, showing where and when he'd gone from one place to another. Abbotsford appeared to be a fairly consistent theme. She picked up the phone and asked Nan, "These notes and things don't have any address or anything. Where did your friend live?"

"Langley," she said, "kind of out toward the Abbotsford area, but not that far."

"So she was what maybe twenty minutes or half an hour from Abbotsford?"

"Oh, I have no idea," she said.

"I just see an awful lot of phone calls from her trucker friend to her from Abbotsford."

"That's if you can believe everything," Nan said. "Don't forget. He could say he's calling from Abbotsford, but that doesn't mean he was. He could have been sitting at a hotel or restaurant just around the corner from her house."

Doreen winced at that thought. "That isn't really something I want to think about. It's kind of creepy."

"Men who want to deceive will find all kinds of ways to do it," Nan said. "You're still working on that case, but I'm not sure it's a healthy one for you."

"No, but when there are so many victims," she said, "it does make you wonder."

"I get that," she said, "and I know there's absolutely

nothing I can say to turn you away from it at this point."

"No, you're right about that," she said, and soon they disconnected.

After talking to Nan and realizing that the case was starting to get a bit dark, Doreen put everything away, locked up her house, set the alarm, and headed upstairs, where she curled up with the animals around her on her bed and watched an old comedy. She was still laughing when her phone buzzed with an incoming email. She took a look to find an email from somebody who she didn't know, asking Doreen if she could help. She quickly opened up the email.

My uncle has been kidnapped in Kelowna. I know he had a very varied and reckless past, but I don't want that to impact how the police look after him. I was hoping you could look into the case.

Doreen stared at it for a long moment, then quickly responded. *How did you find my email?*

Immediately the response came back.

You've been featured in several news stories lately. I just tried your first letter of your first name and your complete last name with Gmail. It's a fairly common way people set up their emails these days.

Doreen winced because that's exactly what it was. *Just what is it you want me to do?* She had quickly replied, then waited for the response to come back.

Investigate. Your success rate is phenomenal, and I would hate to think that my uncle Dicky would be looked upon simply because of who he is.

You'll need to give me more information as to who your uncle is and what you think is going on here. Honestly you might as well call. That would be faster and more expedient. Then she added her phone number. Her telephone rang almost immediately. When she answered, a young woman was at the other end.

"Hello, I'm Denise," she said. "I'm the one who emailed you about my uncle."

"Hi, Denise. I'm not sure how I can help you."

"I know," she said. "I'm desperate though. My uncle has a criminal record, and he found it very difficult to get this job in Kelowna in the first place. But, since he has been there, he's really done very well."

"No more criminal activities?"

"No, in fact, he's been there for seven years. Prior to that he spent ten years in prison in Abbotsford."

Her ears perked up. "A prison is in Abbotsford?"

"Yes," she said, "it's been there for quite a few years."

"*Hmm,*" she said, "interesting. What did your uncle go away for?"

"He falsified documentation for somebody and got caught."

"Like an accountant-type thing?"

"Something like that, though I'm not sure of the details. He doesn't talk about it, and honestly, once I saw how much it upset him, I didn't bring it up again."

"So how do you know he hasn't been involved in anything like that since?"

"I don't know for sure," she said, "but he promised me that he would go on the straight and narrow and that he'd only gotten in too deep because he hadn't really been thinking about what he was doing. He was trying to get ahead in the world, and, once he realized he was in too deep, he knew he was in trouble and had no way to get out."

"Who was he working for back then?"

"I don't know," she said. "Is it important?"

"If he's involved with various people, keeping their accounting records, and some of them are less than savory, doesn't it make sense that they might be the ones who kidnapped him?"

"But why would they?" she asked. "He was in jail for many years. They could have got to him through the prison system."

"Maybe," she said, "but sometimes things take time. Or maybe they didn't know he had something they wanted. Or maybe he went into hiding when he got out, and they've only really been looking for him for the last seven years."

Denise sounded more than doubtful when she said, "I guess you have to look at all aspects."

"Assuming it isn't any of that," Doreen said, "what do you think is going on here?"

"I don't know," she said. "I was thinking he was in the wrong place at the wrong time or something. You know? Like a drive-by shooting or something."

"But what would be the purpose of taking the body away? The fact that there is no body is what makes this very curious."

She gasped. "I'm hoping he's alive and well and that somebody would ask for ransom, but, so far, that hasn't happened."

"Sometimes that can take a while, as they wait to make sure the family is really frantic and losing hope, and then, when the call for ransom comes, the distraught family jumps at a chance to get their loved one back."

"But there is mostly just me now," Denise said quietly. "Everybody else is pretty well gone. We had extended family, but they moved back east when he was jailed, afraid they would be tarnished by the same brush," she said. "But there's just him and me now. My father died a good fifteen years ago now, and Uncle Dicky is the only family I have left."

"And have you kept in touch with him?"

"Absolutely," she said, "we talked every day. He was really happy with his job, was loving everything here. He was enjoying his life here very much. He was learning to do a lot more cooking, which had always been his thing. He's a bit of a foodie," she said in a confidential whisper, as if it were a secret.

"If he was in a nasturtium garden that was for eating, then that would make sense," she said. "What about his boss? Any problems with him?"

"Not that I know of. Uncle Dicky kept telling me how absolutely wonderful his job was and how much he appreciated fresh air and being free."

"Even after all these years?"

"I think, as the years went by, instead of getting blasé about it, it seemed like he was more grateful as time went on. I know he felt like he should do something for others in his world, but he felt like he was handicapped because of his record."

"When you say, *others in his world*, you mean, his other convicted friends?"

"Yes," she said, "an awful lot of them hung out for the first few years, and I don't mean hung out physically because that's always bad news, but I mean they kept in touch."

"So, do you have any names for me, so I can contact them and see if they have any idea who might have done this?"

"Oh, gosh," she said, "let me think. Maybe a couple names that I picked up just from listening to him talk."

"Do you have any contact information?"

"No," she said doubtfully, "nothing like that."

"Can you get into his email? Or do you know his phone number or anything?"

"I do have a little bit of that kind of information," she said. "I'll put it into an email for you."

"That would be good," she said, "otherwise I might lose it."

"I know," Denise said. "Everything on the phone is so hard to remember these days. As soon as you get off, it's a scramble to remember what you were supposed to do," she said, laughing. "Don't worry. I'm writing up an email as we talk."

"Good," Doreen said, "and, while you're at it, put down anything you know of anybody who might have bothered him over the last many years. Anybody from jail who might have scared him, anybody from his previous life in his fraudulent activities who might have not wanted him to have a good life."

"Wow," she said, "that's an awful lot more information than I think I have."

"Give me whatever you've got," she said. "We have to start somewhere."

As Denise gushed out her gratitude, Doreen said, "And remember. I can't promise you anything."

"No, I understand," she said. "I just appreciate you looking into it. Honestly I'm afraid the cops won't give it a fair shake."

"I think you're wrong there," she said. "I know several of the local policemen here, and they don't discriminate."

"I hope you're right," Denise said doubtfully. "But I haven't seen it."

"Have you even talked to anybody yet?"

"No, they won't give me any information."

"Are you the only living relative?"

"I said so."

"Yes, you did, but I'm questioning that because, if you're the only living relative, or even the closest living relative, they will often want to talk to you, in order to ask you some questions."

"I did get a phone message from somebody named Mack," she said, "but I haven't answered it. I just got it a little while ago."

"I do know Mack," Doreen said, with a smile. "And he will give your uncle a fair shake."

"Maybe, but why didn't he call me as soon as it happened?"

"Maybe he didn't know about you," she said. "When did you contact somebody to let them know that you were looking for him? How are they supposed to know that you were somewhere nearby? It's not like there is a directory for that sort of thing."

"You're right," she said in surprise. "I didn't even think of that. I'm probably not listed on his contact information anywhere."

"Exactly." And, with that, the two women hung up.

Doreen realized it would probably be a lot longer than a few minutes for the email to be typed up by Denise and then sent to Doreen, but it was hard to do anything else now, she was so keyed up. "Just because of that," she said, "I may as well look into Abbotsford and the penitentiary there, while I'm waiting."

Doreen found a lot of information, but it read like a government report. It had been around for X number of years. It held X number of prisoners. There was X number of staff who worked there, and all safety precautions were taken, *blah, blah, blah.* Nothing particularly helpful or any data with tangible information, like a list of prisoners from seven years ago. But the fact that it was Abbotsford again just made her antenna quiver. That didn't mean it was connected or that it would have anything to do with Bob Small. But it did make her ponder the possibilities, which is what she was still doing when she finally crashed and fell asleep.

Chapter 13

Tuesday Morning ...

WHEN DOREEN WOKE the next morning, it was with an odd sense of disquiet. She studied her room around her. It was morning. It was light out. The sun was shining, and she'd obviously slept late. With that, the memories rushed through her. She'd had horrible nightmares about a mass grave full of bodies, and serial killers. She shook her head, looked at Mugs, and said, "Maybe we should change our hobby," she muttered. He barked and woofed several times. She looked over at him, smiled, and said, "Please don't tell me that you have to go to the bathroom." He barked again and jumped up on the bed and licked her face, then jumped off and barked again.

"That's a guaranteed 'I need to go outside' cry," she said. Slowly she sat up, rubbed the sleep from her eyes, and pushed her hair off her face, then scrambled out of bed and went to the bathroom. As she looked into the mirror, she winced. "You know what? Only a mother could love this face." She stared at huge dark circles under her eyes and a fatigue in her gaze that she hadn't seen in a while.

As she dressed, she gave herself a pep talk. "Maybe find

something fun to do. Maybe go find something interesting to do, like a sport or a craft or something." She realized that, in the last few days, she hadn't done much in the way of long walks. That always used to cheer her up. The day she'd met Nick over at the eco center was the last walk they'd gone on.

"You know something, guys? After breakfast, I think we'll go out for a few hours," she said. The animals ignored her, as she opened up the back door, and they all scurried outside, as if they'd been penned up for days and days and days. "You could say, *Thank you*," she called out. She turned back, put on her coffeepot, made some toast, and took all of it outside to sit on her pretty little deck. Every time she saw the deck, it made her smile. And to think so many people out there didn't get the same kind of assistance and help that had materialized for her, and it made her feel sad.

"Maybe I should volunteer somewhere. If I can't get a job, at least I could volunteer." Then she winced. She still needed more money coming in. The auction of the antiques would be a good source. She needed to ask Scott about it again, but she hated to be a pest. She might have a shot, a legal shot, at money from Mathew, but who knew how long that would take or how much she might get in the end?

And what was happening with Robin's inheritance? Was it even that much? Mack had listed off a whole pile of stuff, but it didn't feel real because Robin hadn't given it to Doreen directly. For all Doreen knew, it would end up in Mathew's hands. He would probably produce yet another will, one that nullified the one that Robin had written. And even though they had the witnesses to this will, did that make a difference? She didn't know.

As she sat outside, she checked her laptop and realized that, in the wee hours of the morning, Denise had sent through the email with the information they had discussed on the phone. Before Doreen had barely gotten started, a name near the top of the page jumped out at her and just blew her away. Bob Small was a friend of this man who had been kidnapped. She shook her head. That's just way too big of a coincidence. She sent back a reply email.

What do you know about Bob Small?

And she left it at that. She pondered through the rest of the information she'd been given by Denise. And there was a lot of it. A surprising number of details.

Dicky had basically been single, had never married, but had several relationships, to the point of possibly marrying somebody who had been enthralled with his incarceration. That was something else that made Doreen sit here and wonder about a world where women would go after convicted criminals in the justice system. Maybe they thought they could change them? Doreen didn't know, but it all seemed way too bizarre. But she had read somewhere that an awful lot of women liked that concept.

As Doreen kept reading, she looked at the company where Dicky had been working as an accountant, before he went to prison. It was an import/export business, which was in textiles, global textiles.

She laughed. "Oh dear, that could mean anything from stolen property to fine antiques."

And she wondered about that. Maybe somebody in her circle would know about the company. She quickly dashed off an email to Scott, both with the intention of checking up on her antiques and wondering if he knew anything about this company. And nobody was more surprised than her when she got a response back almost immediately, saying that company had gone out of business after it was found to be a front for money laundering.

Stay away from anybody connected. And he continued. *Good news coming your way soon, I hope.*

She stared at that last line. "Everybody is always talking about *someday*," she muttered to herself. "Just what does *someday* mean, and when the heck is it?"

She had just let out a big sigh when she got another email, this one from Wendy at the consignment store.

It's a little early, but I know that you need it, so I've cut you the first check for over $600. Anytime you want to come down and get it, you're welcome.

Doreen stared at the message in delight. "Now I know exactly where we're going for our first walk today," she said, calling out to the animals. Mugs, sensing her excitement, danced around her in joy, not caring what the reason was, as long as he was a part of it.

Thaddeus hopped up onto the table. "Thaddeus loves Nan. Thaddeus loves Nan."

"You better say, *Thaddeus loves Doreen*," she corrected. "Particularly if you're looking for more birdseed."

And, with the uncanny sense of when to shift tracks, he said, "Thaddeus loves Doreen. Thaddeus loves Doreen."

She burst out laughing. "Well, that's good," she said, "because Doreen loves Thaddeus too."

Goliath, never to be outdone, leaped from the ground into her lap, placed his front paws on her shoulders, and gently butted his head into hers.

She reached up and gently stroked his big thick mane. "Aren't you something," she muttered. "You want to go for a walk too?"

Mugs started barking and barking, like a crazy dog. She got up, put her coffee into a travel mug, then checked her watch and realized that, by the time they got there, Wendy would probably have the store open. At least enough to hand over a check, and then Doreen could walk up to the bank and put the money in. And maybe get enough cash to buy groceries. She also had a few bills stacking up that she had been afraid to open. She knew she was supposed to pay them monthly, but, without a monthly income, she didn't know how they could expect her to do that.

"Oh, yeah," she muttered to herself, "everybody else has, you know, a job."

She shook her head because there were no job prospects that she saw. She had been steadily applying to ten jobs a day, even though some of them were in crazy places with no hope of getting them, but still, it made her feel like she was doing something.

"Of course there's a flip side to that," she muttered, as she hooked up Goliath and Mugs to leashes, watching as Goliath immediately threw himself onto the floor and stared up at her in disdain. The flip side was that, by applying every day, it felt like she was seriously searching for a paying job. Yet she got no responses, which made her more depressed.

"First, I need to find out what's happening with Robin's estate. Second, I need to find out what's happening with Scott." Besides Nan's antiques to be sold at a Christie's auction, Doreen still had Nan's antique books and paintings, which, as Doreen remembered, would be sold somewhere else. Just so much was out there to be sold and could be—eventually—converted into cash for her.

If everything ever came to fruition—adding her divorce settlement and Robin's estate to the previous list—Doreen would end up as a millionaire. She stopped and marveled at the thought, wondering if that were even possible. And it's not like she would head back to the same kind of a lifestyle she used to live either. Her days of toting a $1,700 Gucci purse were over. And she had to admit those were on sale at the time she got that one. With her furry and feathered entourage up close, she locked the back door, headed out the front door and on to the front step. Richard was out there at the same time, a cup of coffee in his hand, studying the area. She looked around but couldn't see anything. "Everything okay, Richard?"

He looked at her, then at the animals, and asked, "You're leaving?"

She shrugged. "Just for a few hours."

He nodded. "Good," he said. "Now today is even better."

She glared at him. "You're saying it's better now because I'm leaving?"

He gave her a fat smile and said, "Absolutely." He lifted a hand, then turned and went back inside.

With a note of disdain, she turned and walked away.

Chapter 14

AS DOREEN HEADED downtown, the morning was bright and fresh. Although a little overcast, it was quite pleasant. She hadn't brought a sweater, figuring that it would warm up. Not that today's weather would warm her up, but she warmed up with the exercise. It wasn't long before she was trucking along at a good old pace, wearing a big smile. Several people waved at her, as she walked by. She waved back, not sure who they were and not really that curious.

Doreen found that the animals often loosened tongues and made people a lot friendlier. And, as news spread of who they were and what they'd done to save her, plus all the cold cases she'd been involved in and had closed, the animals were even more welcome most anywhere. She looked at them and smiled. Thaddeus walked on the sidewalk beside them for the moment. He'd get tired soon enough. At the moment, he waddled along quite happily.

"Having a good day, Thaddeus?"

He cocked his head, looked up at her, and said, "Thaddeus is here."

"He is, indeed," she said, with an affectionate grin. They kept walking, until she saw Wendy's store up ahead. She frowned. "I guess you guys aren't technically allowed in all these stores."

She wasn't sure what she was supposed to do about that, but, since she had always gone around to the back of the store before, when she had stuff to sell, she figured she should go that way now. As she rounded the corner, she found Wendy outside, unloading stuff from her vehicle. Doreen called out a cheery good morning.

Wendy was startled, then turned and looked at her and smiled. "Hey," she said. "I have a check ready for you. I cut it last night."

Doreen wasn't exactly sure why Wendy would have cut her check but hoped she hadn't damaged it. Doreen nodded, as if she knew exactly what Wendy was talking about. "That's great," she said. "May I have it then?"

"Sure thing. Let me just unlock everything," she said. "I'm still trying to open up for the day."

"And I came out for a little early morning exercise," she said. She didn't dare tell her that she was here for the check. Mack had paid her for the gardening work at his mom's again, but it sure didn't go far. Especially if both Mack and Doreen were taking in so much coffee that she considered putting some limits on it. But how could she, when it was one of the few true joys she had in her life?

She offered to help, but Wendy brushed away her offer with a shake of her head and a wave of her hand. "I'll be just a minute," she said. And she disappeared inside the store with a huge bundle of what appeared to be clothing. Doreen wondered about what all Wendy sold in the store. Doreen had been inside the store many times but had never really paid attention to the merchandise. She'd been more interested in getting money out of the store, by reselling Nan's clothing, rather than leaving any money behind by purchasing more.

And the truth of the matter was, Doreen didn't need clothes; she had lots still. Some of them were her designer stuff that she probably should let go of and maybe even sell. And that brought to mind her Gucci purse. She didn't have it on her and wondered if that were even something that Wendy could sell. It was all about having the right clientele to pay the right price. And Doreen had yet to get to that other secondhand store, the one that Mack said sold higher-end stuff. When Wendy reappeared, Doreen asked, "Do you ever sell high-end stuff here?"

Wendy raised her eyebrows. "A lot of the stuff that you brought to me was high-end."

"No, I don't mean like that," she said, "but you know? Like expensive little purses. Gucci for example."

"Ah, no." She shook her head. "They just don't sell very well here."

"Okay," Doreen said, with a shrug.

"Do you have something more to sell?" Wendy asked, looking at her. "I thought you got rid of all your grandmother's stuff."

"I got rid of most of it, yes," she said. "But I forgot that I have a couple things of my own from my previous life," she said, with an eye roll.

Wendy nodded. "If you think it's something that I can sell here or if you're not sure, just feel free to bring me a few of the items, and I can let you know," she said. "But I can tell you right off the bat high end Gucci purses are not something I can get much money for. I mean, obviously I can sell them, but you won't like the price. So not sure how high end you have, but consider bringing me something and we'll see."

When Wendy came back out the third time, she had a little more of worried look on her face.

Doreen asked, "Is everything okay? Is someone bothering you in the store?"

"No, not at all. I'm just tired. I've got a few personal problems to work out, but that's all."

Doreen wasn't sure she believed her but nodded as if she did.

Wendy didn't say anything else, and she quickly unloaded more stuff in the front of the car, but Doreen felt slightly apprehensive about it. "Wendy, are you okay?"

"I'm fine," she said, but a notable tremor was in her voice.

"You know you can tell me anything, right?"

Wendy just shook her head and handed her an envelope. "This is your check for the first month."

"Thank you," she said, with a bright, cheerful smile. She opened up the envelope to see the check was $607.63. "This will buy a lot of groceries. I really appreciate it."

"No problem," Wendy said. "I can't exist without selling clothing, so, if you have something you think might sell, feel free to bring it here." Then she peremptorily shut the door in Doreen's face.

Taking the hint, Doreen walked away and headed toward the bank. She studied the check carefully; she didn't quite understand why it was cut or how it was cut, but Wendy had made it very clear she had cut it. She wanted to ask Mack about it badly but decided not to interrupt him. When she walked into the bank and up to a teller, she caused quite a kerfuffle.

The security guard came over right away and said,

"Ma'am, you can't come in here with the animals."

She stopped, looked up at him, then down at the animals. Flustered, she said, "Oh, I'm so sorry. I'm so used to having them with me that it didn't even occur to me that the bank wasn't animal-friendly."

"It's not so much that the bank is not animal-friendly," he said, "but a policy is in place, where no animals are allowed."

She frowned. "Doesn't that mean it's not animal-friendly?"

He stared at her with a bit of a worried look on his face, as if she would be one of *those* customers.

She sighed and said, "I was just hoping to put a check in. I kind of really need the money. And now, since it's been cut, I don't know how long it'll last."

At that, his confusion grew even more. The manager came over quietly and asked in a discrete tone of voice, "Is there a problem?"

The security guard motioned at all the animals. "She is not allowed in here with the animals."

He looked at her and her animals and winced. "He is quite right. We do have a policy."

She nodded.

"She was hoping to deposit a check," said the security guard, who stopped at that.

The bank manager looked at her and brightened. "Why don't we put it in through the ATM?"

Doreen looked at him, surprised. "We can do that?"

"Oh, absolutely," he said. "Come over here, and I'll show you."

He led her to a separate area with a bank of machines, and she looked at each of them and frowned. "I don't even know how these things work," she said, studying them.

"That's unusual," he said. "Automated teller machines have been around for a long time."

She nodded slowly. "I guess I never had any reason to use them before."

"Well, now you do," he said. "Do you have your bank card?" Then he proceeded to walk her through the process and said, "Now see that envelope there? Put the check in it, and you just slide your envelope through those rollers."

She put the check in the envelope, after she had another last look.

He asked, "Did you want to take a picture of it? You seem to be studying it."

She beamed at the suggestion. "Sure," she said, and she pulled out her phone, quickly snapped a photo of both sides, tucked it into the envelope, and then hesitated because she saw the wheels. "What if they hurt the check?" she said, looking at him in worry. "What if it gets lost? What if it gets missed, or what if you guys don't enter it into my account?"

"That's why we went through the process before, where you put in how much the check was, so that, when the check is taken out on the other side, it can be reconciled to that entry."

She frowned, and she really hesitated now.

As she stood here, Richie from Rosemoor walked in, saw her over there, and said, "Oh, look at you, using those newfangled machines," he said. "I can't get a handle on them. I'm always afraid that somebody will steal my money." She gasped. He nodded, gave her a sage look, and said, "That's why I just keep my money under my mattress."

She turned to look at the bank manager, and he immediately shook his head. "No, no, no," he said. "Please don't keep the money under your mattress. What if there's a house fire?" That made sense to her. Still, she held on to the envelope, but he gently took it from her and said, "I promise it'll be safe."

"And you promise that, if it's not safe, you'll give me my $600? Actually $607.63."

"I will. You have my personal guarantee," he said, with a nod.

Feeling slightly better, yet realizing that she didn't have his promise in writing, she let him put it into the bank machine. Then she stood there, shifting from side to side. "How long will it take?" she asked.

He looked at her in surprise. "What do you mean?"

"How long until I can take money out?"

"Oh," he said, "well, it could be a couple days."

Her eyes widened. "Really? Whereas, if I'd just gone to the teller, I could have taken money out right now?"

"Do you have other money in the bank account?"

"I'm not sure," she said. "I think so."

"If you have other money in the account," he said, "you can take money out. Regardless it'll just take a few days for that check to clear," he said, "unless there's a problem with it."

Her heart froze. "What do you mean, *a problem*?"

"If it comes back without sufficient funds."

Now she started to wring her hands. "So," she said, "that check is no good?"

"I'm sure it is," he said. "This is from the consignment store, so it should be written against monies that she sold from goods of yours."

"Yes," she said, nodding. "That's exactly what she did."

And then he proceeded to explain to her the way checks

worked, in that, if the other account didn't have enough money to fulfill the amount on the check, then she wouldn't get her money. By the end of it all, she was supposed to be calm, having further understood everything, but instead she was almost in a full-blown panic. As she stood here, figuring out what to say, she heard a familiar voice behind her. Richie had long gone, and she had obviously attracted attention, with the explanation efforts of the bank manager, who was looking more confused by the minute.

But, as it was, Mack stepped up behind her and placed a hand on her good shoulder. "I'll take it from here."

Chapter 15

Tuesday Midmorning …

THE BANK MANAGER looked at Mack in relief and quickly excused himself. Doreen looked up at Mack and whispered in a hoarse voice, "What if it doesn't clear?"

"What is it?" he asked, leaning forward. She pulled out her phone and showed him the photos.

"What's the problem then?" he asked. "You deposited a check from somebody already once, right?"

"But I didn't understand how it worked," she said. "The manager just said that, if Wendy doesn't have the money, I don't get paid."

"But she wrote you a check with every good intention that she *did* have the money, so that she could pay you," he said, frowning. "It's a typical business transaction."

Doreen looked around at everybody else and then leaned forward and said, "But she told me that she cut the check." He looked at her, saw the dead seriousness in her gaze, and his lips twitched. She watched, narrowed her gaze at him, and said, "Don't you dare laugh at me."

"Not at all," he said, immediately shaking his head. "I'll never laugh *at* you," he said. "So you need to start laughing too."

She glared at him. He pulled her bank card from the machine, gave it to her, and nudged her out of the bank. "Are you trying to get rid of me?" she muttered, staring around, taking one last look to see several other people watching them as they left. "Why am I always the laughingstock everywhere?" she muttered. As soon as they were outside, she turned on him. "What's so funny about her cutting my check?"

"*Cut a check*," he said. "It's just a term that means that she wrote you a check."

She stared at him blankly. "So *cut* means *wrote*? Why would she say she *cut it* then?" she asked, raising her arms in the air. "That's like threatening to take away my money."

"But she didn't mean it that way."

Doreen took several long slow deep breaths, staring at him and wondering if it was safe to believe him.

"Honest," he said gently. "When Wendy said she *cut you a check*, all she meant was that she was sitting down to do the bookkeeping, so she could write you out a check."

Slowly Doreen's shoulders sagged, and she nodded. "So, if that's a stupid question," she said, "then I guess the next one doesn't make any difference either then."

"Remember. There are no stupid questions," he said. "And I'm laughing with you, not at you."

She looked at him and said, "Except I'm still not laughing."

"You should be," he said. "Look. It was a missing gap in your living-life education, which I thought we went over already, but apparently you didn't get it."

She glared at him. "And I also don't get," she said, "why that machine isn't putting the money into my account right now."

"It has to clear first. Remember? They have to put the money into your account, and then they check to make sure the other account—Wendy's—has the money to cover this check to you. Only then does the bank take it out of Wendy's consignment shop account and then put it into your personal bank account. That's the process, and, because you put it in through the ATM, it'll take a bit longer."

"But I need it now," she wailed, "and they wouldn't let me go to the teller."

"Why not?"

She muttered in a slightly lower voice. "Because of the animals."

He looked around and started to laugh.

"There you go again," she said, glaring at him.

"And there you go too," he said, tapping her gently on the cheek. "Most banks won't allow one animal, let alone three of them."

"What difference does it matter how many I have?" she asked.

"It's all about the disturbance to everyone else. A bank is a place of business, where they try to quickly get people through the lines. If there are issues, and the animals become a problem in any way, then it slows down business. Then there is also the hygiene issue."

"My animals are clean," she said in astonishment.

"Sure, but if you're allowed to bring in your animals, the next person must be allowed to as well, and what if they aren't quite so clean?"

She glared at him. "You can't blame me for somebody else."

He groaned. "Okay, this is going sideways already. You

did get the check in, and you do have money still in your account, right?"

"There is some. I just don't know how much."

"You didn't get a balance?"

She shook her head. "No, and I don't have any money on me to get groceries."

He walked her back inside the foyer to the ATMs, all not in use at this time, and went through it again with her card. "Now there's your balance," he said, pointing at the ATM screen. "See? You still have lots in there."

She stared at the amount. "So does that include the money with the check or not?"

"It will include the money with the check, but see where it says Pending? That means it's not cleared yet." She frowned, but she was starting to get an idea of how this worked. "So I can take out money, as long as I don't touch the money that they haven't secured yet."

"Exactly," he said. "So how much do you want to take out?"

She thought about it and said, "I do need to get quite a few groceries."

"What do you want, one hundred or two?"

"I don't want to walk around with a couple hundred dollars," she said. "So maybe one hundred, though two sounds good as well."

He said, "Let's compromise and split the difference."

So she punched in the numbers with his reassurance, then watched in fascination as the machine spat out money at her. When she picked it up, she chuckled. "Does it ever make a mistake?" she asked. "Wow, this is a great way to get money."

"But it only takes it out of your account, and you need

your card and your password," he said. "So how great is it really?"

"Ah, so I can't use it to get into your account," she asked, looking up at him.

He immediately shook his head. "No, ma'am, because I have my own card, and I have my own set of numbers."

"So how does somebody break in and steal something like that?"

At that, his grin flashed. "We've had cases where they came with a forklift and smashed through the front door and took away the entire machine."

She gasped and stared at him, her eyes opening wider and wider as she thought about it. "And what do they do then? Just run down the highway, with this thing in front of them?"

"I believe they tried to dump it into a pickup truck," he said, "but it was too heavy for the truck, and it caused significant damage."

"Oh my." She started to laugh. "That is pretty funny."

"I thought so, but I don't think anybody at the bank really saw the humor of it."

"They should have," she said. "That's hilarious. I really like to hear that."

"Why is that?"

"Because it makes me smile, thinking about the ingenuity of some people."

"Definitely ingenuity was involved," he said. "I only wish people would use that ingenuity while working their job and making money on their own, instead of stealing it."

"Yeah, but you know what people are like," she said. "They're all about making sure they don't have to do much for what they want."

"Very true," he said.

"And, besides, you can't really judge them for that," she muttered, "because I don't have a job yet myself."

"Have you had any breakfast this morning?"

She shook her head. "Not yet. I should have brought something with me."

He hooked his arm through hers and said, "Come on. Let me take you out for a bite."

She looked up, smiled, and said, "Are you just trying to be nice to me?"

He rolled his eyes at her. "Let's not analyze everything," he said. "I want to take you out for lunch. Is that a crime?"

"Nope," she said. "It sounds like a great idea."

And together they walked up toward the mall. He said, "A couple restaurants are around here that we can walk to, if you want."

"Sure," she said. "I'd love to try something different."

"You haven't tried very many of the restaurants in town, have you?"

She shook her head. "No, and every time I get out and walk around, I see something that looks interesting, but then I …" And she just shrugged and held off explaining what he knew already.

He nodded. "A couple are up here. One that serves soups and sandwiches and things like that."

She wrinkled her nose up at him. "Can I get breakfast?"

He stopped and glared at her. "You really had nothing to eat yet?"

She shrugged. "I was thinking about the check."

"Ah," he said. "The check that's now sitting in that machine."

She turned and glared at the bank behind them. "Yes,

that check," she snapped. "I feel like the manager tricked me into putting it in there."

"It's his job to try to get more people to use the self-serve machines and to decrease teller hours," he said. "It keeps the budget trimmed."

"That's another thing that makes no sense," she said, groaning. "You don't trim a budget. You trim a piece of meat, or you trim the lawn. You don't trim the budget!"

"Of course you do," he said. "If it's bloated and costing too much, you must trim it down. Just like cutting off the fat."

She considered that and then said, "Oh. It's not language that my ex ever used."

"Let's keep the day pleasant and not mention him again. How about that?"

"And here I was going to ask if you'd heard anything from him."

"Any reason why I would?"

"No, maybe not," she said thoughtfully. "I'm just not sure what he's up to."

"No good, I'm sure."

"That may well be, and I haven't heard from Nick either."

"That's not necessarily a bad thing. Remember that."

"As long as you've heard from him," she said, looking up at him, slightly worried.

He frowned and said, "So are you worried because you haven't heard from Nick, and you're afraid that he's not doing something for you, or are you afraid that something has happened to him?"

"You can't trust my ex," she said, "and we know the people around him are pretty scary, so I just want to make sure nothing has happened to Nick."

"That makes me feel better."

She frowned. "You weren't really thinking that I was worried Nick would cheat me, were you? Though it's not like I'm paying him. However, I did give him the change from my purse."

He groaned. "Forget the change," he said. "Come on. Let's try this one over here. It has outdoor seating, so we should be allowed to take the animals in, or we can try at least."

She looked up and said, "Oh, it's Indian."

"Yes," he said, "it's fairly new. I haven't tried it yet."

She nodded and said, "I'm more than happy to try it, especially if you're paying."

"That's what it means when I invite you for lunch," he said.

"So is this like a date?"

He stopped, looked at her, and asked, "Does it matter?"

She frowned, shook her head, and said, "Well, no, I guess I was wondering."

"And I guess I'm wondering if it matters," he said quietly.

She smiled up at him. "Only in that I would tell Nan that I went on a date with you."

"Do you tell Nan things like that?" he asked curiously.

"It would help get her off my back," she muttered.

He started laughing. "So is she for or against us having a date?"

"For, definitely for. She says that I should have been pushing you a long time ago." She shook her head, her palms up. "I've told her at least one hundred times that I'm not ready, and she told me that I'm just making excuses."

They continued to walk, until they reached the patio area. As they walked in, he asked, "And are you?"

"Am I what?" she asked, already having moved on in the conversation.

"Making excuses?"

She frowned at him. "I don't think so," she said. "Seeing my ex just brought back a lot of unpleasant memories that I don't really want to recall."

"But you wouldn't have to," he said. "It's a whole new ball game."

"I guess," she said, and obviously something shifted, as she smiled. "Because you're taking me out for lunch." And, with that, she turned and smiled at the waitress coming toward them. "This is lovely here," she said to her. "Are we okay with the animals?"

"Sure."

Chapter 16

THE WAITRESS DROPPED off the menus and took off again.

"She looked fairly distracted," Mack noted.

"I wonder if there is something in the water," Doreen said, "because Wendy looked upset too."

"Wendy?"

"Yeah, Wendy, who gave me the check."

"*Hmm*, did she say why?"

"No, but every time she went back into the store and came back out again, she looked a little more disturbed."

He stopped and looked at her. "That doesn't make any sense. Tell me again from the beginning what you saw." And she did. He frowned and said, "As long as she is okay, and nobody was inside."

"She came out every time, quite willingly."

"Maybe I'll stop by this afternoon," he said. "No, let's nip this in the bud now."

She frowned. "I guess I should have asked her more."

"You had something else on your mind." He pulled out his phone and placed a call but put it on speaker so she could hear Wendy's voice on the other end. She seemed to be fine and answered his questions without hesitation. "I'm just checking that all is okay," he said smiling at Doreen. "Doreen was worried about you."

After several assurances he ended the call.

"Oh dear," she said. "Am I a terrible person?"

He looked at her, smiled, and grabbed her fingers. "No, you are not a terrible person."

He said it so firmly that she relaxed slightly. "I mean, it was obvious she was upset, but I couldn't really tell why," she muttered to herself, trying to think back. "When she came out with the check and handed it to me, she looked the most visibly upset then. You know what? It never even occurred to me, but maybe she didn't have the money to give me." And then she glared. "And maybe that check will bounce. See? She shouldn't have cut it, if it would bounce."

"That's good advice for anybody," he said. "But you don't know what's going on, so let's not jump to conclusions."

But it was hard not to. But the phone call convinced her to ease off and to relax about it. She shrugged and sank back into her chair, and then Mugs started to bark. She immediately tried to shush him, but he wasn't having anything to do with it. She looked around to see what the problem was and saw another big dog coming toward them at full speed.

"Oh my," she said, just a small railing between her and the approaching dog. Mack immediately stood and looked around for the owner of the big dog, still racing toward Mugs, who, instead of being aggressive, was now under Doreen's chair, staring out between her legs. She immediately reached a hand down and said, "Yeah, you stay safe."

As the big dog jumped up against the railing, Goliath jumped up onto the table, then reached out and whacked the big dog across the face. Almost immediately it turned, howling, and it took off. Mack looked at her, looked at Goliath, looked at Mugs hiding under the table. "Wow."

"Right," she said, reaching over and petting Goliath. "Thanks for defending Mugs." But instead of looking appreciative of her gratitude, Goliath sprawled out across the table, almost knocking over her glass of water.

She stared at the animals and groaned. "Just when I think I understand them, they do something that makes me not understand anything."

"That wasn't hard to understand at all," he said, taking his seat.

"Wonder whose dog that was?"

"Some dog that got away from his owner for a few minutes," Mack said, with a shrug. "I wouldn't worry about it."

"No, but I certainly haven't had any dogs try to attack Mugs either. I don't like it."

"Another reason to stay closer to home," he said. "The farther away you get, the more opportunity for getting into trouble."

She glared at him. "I can get into trouble anywhere," she announced.

He stared at her and started to laugh. "No truer words were ever spoken," he said.

Then she realized what she'd said. Her grin flashed. "See? I like that about you," she said. "You do help keep me off-balance."

"Is it good that you're off-balance?" he asked curiously.

"I think so," she said. "Nan would say it keeps me on my toes."

"And that's good because it keeps your mind going?"

"Yeah. Except my mind needs to slow down," she said. "Between the Bob Small thing and the gardener who got kidnapped and all the Abbotsford connections, it's definitely worrisome. And then, of course, there's Denise."

He stared at her. "What are you talking about?" As she winced, he leaned forward and said, "Doreen?"

She sat back, flummoxed. What was she supposed to tell him now? "She contacted me. It's not my fault," she muttered.

"Contacted you how?"

"Email. About the gardener who disappeared," she said.

"Right. Of course she did," he said, pinching the bridge of his nose. "And what did she have to share?"

Doreen explained everything Denise had said and then added, "Really, she doesn't know a whole lot."

"No, but she knows enough," he said, "and obviously we'll track down all those people."

"That would make sense," she said. "I don't know why you haven't done it already."

"Did you give us the list?"

"Um, no," she said, "and I should have. It completely skipped my mind."

"Wow," he said. "That's the one good source of information we have."

"You can call her."

"Give me a minute." He stopped. "And, Doreen," Mack continued, "stop taking in all these strangers, asking you for help. The least you could do is give me a heads-up, so I can run a background check on them."

"Why? You never share that information with me. And maybe you should."

"And maybe you should stop letting these people into

your house, who then attack you." He got up, about to walk away, but, just before he did, he leaned over and said, "Order me a burger with everything." And he disappeared around the corner.

She stared at him, wondering what was the point of coming to a new Indian place and then ordering a burger. Just then the waitress came back. Doreen checked out the menu, glanced at the waitress ready for her order, then looked at Mack and shrugged. "We'll both have the special."

With that, the waitress scooped up the menus and disappeared. When Mack came back, he said, "I did connect with Denise, and she is definitely overwrought about the whole thing."

"It's her uncle," Doreen said. "Of course she is."

"But, without any good leads, it's really not much help."

"But it could be," she said. "We just need to figure out more about whether any of these people would have any idea what was going on. And you've also got to figure out if they were both in the same prison at the same time."

He stared at her. "Who is *they*? Who were the two in the same prison?" he asked, shaking his head.

"Bob Small … and the gardener."

Mack stopped and stared. "Did you say Bob Small is in that prison?"

"He was," she said. "Apparently, per Denise, her uncle and Bob Small were friends."

"Good Lord," he said. "How do you manage to get this stuff all so confused?"

"Me?" she said. "I didn't get anything confused."

"Says you," he muttered, shaking his head. "We had absolutely no reason to bring Bob Small into this."

"Now you do," she said triumphantly. "So now you have

some leads."

"That's not a lead," he said. "That is a spider's web."

"And one that needs tearing apart," she said succinctly. "I get that it's complicated and a mess, but we still have to sort through it."

"Do we now?" he asked, staring at her in fascination. "How do you figure that? We don't have very much information at all."

"I know. I'm going through all Hinja's letters now," she said. "And, I mean, outside of everything I've told you, I haven't found anything new. The Abbotsford angle keeps coming up though."

"So, Bob Small was in Abbotsford. Big deal."

"Maybe they were in the penitentiary at the same time."

"Some of that information is public."

"Right, so it's not like I would get into trouble checking it out."

"No, not this time," he said, "but it's still not the easiest thing to sort out."

"No, it just means, when you go back to the office this afternoon, you'll have some work to do."

"I always have work to do with you around," he said, groaning.

Just then, the waitress returned, setting their full plates before them and promptly leaving them alone.

Doreen looked at it in delight. "Wow, this looks awesome."

He stared at his, at hers, and asked, "What happened to my burger?"

She winced. "I figured that you had absolutely no reason to come to a place like this and order a burger. I'm not even sure it was on the menu. Really, if you come to an Indian restaurant, you should get Indian food."

He stared at her, then shrugged and said, "Good point."

And he dug in.

Chapter 17

BY THE TIME Doreen and her animals got back home, she was tired and worn out. Mack had offered them a ride, but Doreen had declined, knowing he had work waiting for him. "Our walk ended up taking longer than we thought, didn't it, guys?" she said, as she made her way up the front steps. As she entered her living room, she realized she hadn't set the alarm.

"Uh-oh, we're sliding on that point, even with all the danger around. We were doing really good, but now, every time we go out, we tend to forget," she muttered. And that made her feel even worse.

But she walked in, checked everything out and realized that it still appeared to be completely fine. Too bad Mack had to return to the office. But then he had a lot of work to do, and she needed to get busy on this case. As she walked into the kitchen, she thought she heard something and looked out to the backyard, just in time to see somebody scrambling down the pathway past her property. She frowned, looked over at Mugs, then opened up the back door. He wandered outside but appeared to have missed seeing the guy.

"Trouble is," she said, "we have such a suspicious nature by now that we don't know if that was just somebody innocently walking or not." It's not like they couldn't walk along the river, like she and lots of other people did. She just wasn't used to seeing very many on her property. And, of course, because of all the new stuff she'd been looking into, she was a little on the suspicious side.

She also realized she was looking around every corner because of Mathew and all the recent drama surrounding him, Robin, and Rex. She pulled out her phone, and, determined to make the most of this moment of courage, she texted Nick and asked if he had any news. Instead of texting back, he phoned her.

"I do have a document drawn up," he said. "I need to come by and get your signature on it."

"What is the document?"

"Divorce papers," he said, "so we can get the divorce done."

"That would be lovely," she said. "Is it, uh—" Then she stopped.

"Is it what?" he said.

"Will it piss him off?"

"Possibly." And he waited.

She winced. "I'm really not into long-drawn-out battles."

"Once you sign this," he said, "then I handle the battling for you."

"Unless Mathew comes up here, angry," she muttered, "and finds me alone."

"Are you physically afraid of him?"

"No," she said slowly, "and yet …"

"You don't want to confront him or to see him get angry."

"Exactly," she said.

"Why don't I come over right now?" he said. "We'll get this signed and get the process started."

"After I just told you that I didn't want to deal with anything ugly?" she asked in disbelief, then blew out a huge sigh. "Okay," she said.

"Put on some of that absolutely divine coffee of yours," he said, "and I'll be there in about twenty minutes."

He hung up on her, and she stared down at the phone. "*Divine* coffee?"

Nobody had ever called her coffee divine before. Bolstered by that, and still smiling about the lunch she'd had with Mack, she headed to the kitchen and put on a pot of coffee. As it finished dripping, Nan called.

"How was your lunch?" Nan asked.

Doreen rolled her eyes. "Which one of your spies tattled?" she asked, with a laugh.

"Does it matter?" she said. "You know nothing happens in this town without me knowing about it."

As it turned out, quite a bit had happened in this town without Nan knowing about it, but Doreen wasn't about to burst her grandmother's bubble on that one. "I'm glad you're having so much fun," she said.

"But the real question is," Nan said, "are *you* having fun?"

"It was nice. It was a restaurant I haven't been to before, and I don't get to go out very much on nice luncheons like that."

"Ha, so it was a date, wasn't it?"

"It was a date," she confirmed, and Nan went off, crowing and crowing through the phone. "Calm down," Doreen said. "It doesn't mean anything. Mack and I have shared a lot of meals together."

"Sure, it means something. You finally let him into your life, and he stepped up to the plate. Good man, Mack."

Doreen groaned. "Don't you push us, Nan," she said. "I won't be happy if you do."

"Oh, never," she muttered cheerfully. "It's way too much fun this way."

And, with that, she hung up.

Doreen didn't have a chance to ask her grandmother any questions. But, with Nick on his way, Doreen figured it was probably just as well anyway. And, sure enough, just as she turned around, she heard a vehicle coming up the driveway. She walked out to the front porch, where she waited on the top step for him to get out of his vehicle and to come toward her.

He smiled. "Waiting for me, were you?"

She shrugged. "I heard the vehicle."

"Good," he said. He had a sheaf of papers in one hand and an envelope in the other.

"I really would like to see an end to this soon," she muttered, staring at the envelope worriedly.

"Me too," he said.

She winced. "I'm not being very grateful, am I? I really do appreciate you doing this."

"And I'm glad," he said, "because I don't want you backing out at the last minute and putting all my efforts to waste."

"No, that wouldn't be very good, would it?" she said. "Okay." She groaned. "Let's go in and take a look at it."

As they walked inside and into the kitchen, he looked around and said, "You could really use some money to fix this place up, huh?"

"I could use money to eat," she said bluntly.

He looked at her and asked, "Is it that bad?"

She shrugged. "It depends if the machine eats my check or not."

He stared at her silently.

She laughed. "Apparently it's normal, but I don't know," and she explained about the check that was *cut* for her today. He laughed. "Mack had a similar reaction," she said. "How was I supposed to know *cut* didn't mean *cut*?"

"The lingo of any industry is always fun to learn," he said. "But you've been a good sport about it all, so keep your sense of humor."

"I'm trying," she said. She poured two cups of coffee, and, as he held the back door for her, they walked out to the little table on the deck, with its four chairs.

"Mack told me that he had snagged the patio set for you."

"Isn't it wonderful?" Doreen asked.

"But still just the one rocker, huh?"

"Yep, it takes money to buy a second one," she muttered. "Plus, I would love a couch and maybe a side table on the new poured patio."

"Understood," he said. "So what do you say that we go about getting you some of that money?" And, with that, he handed her the papers.

She looked at him and winced. "I feel like I need to read all of these because of what happened last time, but I do find legalese very difficult, and it brings up all kinds of ugly memories."

"Why don't we go page by page?" he said. "That way you can read as we go."

Then, true to his word, he led her through what appeared to be a fairly simple document. When she got to the part that really counted, she said, "Half? Seriously?"

"You were married for fourteen years. He had no business prior to your marriage, and you helped him develop it afterward."

"Mathew had some money before," she said, "so I'm not sure that's fair."

"I'm only asking for 50 percent from the time that you were married."

"Okay, well, I guess that's fair, although he won't think so."

"You let me worry about that."

She nodded slowly and, with the pen he gave her, she signed. Even as she did, the action felt like something momentous. "How long before we hear back?"

"Probably pretty fast," he said, "mostly because he won't like this."

"Of course, and what happens if we can't come to an arrangement on our own?"

"Then we go to court," Nick said cheerfully, "and the judge will help divide the assets. And you can bet your ex will know that."

"How will the judge divide it?"

"In this case, I highly suspect it will be 50/50, just like we've got here."

She shook her head. "Is that what normally happens?"

"Absolutely it is," he said. "That's very common."

"If you say so," she said. "I don't want to take anything more than is rightly mine."

"I know that," he said. "It's one of the reasons why I'm helping you out."

She wasn't sure exactly what that meant, but she was happy to let it go.

By the time he was finished with his coffee and had packed up his papers, she felt sick and looked at him almost with loathing. "Do you think he'll contact me?"

"If he does, just tell him to contact your lawyer and hang up," he said comfortably. "That's all you have to do."

"And what if he doesn't want to?"

"He has a lawyer I'll be dealing with. So, once we get that going, it becomes a very different problem."

"If you say so," she muttered, and she walked him out and waited at the front door for him to drive away. Then she turned and looked at the animals. "Fun times coming up, guys." Mugs barked. Just then another vehicle drove in her driveway, and she groaned. "We won't really get any peace and quiet today, will we?"

A woman hopped out, looked at Doreen, and asked, "Do you have any news on my uncle?"

She winced. "No, I don't. I am looking, but I don't have anything so far."

She nodded. "That's one of the reasons I came by. This is the other. It came in the mail today," she said, as she brought something over.

"Did you take it to the police?"

"Not yet," she said. "I wanted to show you first."

Doreen looked at Denise and said, "If it's got to do with your uncle's kidnapping," she said, "we need to get the cops involved."

"And I will," Denise said, "as soon as you see it."

They opened it up, and Doreen winced as she read it.

You need to give back what you've stolen, but I'll take $100,000 instead.

Doreen quickly took a photo of it and said, "We need to get this to the cops." She immediately dialed Mack. When he answered the phone, and she quickly explained, he started to swear.

"I'll be right there."

"Okay," she said. "I took a picture of it too, so I'll send it now." She looked at Denise. "The cops are coming."

"Good," she said, rubbing her arms. "I shouldn't have even opened his mail."

"It's not like it was addressed to anybody in particular, just To Whom It May Concern. See?" Doreen flashed the envelope to Denise.

"But why would they put it in his mailbox? I figure that's from the kidnappers. But shouldn't the kidnappers already have Uncle Dicky? They could just tell him directly."

"Because the kidnappers knew that that mailbox would be monitored by the police," she said quietly. "That's how it works. The authorities track everything from Dicky's mail to his emails, and, if they can, they even get into his phone calls and financial records."

Denise nodded. "I guess," she said. "It's just that the whole thing's so horrible."

"I'm sorry," Doreen said. "You're right. It's tough news right now. So did he ever mention Bob to you? Bob Small?"

She nodded. "He was good friends with a guy named Bob. I think that might have been his last name. Wasn't that one of the guys I listed in the email I sent to you? I don't know for sure. They were good friends in prison," she said. "I know my uncle believed that the cops didn't know anything about what Bob was guilty of."

"Was he in for murder?"

She looked at her in surprise. "Oh my, no. No, not at

all. I think he refused to pay a whole pile of parking tickets or something, and they finally jailed him because he wouldn't make good on it."

Doreen started to laugh. "Seriously?"

"Yeah, seriously."

Chapter 18

IT WAS ALMOST too much irony. Enough so that Doreen had to wonder if Denise had any idea what her uncle really had done.

"He did drive a big truck," Denise explained, "but I can't imagine how many tickets he had to accrue for them to get pissed off enough to charge him."

"I don't know," Doreen said, turning to look around.

"How long will the cops take?"

"Hopefully not too long," she said. "Mack said he'd be right over. Do you have any idea what your uncle supposedly stole? Particularly if it's worth the six-figure mark."

"I don't know," she said, looking at the letter and shivering. "He said he'd been on the straight and narrow ever since, but obviously somebody doesn't believe him."

"Or somebody thinks that he stole it back then and still either has it or already converted it to cash."

"Maybe. I can't imagine what he was working on."

"He could have siphoned money from various accounts he had access to, you know, before he got caught," she said.

"If he did, I sure never saw it. He's always lived very frugally. As a matter of fact, I know he needs this gardening job."

"I'm sure he does, but that doesn't mean he doesn't have a money stash that he's still too afraid to spend."

Denise stared at her in horror. "I don't think you realize what my uncle is like."

"No, I have no idea," she said. "As far as I know, I've never met him."

"He's a good man, and he's very honest."

Doreen stared at her.

Denise blushed. "Okay, so he made one mistake in his life."

"But what you're saying is that you firmly believe he's innocent of being in trouble this time."

"Absolutely," she said, "almost fervently."

"So you've never seen him show any signs of having any money of the level this guy is looking for? Why would they expect him to have even one hundred thousand dollars?" she said, marveling at the figure. "How many people do?"

"I don't know," she said. "I certainly don't."

"Neither do I," Doreen said, shaking her head.

"Don't you?" Denise asked, looking around. "You have your own house."

"Sure, I do," she said, "but that's because I inherited it, yet I don't have any money to fix it. As you can see, it's not exactly the Taj Mahal."

"No," she said, "but you could sell it, and then you would have more money."

She winced. "I can't even imagine," she said. "It was given to me by my grandmother, and she's still alive and living in a home for seniors nearby. She would be absolutely devastated if I sold her home."

"That's the thing. Gifts like that, they come with

strings," Denise said.

"And have you been helped by your uncle to the point you feel indebted to him?"

"He has helped me," she said immediately. "Honestly he's a good man."

"And that's good," she said. "I'm really happy to hear that. The question is whether someone knows anything different about him and can explain why somebody expects him to have one hundred thousand dollars to give them in lieu of what was supposedly stolen."

"Because they obviously don't understand what happened way back when," Denise said.

"And that certainly won't be something your uncle or his kidnappers would share either, is it?" she said, trying to give Denise a bit of an easier time.

"Exactly," she said. "And, if you think about it, all he has been concerned about is staying on the straight and narrow ever since."

"Any chance he's been afraid that somebody would find him or that maybe he's been in hiding?"

Denise looked at her thoughtfully. "I wouldn't have said so," she said, "but he didn't go out, and he didn't have any friends really. He kept in touch with hardly anyone."

"Who is the hardly anyone?"

She shrugged. "I don't know if it's anybody. He worked here in town, and, when he wasn't working, he really enjoyed cooking. He was looking at doing more chef's training, so he could work in professional kitchens. But I don't know that he would have gone back to school. Or if he would have even been allowed to. Are criminals allowed back in school?" she asked Doreen.

"I have no idea. But you would think it would be a good

thing for them to do, so they could get out of their wayward life and get into something honest and self-supporting."

"That's what I thought, but he didn't seem to think he had a chance."

"We never really know until we try," Doreen said.

"Well, I know he was trying, and he was certainly applying to places. But what he really wanted was to get into cooking school."

"At the college level?"

"I really don't know, but that would have been a smart place for him to start, right?"

"Well, yes, it would have been. I'm sure the police can check to see whether he applied at the college here. I know they have a really good cooking program. I don't know if they still have it, but I remember Nan talking about them having a restaurant, almost like a little buffet, and you could go in at noon all the time. Even people who didn't go to the college and more than the profs and the visitors liked to go. It was open to the public, and I remember Nan telling me how wonderful it was."

"That would have been great," Denise said, looking pleased. "I've never even heard of that."

"I think they closed it down or changed the format here a few years ago. Which is kind of too bad, since Kelowna doesn't have very many buffets."

"I've never been one for buffets," Denise said. "I'm not a big eater, so, if I go someplace, I just pick up a salad."

"But I can make a salad myself," Doreen said. "I've come to learn and to appreciate that going out for a meal should really be something that you'll enjoy, be something you can't make for yourself."

"Or it should be something that's expedient," Denise

said, with a laugh. "Sometimes I just don't have time, so it's easier to pick up something."

In the distance Doreen heard a truck. She smiled and said, "That's Mack."

Immediately Denise spun around to look. "I don't see him," she said. She had not even finished speaking when Mack came barreling up the road and turned into the cul-de-sac.

"That doesn't look like a cop," Denise said, turning to look accusingly at Doreen.

"He's a detective," she explained. "So he's in plain clothes."

"Oh. So he's RCMP?"

"Yep," she said. "There's no city police in town, which was something that took me a while to figure out. I guess only certain suburbs in the Lower Mainland have them."

"Vancouver does, and I think West Vancouver does now as well," Denise said, muttering.

"Do you spend much time down there?" Doreen asked.

"I went to school at SFU," Denise said. "That university was a godsend for me." And she turned to look at Doreen with another accusatory look. "My uncle helped me to get through school."

"What did you take?"

"Bookkeeping," she said.

Doreen nodded and gave her a brilliant smile. "That's good," she said. "You shouldn't ever have a problem getting a job."

"No," she said. "I do work in the retail industry for a company that manages several retail fashion designers."

"Wow," she said, "that would be nice."

Denise shrugged. "It's just numbers and figures. It's not

like I get to walk down the runway, wearing any designer clothes."

"Would you want to?" Doreen asked curiously. She never really understood the appeal of stripping down to almost nothing and wearing the very bizarre clothing they were asked to wear.

"Sure," she said, "it would be a lot more exciting than my current life."

"Well, maybe," Doreen admitted. "I guess numbers aren't terribly exciting."

"Nope, they sure aren't," she said. "They're boring, and it's pretty well the same, day in and day out."

"Not necessarily a bad thing—at least you can count on it," Doreen said. "Something that happens day in and day out that you can depend on, instead of waking up and wondering what'll happen, you know?"

"And that's boring," Denise said, with a smile.

Mack parked, shut off the engine, and hopped out. He walked out, his gaze assessing Doreen, who gave him a big fat smile. Then she introduced the two of them. He nodded, looked at Denise, and asked, "Why didn't you bring that to the police?"

"Honestly I figured your hands were full," she said, "and I wanted Doreen to see it first."

A thunderous expression filled his face, as he turned to look at Doreen. She shrugged and said, "Hey, I called you."

He nodded slowly and said, "And I appreciate you doing that." He held out his hand, and she gave the note to him, holding it gingerly between two fingers. "Do you think there's any chance of fingerprints, after you two have handled it?"

"You've already got mine on file," she said, "so you can

easily knock mine off."

Denise looked at her in shock. "Are you a criminal too?"

"Nope," she said, "but, in the line of my cold-case hobby, I've had my fingerprints taken, just to understand all the prints that were at a crime scene."

"Oh, I get it," Denise said. "I wondered there for a moment if I was doing the wrong thing by bringing it to you."

"Yes," immediately Mack said, only Doreen's voice was louder.

When she said, "No, of course not," Mack just glared at her. "Because I understand that I need to give it to Mack too," she said immediately.

Mack rolled his eyes at her and said, "I'll take this back and see if we can get anything off it."

"Don't you want to read it first?" Denise called out anxiously.

"Doreen gave me a photo of it," he said. "I already know what it says." He turned, looked at Denise, and asked, "Why don't you come down to the station, so we can ask you some questions about it?"

Her eyes wide, Denise shook her head, stepped closer to Doreen. "I don't have any answers," she said, shifting back and forth, like ready to take flight. "I don't know anything."

Mack frowned at her initial response and glanced at Doreen, before facing Denise again. "You haven't yet heard our questions, so we would like to ask you some."

She immediately turned to Doreen. "Could you come along?"

Doreen stared at her in surprise. "Um," and she looked over at Mack for help.

He shook his head. "Doreen doesn't need to come. We're not accusing you of anything. We're not attacking you. We're not charging you with a crime. We just need to ask you some questions."

"Maybe so," she said, "but I would feel better if she came. I don't really know anybody here."

"Fine," Doreen said impulsively, "I'd be happy to come." Mack groaned. She added, "It can't hurt, can it?"

"No, maybe not, but you have to stay out of the questioning," he warned.

"Of course," she said, with a brilliant smile. "Of course I will."

He said, "I know that's a lie. You haven't managed to stay out of anything yet."

"I could now," she said, as she looked at her animals.

Mack shook his head. "Leave them behind."

She glared at him. "You know I don't like doing that."

"You're coming to the police station," he said. "I highly doubt you'll need them for defense there."

"No, but I may need them for support," she said, giving him a smile.

"That won't help," he said. "You're supposed to be the support."

Doreen could really say nothing to that. She looked over at Denise and said, "Go ahead down to the station. I'll follow along."

Denise immediately nodded and reached out to grab Doreen's hand. "Thank you. Thanks a lot." Then she dashed to her car down the driveway and called out to Mack, "I'm on my way."

He looked over at Doreen and asked, "What was that all about?"

"I have no idea," she said. "I really don't."

"You better get down to the station fast," he said, "because I'm not sure where this is going."

"Me neither."

As he drove off, she walked back inside, looked at her animals, and smiled. She wondered if it were possible to have the animals turned into therapy animals. "You know something, guys? Maybe, just maybe, this is a career move we could make. All four of us together."

Mugs barked. Thaddeus looked at her, tilted his head to one side, and said, "Thaddeus has a job. Thaddeus has a job."

She laughed. "One of us needs to, big guy, because I sure don't."

She went upstairs and quickly changed, then fed the animals a little to get them settled in and locked up the house. Could she really get behind that therapy-animals idea? Maybe she could take them to the hospital for the kids who were sick or could go to the police station as support animals for other people being interviewed. She'd talk to Mack about that. But then, she really didn't need to talk to Mack at all. She could maybe do something on her own. At least she could do the research into that; she was good at research.

As she locked up the front door, Goliath wandered through the curtains in the front window, and Mugs jumped up on his hind legs, trying to see out. She winced because she hated to leave them all home. But she didn't dare take them all down to the station for this. Mack was right; Doreen was supposed to be focused on this woman and helping her. And that brought up another whole issue too.

Doreen walked to her car, mulling it over, as she opened up the garage, got in, and backed out, so she could close the garage door again. Then she reversed down to the cul-de-sac and slowly headed to the station. She saw why some people would want someone there for support, and maybe, because this woman was alone and the missing man was her only living relative, Denise wanted Doreen there. But it still seemed a little off.

The minute she'd been asked to go to the station, Denise had almost panicked. And maybe for good reason. Maybe she had bad memories from her uncle being sent to prison, or maybe she'd had some kind of trauma herself. Maybe she was a criminal in her own right.

Doreen had to stop and think about it. An awful lot of elements here were starting to twist in on themselves. The fact that Abbotsford—the city and the penitentiary—Bob Small, kidnapping, and ransom were all now involved was definitely intriguing. But the fact that Denise wanted Doreen as support while at Mack's interview and that Denise had sent the information to Doreen instead of the police was fascinating.

With a big smile on her face, Doreen pulled into the station and parked.

Chapter 19

DOREEN WALKED INTO the station, waving at Chester, who stood on one side, among several of the other guys that she recognized. The captain leaned against his doorjamb, talking to two officers, his cup of coffee in hand. As she walked by, she patted him gently on the shoulder and kept on going.

"Doreen?" he asked. "What are you doing here?"

She looked back at him, flashed him a bright smile, and said, "A request from somebody who's come down to give a statement."

He nodded in understanding. "Got yourself another case, have you?"

"No," snapped Mack, from the other end of the hallway, where he waited for her.

The captain looked at him, one eyebrow cocked.

"You won't believe it anyway," Mack said, "but I do need to fill you in."

The captain detached himself from the group to walk toward them, just a few steps behind Doreen, and said, "Okay, tell me more."

Doreen listened, while Mack quickly explained.

The captain looked at her and said, "Why would she come to you?"

"I really don't know," she said, her voice low. "It's very odd."

"It is," he said. "I know you're getting a heck of a name for yourself as somebody who champions the underdog and all, but this is an interesting twist."

"And I don't know if it's just out of a concern that you guys won't look after her uncle's case because he was a criminal or what," she said. "I could understand, if she's had some bad experiences, that maybe she needs to push her uncle outside of regular law enforcement channels."

"But that's not the case," the captain blustered.

Doreen shrugged. "We can say that," she said, "but this person obviously feels very differently about it."

"Yeah," he said, with a nod. "I can see that."

Mack nudged her forward. "Let's go to the interview room," he said, nodding to his captain.

She looked around with interest and then whispered to him, "I've never been down here before."

"Really?" He looked at her with interest, as he contemplated it. "You've been down here a number of times."

"I have," she said, "but usually I'm on the other side."

"You might be this time too," he said in a grave tone.

She stopped and shook her head. "Surely not," she protested. "I haven't done anything wrong."

"No, but I'm not sure who this Denise person is and why she is aligning with you."

"And that just makes it sound like something is wrong with me."

"No," he corrected again, his tone firm. "Something is very right about you, and I think Denise's trying to hook into that."

"Oh." His explanation left her momentarily speechless because she didn't have a clue what to say to that. Mack motioned her into the room, and she saw Denise, sitting there nervously. Doreen walked over, giving Denise a big smile. "See? I said I'd be here," she said, then pulled up the second chair and plunked down beside her.

Immediately Denise leaned forward, her face a wreath of gratitude. "Thank you," she said. "Police stations, the courts, the whole law enforcement thing, it all just gives me the heebie-jeebies in a way."

"Because of your uncle?"

"I don't know if it's so much my uncle. My father was always in trouble with the law, and he kept getting carted away, time and time again, and it left a really weird feeling. It's almost like it's major trauma for me."

"If you didn't do anything wrong," Doreen said, "it shouldn't affect you."

"Easy to say," she said, with a half laugh. "Some of the darndest things trigger memories that just make life difficult."

Doreen had to remind herself that she had a few of her own skeletons. "No, you're quite right there," she said, "but today it's more about just asking you questions."

"But the questions get personal, and they get difficult. I always feel like I'm writing an exam and that they're looking for specific answers. If I don't know what the answer is or if it's one that I should even give them because I don't know what they truly have for an agenda."

That was such a thought-out answer that Doreen could only stare at her in wonder. "Sounds like you have been on this side before."

"Oh, absolutely. Every time my father got in trouble," she muttered. "I had to explain where he was, what he'd done, why he was where he was, where I was, what I was doing—that whole feeling of being a suspect too," she said, "and it's not fair."

"No, that sounds awful," Doreen said.

Mack had been standing at the doorway, just watching the two of them interact with each other. He entered, sat down with a pad of paper and a recorder, and said, "Honestly we're not here to terrorize you. We're just trying to figure out where your uncle has gone and help you find him."

"That would be lovely," Denise said, "but it never seems to be quite so easy."

"Let's start with the basics." And Mack went through a whole pile of questions that Denise answered readily enough. And then he asked, "Why did you go to Doreen with the note?"

"Honestly because I didn't think you would give my uncle a fair shake."

He looked at her, frowning. "He's just a missing man," he said. "I don't mean to make that sound like he doesn't matter or that missing men don't matter. And, while his history gives us more leads as to why somebody may have taken him, it doesn't make him any less of a victim in this case."

"And I want to believe that," she said earnestly, "but it's not the easiest thing, if you're me."

"Understood, but you know there could have been fingerprints on that letter, and there could have been some kind of trace evidence maybe."

"I don't think so," she said, "and I don't understand why it was addressed To Whom It May Concern. I mean, if somebody knew about him, they should have known that I was around."

"But you didn't live there, did you?"

"No, I moved out a few weeks ago, but I was over all the time, visiting," she said. "And because my mail was still delivered there, I was the one who always checked the box."

"Which means the sender likely knew that but maybe didn't know who you were," Doreen suggested.

Mack nodded. "Both are possible. And we'll make a note of that. So you never saw it delivered, correct?"

She shook her head. "No, I just opened the mailbox, and it was there."

"I'm sure you noted that no stamp is on it. So it didn't go through the regular mail system."

She stared at him. "You know what? I didn't even think of that. I guess it makes sense, and that probably means it was hand-delivered." She frowned. "The mailbox sits on the edge of the fence, so anybody could have put it in there."

"Are there any cameras around?" Doreen asked Mack.

He shook his head. "No, it's not a very common thing in town, as it is."

"I wonder," she muttered. "It just seems like such an opportunity is there for either our kidnapper or for somebody else close to Dicky to have availed himself of this method for a blackmail note. But for a ransom? 'Give back what you stole, or I'll take $100,000,' I'm not sure I buy it."

"I wonder just what the value is of the item this person supposedly lost," Mack said to Doreen.

"Meaning," Denise asked, "he's asking for an equivalent amount or for so much more that it'll be easier to give back the item they have?"

"If the thieves even still have it," Doreen said. "Especially if this is something nicked twenty-odd years ago."

At the use of the word, his eyebrows shot up. He looked at her and said, "*Nicked*?"

She shrugged.

"But he didn't take anything," his niece said in a determined voice. "And I can't have you thinking he did."

"Okay," Mack said, looking at her dubiously. "But think about this. Dicky was guilty once, so you know that's possible. You just don't know why he would do it again."

Denise slumped in her chair and nodded slowly. "I guess that makes sense."

Chapter 20

THROUGHOUT THE WHOLE conversation, Doreen kept getting an odd vibe off this young woman, studying her intently. She couldn't figure out what it was. Finally Doreen settled back, aware of the concerning look in Mack's gaze as he focused on Denise too. Doreen gave a one-arm shrug and said, "Are there any other questions you need to ask Denise?"

The young woman looked at her gratefully. "I really would like to get out of here," she said, waving her hand as if it were a fan. "It's really hot, isn't it?"

Mack stared at her. "No," he said, "it's really not."

She just frowned.

"I'm sure it'll be fine," Doreen said in a gentle voice. "Is there anything else you can offer?"

The woman immediately shook her head. "No, I got this letter, and that was it," she said. "I don't even know why I have to be here." She jumped to her feet and asked, "Can I go?"

Doreen immediately hopped to her feet and said, "Yes, of course we can go."

Denise looked at her hopefully and said, "Really?"

"Yes, of course." Doreen looked to Mack and asked,

"You know how to get ahold of her if you have any other questions, right?"

He nodded. "I sure do." He walked to the door, opened it, and said, "Thanks for coming in. As soon as we get any more information on this, we'll let you know."

Denise nodded and basically ran from the room.

As Doreen went to follow, Mack grabbed her hand and said, "What was all that about?"

"Depends on who you're asking," she said, "because I have no idea. I just get a weird feeling from her."

"Me too. I'm really not sure what's going on here. I'll check into her background a little bit more."

"Which is why people don't like to come in to the cops," she said, with a note of humor. "She came in to help out, and now you'll investigate her."

"It's what we do," he said.

"I get it, but you can also understand why she's hesitant to come in."

"If she has nothing to hide, it won't matter."

"She's related to a criminal," she muttered gently. "I don't think that it's even an issue that she has a criminal record but that she'll obviously be nervous because of her uncle's record. And her father's."

"Maybe, but there's been no sign of Dicky yet."

"What are the chances that he took off on his own?" she asked.

"No, we don't think so," he said. "We have an eyewitness report that he was forced into a car."

She nodded slowly. "Who is this eyewitness?"

"I can't really discuss it," he said, "but it's reputable."

"Maybe, but somehow you know very well that we don't always see what we're supposed to see, or we're led to see something that is different."

"Meaning?"

"What if he staged it? What if he's trying to get away from whoever and whatever and staged it to make his own getaway?"

"Why would he do that?"

"If he stole something worth $100,000 and spent the money after selling the thing and knew he would be found out sooner or later, he's probably figured out his escape plan," she said. "Regardless, if you think about it, it worked. Nobody has a clue where he is. He's off doing his own thing, and, outside of his niece, nobody seems to care."

"We care," Mack said.

"I'm sure you do," she said, with a nod, "but it's not like he's overrun with crying relatives, is he?"

"And?"

"I don't know," she said. "I don't know." With that, she turned and walked out of the station. "Next time, I'm bringing the animals," she called back.

The captain hollered from his office, "Do it. I really like that dog."

"It's the bird that's awesome," added one of the other detectives from across the hall.

She laughed. "Glad you guys like them. I was thinking about making them therapy animals."

"Wow, I don't even know if you can do that," Mack said, looking at her in surprise.

"I don't know either," she said, "but it's a job for those of us who don't have any."

"There you go," Arnold said, sniggering. "Put the animals to work, so you don't have to."

She beamed. "Right. Isn't that how it's supposed to

work?"

"It does with kids, or at least it's supposed to," the captain said, with a smirk. "But it never really works out the way you expect it to."

"You know what? I can kind of see that too," Doreen said, some of her hopes falling. "It's not like Mugs and Goliath and Thaddeus will be the easiest to get to do my bidding. They seem to think they can do their own thing."

"That's because they do," Arnold said, with a grin. "Your research findings keeps us all busy in the meantime."

She smiled and said, "I'm not really hot to trot on any real case right now. I'm kind of bored." She looked at the captain hopefully. "You don't have anything for me to look at, do you?"

He shook his head. "We're so overwhelmed with all our current cases," he said, "nobody has had a chance to even look at our cold cases."

"That's sad, isn't it?" she said.

The captain nodded. "It's beyond sad because we don't want them to be cold in the first place. So to think of them sitting there unsolved all this time makes it even harder. We need to find a way to get in touch with each one and just do a reassessment to see if there's anything, like new technology, that we can look at."

"And this is where I wish I were a cop," she said, with a nod, "because that would be right up my alley."

"And I see that," the captain said. "You appear to have quite the problem-solving mentality."

"Or just the problem-making mentality," Mack said, coming up behind her, joining the group. He laid a hand on her good shoulder and said, "I thought you'd gone to the parking lot with Denise."

"No," she said, looking up at him. "I just wanted to put a little distance between us."

"Any reason why? What was bothering you about her?"

She shook her head. "I don't know. It just seemed odd. Something was off, but I can't put my finger on it. The whole time I was in there, it was bugging me."

The captain nodded sagely. "Sometimes you've got to honor that part of you too," he said, "because instinct is huge in our business, and it has saved many lives."

"That's good to know," she said. "I've had a lot of close calls, but I'm not sure how much of that was instinct versus my animals."

"Doesn't matter," the captain said, "as long as they were just close calls, and you've managed to get away from it all."

She smiled. "Anyway I'll head home. I miss the animals already." With a wave to everyone, she turned and walked out. As she got to the door, she saw Mack racing up behind her. She stopped and waited for him. "What's up?"

"Just wondering if you're okay."

"I am. Like I said, something is off about that young woman."

"I know," he said. "I felt it myself, but you know that it could be nothing. We're always looking for the boogeyman, and, when we can't find any, sometimes it's easy to make them up."

"Maybe, and maybe it's more that she is hiding something, and we just don't know what it is. That bothers me though. It could be anything—from having walked out and not paid for her lunch to who knows what else," she said, with a half smile. "It's just enough to be unnerving."

Chapter 21

Tuesday Late Afternoon to Wednesday Morning …

DOREEN GOT HOME to find all the animals curled up in the living room. She managed to get up on the porch and peek in the window, before they heard her. Of course they jumped up excitedly when they saw her. She unlocked her door and disarmed the security system, as she shook her head and said, "Hey, Mugs." She reached down and scrubbed his ears. "I know you know it's me, but still a little bit more guard-dog alert would be nice."

Yet she understood that Mugs needed his downtime too, what with the last few months being so exciting. Maybe he needed a little extra sleep too. She went into the kitchen and put on the teakettle, deciding that it wasn't time for coffee at the moment. When her tea was brewed, she took her cup out onto the deck, where she sat down on her rocking chair to enjoy the day.

Mugs immediately came to her side and rubbed his head against her leg. She bent down and picked him up. He was a good armful, and she groaned with an *umph* as his weight settled into her lap. But he turned and immediately licked her neck and tucked in close. She held him against her heart for a long moment, just enjoying holding him close to her, so grateful that he was in her life. "We've had quite the time, haven't we?"

Mugs woofed and Goliath purred.

Her phone rang beside her and, shifting the weight of Mugs to her other arm, she pulled out her cell and took a look. "Hello, Nick."

"Have you heard anything from your ex?"

"No, though you told me that, even if he did try to contact me, to not answer him."

"Good," he said, "you got the message then."

"What message?"

"About not having anything to do with him."

"Why are you calling me again?" she asked in confusion.

"Just checking. Has he responded at all?"

"Nope, nothing. Complete silence. So what happens if he doesn't respond?" she asked.

"That's a good question, but we do have ways and means, if he refuses to negotiate," he said. "Then we'll go to the judge, if need be."

She winced. "I can't say I'm looking forward to anything that involves going to court," she muttered. "He's quite intimidating that way."

"Nah, not for you," he said. "You're the woman solving all these cold cases. You will fight for everybody but yourself. How about sticking up for yourself, just this once."

She gasped. "That's not fair."

"Maybe not," he said gently, "but it's true." With that, he hung up.

She frowned as she put down the phone. Was it true? Was she the kind of person who wouldn't look after herself, but the minute somebody else was attacked she'd defend them? She realized that a lot of truth was in his words. She sat here for a long moment, contemplating how much she'd changed in some ways and how little she had changed in others. "You know what, Mugs? Here I thought I was doing great, but maybe I'm not doing as well as I thought."

She was still thinking about that when she made herself a simple salad for dinner—and even later when she got ready for bed. She brought out her journal and took a look at it and realized how much confidence she had gained with all these cases and dealing with people.

After staying as many months as she had in Nan's house, managing to pay some bills and surviving okay, even though she wasn't necessarily thriving, at least financially she had managed to squeak by okay. So she'd gained a lot of confidence. But not gained a ton of self-worth, and that was something she hadn't even realized. It was a little disconcerting to consider it also.

She looked at Mugs and frowned. "I'm not sure what we're supposed to do with this," she muttered. "It's a bit of an eye-opener to even consider that I've made so little progress in that department."

And it all surrounded her marriage to an abusive and controlling man. Just as she was about to set it out of her mind, she got a text from her ex. She looked at Mathew's text in confusion.

No way!

She responded. **No way what?**

No way am I giving you half.

She stared at it, aware that it was late at night and that she was all alone in the house. It was communication with the person she wasn't supposed to communicate with, and she'd already done what she wasn't supposed to do. For some reason, his response struck her as funny, and she started to giggle and laugh. She took a screenshot and send it to Nick, with an apology. **Sorry, I already forgot.**

And, when her phone rang, she expected it to be him. But instead it was Mack. "Wow," she said. "What are you doing up so late at night?"

"What am I doing so late at night?" he said, with a chuckle. "I'm just checking up on you, what else?"

"Why is that?"

"Is it wrong?"

"No."

"Besides," he said, in a quiet voice, "this isn't for public announcement, but we found a body."

She immediately gasped. "Oh no. Is it the gardener?"

"We're waiting on an ID," he said, "but I can tell you that he didn't die in the last few hours."

"Wow, so he was probably killed shortly after he was picked up. Which means that he obviously didn't stage all this himself."

"We also have to consider that," he said, "which I never considered that seriously anyway. That was all you."

"Oh, fine," she said. "It was just a theory. Brainstorming, you know? So how will you get the positive ID?"

"A couple avenues," he said, "but one will be to ask Denise."

"Ouch," she said. "How was he killed?"

"You'll have to wait on that," he said. "I just wanted to warn you, in case Denise contacts you."

"Right," she said. "It'll be hard to go to sleep now anyway."

"I just wish I knew what was going on behind it all and who would have killed him," he said.

"And was it deliberate or accidental?"

"Since when is murder accidental?"

"The death, I mean. Like, if he was involved with somebody else, and they tried to make it look like a kidnapping. Maybe something went wrong, and he ended up dead. Just a thought."

"We're still not sure that it's him, for one thing," he said. "First things first." They rang off very quickly after that, and she went to sleep with troubled dreams.

When she woke up the next morning, she got out of bed slowly, remembering the news from Mack and Mathew, checking her phone for messages. Between Mathew and Denise and now potentially the kidnapped uncle being murdered, things were heating up. But it still didn't have anything to do with the Bob Small cold cases. And were there threads involving Bob Small to the kidnapped gardener or was there absolutely no connection? Just ones she was looking to find?

The fact that Denise's uncle Dicky and Bob Small even shared time at the same prison was interesting for instance—if Denise could be believed because Doreen couldn't confirm that herself. Still, was that enough of a connection to call it one? Hundreds of prisoners had to be there, and any criminal who went into the penitentiary system had to be one of only a few in BC, unless they were sent across Canada to other prisons. She frowned at that, wondering just how anybody would connect these cases, when she got a phone call from Denise. "Hello," Doreen said.

"Hi," the woman said, crying unashamedly into the phone. "I have to go identify a body. They think it's my uncle."

"Oh no," Doreen cried out, "but they don't know for

sure?"

"No," she said. "They want me to go, you know, take a look at it."

"Ouch," she said, "that would be terrible."

"And they're not even sure it's him," she said impossibly.

"Do you want me to come?"

A break came in her sobbing, and then her hopeful voice asked, "Would you mind?"

"No," Doreen said, as she stared at herself in the bathroom mirror, wondering what was wrong with her that she'd even made the offer. "I'd be happy to."

"Oh my," she said, "that would be awesome. I don't really want to go all alone."

"No, of course not," she said. "That sounds terrible." And then she made another offer, again not knowing where it came from. "Do you want me to pick you up? It doesn't sound like you're in any shape to drive."

"I should be okay," she said. "I'll meet you there, if that's all right."

"That's fine," she said. "How soon will you be there?"

"I guess I should let you get coffee at least."

Doreen was nodding crazily into the mirror. She definitely needed coffee first.

Then Denise went on and said, "But I'd really rather get it over with."

Doreen closed her eyes and said, "So when then?"

"Do you think you can meet me there in, say, fifteen minutes?"

She opened her eyes and glared at the mirror. "Sure, I can do that." As soon as she hung up the phone, she stood there, hung her head over the sink for a moment, and whispered, "Why? Why would you do that?"

But she had no time to understand her own actions, as she threw on her clothes, set the alarm system, and drove. She didn't even have time to take the animals outside, and, for that, she was very sorry. As she made it to the morgue, she hopped out of her vehicle and waited.

When she saw a woman walking up from the other end, she knew it was Denise. She walked toward her with her shoulders hunched, and it didn't look like she was still crying but more like she was shocked. "Let's get this over with," Doreen said bracingly.

Denise just nodded, and together they walked to the door, where, sure enough, Mack stood in the open doorframe. When he looked at Doreen, she shrugged and said, "I offered."

He gave a partial headshake and ignored her. Then they went through an interesting process, where the body was viewed behind a screen.

Denise stared at it and then shook her head. "That's not my uncle."

Mack looked at her warily and said, "It isn't?"

She said, "No, not at all." She frowned. "It might be his friend, but I can't be sure."

"Which friend is that?"

She looked over at Doreen. "I think it's his friend, Bob. The one you were asking about."

Mack stared at Doreen. She stared right back, then faced Denise to ask, "Bob Small from Abbotsford penitentiary?"

"Yes," she said, "that's the one." She stared at the body again, shrugged, and said, "At least I think it is, but I haven't seen him in a few years." But she beamed with a broad smile and said, "Regardless it's not my uncle, so good news, right?"

"It's good news in that your uncle is not deceased,"

Mack said, "but not good news in that we haven't gotten any closer to finding him."

Denise motioned at the guy on the table. "Check his handwriting against the handwriting on that note," she said. "I bet they're a match. I thought they were good friends, but you know what? He's just as likely to have tried to blackmail my uncle."

"Did they ever do any jobs together?" Doreen asked her.

She frowned, shrugged, and said, "I don't know. I don't even want to think about that question."

Mack nodded and said, "But they did have a history."

Denise laughed. "They certainly did in the penitentiary but before that? I don't really know," she said. "My uncle did not talk about his crimes."

"Good enough," he said. "Thanks for that bit of help. We'll run his DNA and see what we can come up with."

"Okay."

Mack said, "Thanks for coming."

"It was an experience," Denise said, taking a last glance, then she turned and left.

Mack looked at Doreen and asked, "I wonder what's going on here?"

"I'm not sure," she said, looking back at Denise. "I'm also not sure I believed her."

"What do you mean?" he asked, turning toward the body, now covered by a sheet.

"I don't know," she said. "I can't get a read on her."

"When she looked at the body," Mack said, "she expressed no grief, no recognition."

"No," Doreen said, "there wasn't any, but there also wasn't any joy."

"Meaning?"

"Meaning that it felt—" Then she stopped. "I can't explain it. I just can't explain it."

"You don't like her?" he asked.

"*Like* has nothing to do with it," she said. "There's just a lack of authenticity that I'm having trouble wrapping my head around. And, for all I know, it's because she's very closed off or protective. Maybe she has just shut down because of all this fear. I don't know. Obviously I don't want to say too much and make it look like she's guilty, especially when she's not."

"Interesting," he muttered. "But now we have a body that we need to identify."

"Right," she said. "Any way to check if it is really him?"

"But Denise just said it wasn't."

"I know," Doreen said, "but maybe you should check anyway."

He raised his eyebrows, tilted his head, and shrugged. "I can do that. It would be nice to know why Denise wouldn't ID her uncle though."

Doreen looked at him, nodded, and said, "I'd really like to know why too."

Chapter 22

Wednesday Late Morning ...

AS SOON AS Doreen got home, she put on coffee, desperately in need of the caffeine. Her mind was in chaos. And finally, with her coffee in a travel mug, she reached for the dog's leash, and soon, with the animals at her side, she stepped outside, this sense of confusion, chaos, and tension coiling through her. A good walk would help. At least she hoped it would.

She wandered the streets, not really watching where her path took her, struggling to sort through all the conflicting thoughts and emotions running amok in her mind. Of all the cases that she had seen so far, this one was the one most puzzling. And she thought it was because of Denise herself. It made no sense; none of it made any sense. Mack had mentioned she had a brother, ... but, as usual, had another call and abruptly ended their discussion.

For that reason alone, Doreen was trying not to think about Denise but to view the whole thing from a completely different perspective. While Doreen was out wandering around, she found herself in the back of Mission Creek, on the pathway going up and down the hills. When her phone rang, she was surprised to see it was her ex. She answered it. "I'm not supposed to talk to you," she said, without preamble.

He snorted. "You never were very good at listening."

She frowned. "Did you have a reason for calling?"

"If I called you, then I did, didn't I?"

She hated that tone in his voice. "Then speak up," she snapped.

"I thought you weren't allowed to talk to me."

She pinched the bridge of her nose and glared into the phone because, of course, she wasn't supposed to speak with him. She shouldn't have answered the phone call to begin with, and now he was reminding her of how much of a jerk he could be. Just something in his tone suggested he knew something she didn't and that he would always know something she didn't because she was simply too stupid to understand.

"I'm hanging up in three seconds," she said, "if you don't start talking."

"Wait," he said, the first sign of alarm entering his voice.

"Wait for what?"

"I think you need to rethink this document."

"I haven't got any document here in front of me," she said, "so what are you talking about?"

"The divorce papers," he said, his voice turning surly. "No way you're getting this much."

"Well, look. If you hadn't tried to cheat me out of everything," she said, "it wouldn't have come to this."

"Hey, I didn't cheat you. That was your lawyer. You're the idiot who got the lawyer involved."

"I had to get a lawyer involved because you had a lawyer involved."

"Yes, but it was our family lawyer," he said, his tone turning persuasive. "You could have just left it at that."

She laughed. "Really? Is that what you think? Personally I think my lawyer couldn't have been any worse. But then, of course, you were sleeping with her as a way to get her even more on your side."

"I didn't have to even sleep with her," he said. "The woman was a psychopath."

"I'm not sure you're any better," she said cheerfully.

"You can't mean that," he said, his tone injured.

She frowned, then shook her head, warning herself not to even get involved in this. But knowing she'd already made that mistake, she said, "Speak up, if you're going to."

"I just want you to rethink things," he said, trying for a convincing tone. "We had a lot of good times together."

"What's that got to do with the divorce?" she asked. "You cheated on me. You ousted me from the house, and you got my lawyer to cheat me too. So where in all of this do I owe you any loyalty?"

His voice darkened, deepened into a threat. "You better, or you'll regret this," he said. "You haven't heard the last of me." And he hung up.

Knowing that she would get in trouble for it, she quickly texted Nick and said that Mathew had called, giving Nick the gist of the conversation.

And why did you answer?

The truth? Out of habit.

Her phone rang then, and, as she wandered up and down the pathway, she saw a beautiful fallen tree trunk up ahead, and she perched on it, while she answered. "I know I wasn't supposed to," she said, "and I really did try to get him to make his point, and all he would say is, he wants me to rethink the document, and I don't deserve half. At the end though, it sounded more like a threat."

"What kind of a threat?"

"Something about I'll regret it."

"Yeah, that's a threat," Nick said, obviously writing something.

She heard scratching on a pad. "Are you taking notes?"

"Of course. It's all powerful information to give to the judge."

"*Ugh*," she said. "You know how I feel about a court and a judge."

"Doesn't matter how you feel," he said. "You still have the process to get through."

"I could just walk away."

"You could, and you could go back to living on the streets and having nothing to eat too. Is that really how you want to live your life? This isn't money you're stealing from him. This is money he is stealing from you. If you put it in perspective, it makes things a whole lot easier."

"But he's one scary dude," she said.

"And yet you had dinner with him," he said, but no rancor was in his voice, no judgment, just curiosity.

"I was trying to help Mack," she said.

He stopped and said, "Oh, that explains it."

"Explains what?"

"Nothing," he murmured in a much more cheerful voice.

She frowned. "Don't you read more into this."

"I won't," he said on a burble of laughter.

She frowned. "Why does everybody think there's more between us than there is?"

"Because there is," he said. "You're just taking some time

to figure it out."

She frowned. "I'm really not stupid, you know?"

"Absolutely not, and no way I would ever think that," he said. "That's not the kind of person I am, and you've shown that you're very intelligent. Look at how many cold cases you've solved."

As soon as they hung up, she hopped off the log to her feet. Feeling the tension inside her increasing, and, with the animals in tow, she raced down the big set of log steps. She raced back to where the eco center was and then headed up the pathway about half a mile. Up there was another set of steps, which she took on up. Wandering aimlessly, her mind still confused, she found herself on a deserted road, surrounded by orchards and country homes.

She smiled in appreciation, as she saw the apples and the pears on the trees all alongside the road. "That's the wonderful thing about Kelowna," she said out loud to the animals. "Beautiful fruit trees. It's a really great temperature for growing them."

There were so many good things about being here in Kelowna, starting her new life. She stood still, thoroughly admiring the countryside. She eyed the view behind her and stopped for a moment to admire the city laid out before her. Hearing the sound of a vehicle, she walked to where the road was, then stepped out of the way as she came up upon it suddenly.

A car whipped past, and she surprisingly recognized the vehicle from her recent trip to the morgue. It was Denise. Frowning, Doreen wondered what Denise was doing up here. She headed down the same road that Denise had taken, not even exactly sure where Doreen was at this point. She was also afraid to get herself caught up too far away or with too long of a walk to get back home.

But then she automatically felt comfortable, knowing that, if she called Mack for help, he'd come and pick her up. Still it wasn't the smartest idea to get lost, and there were plenty of places in town that, if you weren't driving, were quite a distance away.

Chapter 23

DOREEN AND HER animals had come already quite a distance, and she hadn't brought any food, water, or treats. She shook her head because she should know better. Still she wondered if it would be okay if she took an apple from one of the trees beside her. Even as she watched, one fell to the ground, and she picked it up, checked it over, and then took a good bite. She laughed.

"This is awesome," she said. She wondered about Denise showing up here, but Doreen didn't even know where the woman lived or who her friends or family were. It made no sense that Doreen would run into Denise out here, and it must just be a crazy coincidence. But then she heard Mack's voice in the back of her head, snorting at the concept.

"In law enforcement we don't like coincidences," he used to mutter to her.

Shrugging and chomping on her apple, she walked in the direction where Denise's vehicle had disappeared to. No sign of it was up ahead, and that had been the only vehicle on the road that Doreen had seen since walking around here. Or maybe this was just a rural road, with not a lot of traffic. It wasn't scary, and nothing made her nervous, even when her GPS function on her phone didn't work, telling her that she had no internet connection out here. *Probably all these trees blocking the signal.*

But yet she had some bars. So she could call someone—Mack—if needed.

The sun was shining up high. The sky was blue, and it was a beautiful day. And the walk had been really good for calming down the tension she'd felt. As she continued to walk, she looked at the big beautiful farmhouses, except that they looked more like estates. Obviously a lot of money was in them. They had large acreages, and most had fruit trees.

As she kept on walking, she saw a few more dilapidated-looking houses, some older ones that had obviously not been torn down and rebuilt, like the previous ones she had just passed. She thought she saw Denise's car up ahead, parked outside one of them, so she noted it and kept on walking closer.

As she neared the vehicle, somebody hopped into the car and raced down the driveway, turning onto the main road ahead of her. It was a guy, one she didn't recognize. But he looked like he was quite pissed. She sent a text to Mack, asking if Denise lived alone.

Mack called her a few moments later. "Why?"

"I'm not sure it's her exactly," she said, "but I'm up on the top of a hill behind the eco center, just walking. Now I seem to be where all the orchards are," she said. "I might need a rescue later too," she muttered, "but the point of why I'm asking is that I thought she passed me in her car. I mean, it was kind of hard to see her, but I recognized the car."

"Right, and?"

"Just now I saw it parked up here in front of one of the homes, and then the car came down the driveway fast and took off, and a guy was driving, and I didn't recognize him."

"So now you're investigating her?" he questioned humorously.

"No, but that guy could be her brother that you mentioned earlier, but you never shared a picture of him. Maybe if you shared more with me, then I'd be more willing to share more with you," she said, point-blank.

Mack sighed loudly.

"I'm just out for a walk to clear my head. I found it hard to settle at home, and I just wanted to get out."

"Hopefully you had breakfast first."

"No," she admitted. "That's why I might need a rescue later."

"You know better than that," he scolded.

"I do, but, like I said, I was just trying to get out."

"You've had a pretty unsettling couple of days," he muttered, "so okay."

"How about a couple of unsettling months," she responded back. "Plus, my ex called, and then I had to call Nick and then—" She stopped, with a wave of her hand. "Anyway, does Denise live alone?"

"I'm not sure we've ever asked her that."

"Who else would be around in her world? Do you have an address? Do you even know where she lives?"

"Do you think something's wrong there?"

"It feels wrong," she said, "but again I don't have any reason to question it."

"But you just feel like you can't stop questioning it?"

"Feels wrong," she said, with a shrug. She walked up to the driveway and then stopped. "See? I'm at the driveway, but I don't even feel like I can walk past it."

"Don't you dare go up there," he warned.

"But why not?" she asked. "I mean, I'm just out in the neighborhood, and I saw her. At least I think I saw her. Why can't I just stop in and say hi?"

"Because that's not how this works," he said.

"But it could be," she said. "I mean, if it were anybody else—if it was you, Nan, your mom, or Nick—wouldn't I be welcome to do that?"

"Sure, but it's not like you even know who this Denise person is."

"Maybe not, but, at the same time, I have been invited to the police station and to the morgue with her," she said. And then Doreen stopped. "Wait. You know something? The guy who just drove away looked kind of like the guy in the morgue."

"What?"

She nodded. "I know it makes no sense. All I can tell you is that's what I think."

"No, you're right. It makes no sense," he said. "Exactly where are you right now?"

"I'm not sure," she muttered. "No street signs are up here."

He said, "I've got a map of Kelowna in front of me. So where did you start from?"

She gave the landmarks she had passed on her walk. "But I really don't know precisely where I ended up. I just know that lots of big fruit trees and big houses are here."

"Sounds like east Kelowna. You probably went up the ravine, using some of those old steps there."

"I did take a bunch of steps up, yes," she muttered.

"An awful lot of land is up in southeast Kelowna."

"When does southeast become east Kelowna?" she asked. "Does that mean there's a north Kelowna and a south

Kelowna?"

"Yes," he said, his voice serious. "It absolutely does. If you ever want to see how the division of the property goes, look at the realty site for the area, and it will show you a map, where it's all broken down."

"Oh," she said, "I've never even thought of that." She looked around. "I don't see any house numbers either."

"No? So do you need a lift?" he asked. "You're quite a long way from home."

"I just thought maybe I could ask Denise," she said, looking back at the house, "except that I think her car just disappeared."

"But you said a man was driving, right?"

"Yes, yet I didn't really recognize him. Just that he looked familiar. Familiar, like the guy in the morgue. Listen. Did you ever think," she said, "that Denise and the guy in the morgue looked a little similar?"

"Yeah, which is one of the reasons we thought that maybe he was the uncle. But he wasn't, right?"

"Have you got the DNA test back?"

"We're running fingerprints first," he said, "because we have prints and DNA for everybody in the penal system. It's just that the DNA can take longer," he replied.

"If he is on file, if he has a criminal record, we should find him pretty fast then."

"But everything takes longer than expected," he warned her.

"I know," she said.

He added, "Just keep on walking home, and, if you get too tired, give me a shout, and I'll come pick you up."

"Oh, I'm walking all right," she said, "right up the driveway." And, with that, she hung up the phone. With the animals in tow and perfectly content to wander along, to smell the flowers, and to sniff the fallen fruit in the air, they all were enjoying the walk.

"We haven't done one this long in forever," she muttered. She wasn't even sure that she'd done one this long ever. She knew, in the back of her mind, that they were too far away for common sense, but she wasn't even sure how to get back home at this point, if she were honest. She might retrace her steps, but there was a good chance that she would miss the turnoff to the steps again. She felt like she was committed to keep going, even if she didn't know where it took her.

"You think we're okay, Mugs?" she asked. He woofed at her. She nodded and said, "Yeah, me too."

And they kept on walking up to the house. She studied it because it wasn't one of the big fancy mansions, where somebody had put some time and effort into its upkeep. Like her own home, this one needed some repairs. She walked up the front steps and knocked on the door.

When a young woman opened the door, she stared at her.

"Hi," Doreen said. The woman in front of her wasn't Denise. And that, in itself, was disappointing but also reassuring.

The woman nodded back at her. "Hi, what can I do for you?"

"Actually you could tell me where I am," she said. "I've been walking for quite a while, and I've managed to get lost."

The young woman smiled. "You are on the Southeast Kelowna Road," she said. "Not sure where you're trying to get to, but most people aren't up for walking in this area. Still, if you're walking in any direction, and you're hoping to head back to town, go that way," she said, pointing as she spoke.

"That's the way I've come," she said. "I took some steps up a hill and just kept on going, and now I'm a bit lost." Doreen smiled at the woman and said, "Thanks. I mean, I figured that, if somebody were here, I could ask for directions, so it's much appreciated."

"No problem," the woman said cheerfully.

Doreen stepped back, not sure what else she could say. And the door closed in front of her. With no other recourse, she followed the driveway back to the road. When she got there, she called Mack. "Apparently I'm on Southeast Kelowna Road," she said. "I just asked for directions, and she told me to go back the way I came."

"So was it Denise?"

"No," Doreen said thoughtfully. "And again I saw a bit of similarity in the other woman, but it's really hard to confirm, until I see the two of them together. Maybe she's just a friend."

"Which comparison you're not likely to do," he reminded her, "because Denise isn't there."

"Not that I know of," she said. And then, with a shrug, Doreen said, "I don't know. It's all just kind of weird." She turned to look back up at the house, while still on the phone with Mack, and said, "Some man is out on the side porch, watching me."

"How many times in a day does somebody walk up a country road like that, with a menagerie of animals, asking for directions because they've gotten lost. Kelowna is not that big."

"It's big enough on foot," she muttered. Just as she looked back at the house, she saw the same woman, who had earlier answered the door, step up at the side of the house, as if she were walking to the front, who said something to the man now in the front yard. Then the man immediately turned and bolted back around the house. "Now that's interesting," Doreen said.

"Uh-oh," Mack said. "What's interesting?" She told him what she just saw. "Any idea who the man was?"

"No, I'm a little bit too far away. But the woman seems to be the same one who gave me directions."

"Good," he said. "Now you stay away from them. They are strangers. Remember that."

"I got it." But, even as Doreen said that, she studied the area around her, wondering if she had a way to come around and take a look at what was going on at that house from another perspective.

"Remember. No trespassing," Mack warned. "We have laws against that."

"Sure, but what if they're part of the kidnapping?"

He stopped and said, "What led you to that notion? So far, all you've said is that you've walked up onto a stranger's driveway and asked them for directions. What on earth makes you think they have anything to do with the kidnapping?"

"I don't know," she said. "Instincts?"

"Not good enough in this case," he warned. "I can't get a warrant on something like that."

"I know," she said. "Never mind. Just let me think about it."

"No, you don't need to think about it," he said. "You should walk home or at least get back to the steps, so you know where you are. You're lost. Remember?"

"Not necessarily lost," she said. "I am in Kelowna."

He groaned. "Do I need to pick you up?"

"You can if you want to," she said. "My feet are a little sore, but it's my own fault, so I'll keep going."

And, with that, she hung up and kept on walking a few paces down. She turned to look back to see that the woman she'd talked to was halfway down the driveway and following Doreen's progress. Doreen turned and kept on going; at least she was following the direction that she'd been told to go, but still it felt kind of creepy. As if the woman were making sure Doreen was leaving. And that in itself was strange as well.

At the corner, and out of sight a little farther, Doreen kept turning back to make sure she wasn't being followed, and, when she realized she was free and clear, she went cross-country, through the apple trees up the side of the property—or the neighbor's property perhaps. She wasn't even sure whose property she was on. It seemed like these orchards just kept on going from place to place. She couldn't see any division in the land, so she wasn't sure if it were all one big orchard or if nobody had bothered to fence them individually.

She saw a deer in the distance and thought it would probably have a heyday in a place like this. She hadn't really had to deal with a deer just yet, since moving to Kelowna. And she wouldn't mind if she had that opportunity; she did love animals. She wasn't sure she would get the experience that she was hoping for because a lot of people said some of the deer were quite aggressive. That seemed odd to her, but she didn't have any firsthand knowledge otherwise, so what did she know?

By the time she wandered up through the trees, still keeping a wary eye on her surroundings, she saw the house in question ever-so-slightly ahead of her and down a little bit. Apparently she had climbed a hill without realizing it, though she wasn't very high up. It was just enough to give her a little bit of a lift, so she could look down. Seeing yet another rise off to the side, she changed direction and climbed up what appeared to be more of a hillock area, with more trees on a plateau above it. She nodded approvingly. "They've made good use of this space."

Indeed, they had, and it was amazing to see how enterprising the original people who planted these trees had been. But she really appreciated the use of all the land. As she took another look back at the house, she shook her head because, right in front of her, she saw several people, and they were arguing. She hunkered down, with Mugs and Goliath tucked up close. Thaddeus had been snoozing for the last while, tucked up against her neck, but, as soon as she stopped moving and sat down, he perked up and cried out, "Thaddeus is here. Thaddeus is here."

She immediately shushed him. "We're on a mission. Let's not let anybody know we're here."

He stared at her with this wide-eyed look, flapped his wings, but stayed quiet. In fact, he curled up against her neck and nodded off again. She worried about him for a moment; then she realized that all this fresh air was likely to have had just as big of an effect on her as it was on the rest of them. Goliath immediately stretched out below her, looking for all the world like he was ready for a good snooze too. She smiled at Mugs. "We haven't done a long hike like this in forever, have we?"

He woofed quietly, then snuggled up against her and stretched out, nodding off too. "Okay, so I guess this is a very necessary break," she muttered.

With the sun up, it was definitely pleasant. Sure, she was trespassing, but she wouldn't focus on that. And she had no reason to believe that anything was really wrong down below, but, when she'd seen the guy disappear around the corner of the house earlier, that had made her immediately suspicious, but apparently she had a suspicious mind.

Just as she was about to settle back and close her eyes for a bit of a rest for herself, she heard a loud noise as somebody yelled. She looked at the house, wishing she could have gotten closer, but, with so many people around, it was hard. She watched as the man she had seen earlier hit another man. The fight went on, and nobody appeared to be stopping it. She leaned forward, looking around the area to see if she could find a better vantage point.

Seeing one, she hopped up, and, dragging the animals with her, she quickly snuck a little closer. The yelling was still going on, but now it was more like cries of pain. She held out her phone and tried to get a video, but it was hard because they were still just that far away. She also didn't know who was involved, and, of course, she had no right to be here, but that wouldn't stop her.

Somebody was hurting somebody else, and Doreen didn't know whether she should get involved in it or not. Mack would no doubt say no—or perhaps something stronger—but she had yet to listen to him. Although that voice of reason was telling her it might be a good time to begin. Finally in her new vantage point and having taken advantage of all the chaos below to make the move, she studied the players, and, sure enough, there was Denise, standing by the fight, a hand over her mouth as she watched it. Doreen couldn't identify the two men involved, but surely one would be the uncle.

The one who had supposedly been kidnapped.

As she watched, all of a sudden, the one man seemed to have exhausted himself, and he pulled back, then took another step back, as if distancing himself from the mess. "You can't do anything right," he roared at the man. "This was as simple as disappearing for a while and have them not find you. You know? Like take off and get a new life somewhere else. Instead you kill your brother and put him on a slab in the morgue."

The man on the ground said something, but Doreen couldn't hear what it was; she just hoped that something was being recorded on her phone that Mack could amplify somehow. She quickly sent Mack a text, explaining what was going on, saying that it looked like the uncle was here. But no sooner had she sent it, when the conversation below got even more heated.

"It wasn't me who killed him," the supposed uncle roared. "That was you."

"I didn't kill him," snapped the other man, who had beaten him up. "That was you. You and your stupid plans."

"He was my brother," he whined.

"That's nice. Too bad you didn't give a shit about him."

Both men just glared at each other, but it appeared as if the fisticuff session was over for the moment. Doreen had never really understood how someone could pound somebody into the ground, then, all of a sudden, have it over with. Why didn't the guy on the ground just get back up and punch him out?

Perhaps he would just take another beating, since he clearly couldn't defend himself in the first place. As she watched, the one man who'd done the beating stormed into the house and slammed the door. Denise walked over to the man on the ground and asked, “Are you happy now?”

He struggled to his feet and glared at her. “It’s not my fault,” he retorted.

“I had to go to the morgue,” she snapped. “And I said I didn’t know who it was.”

“Good,” he roared. “You don’t know the man. Just because he’s my brother doesn’t mean you’ve had anything to do with him.”

“But he looked enough like you that I’m sure it won’t take them very long to figure out who it is.”

“I still didn’t kill him,” he snapped.

“No, but which one of your cronies did? He did time for you. You owe him something.”

He looked at her, then shrugged and said, “It’s the life. It sucks it out of you and makes you into this cheat.”

“You don’t have to be a cheat,” she cried out. “You can be whoever you want to be.”

“Not if I ever get caught,” he said. “I’m living a completely different life now. I’m not going back to that.”

“Until you get caught,” she warned, and, with that, she turned and headed back inside herself.

Stunned, Doreen could only sit here in shock, as she tried to figure out the new pieces of the puzzle. When her phone rang, she quickly answered it to make sure that the sound didn’t carry.

“What are you talking about?” Mack asked. “I got that text but half came out garbled.”

“Yeah, no wonder,” she said. “Hang on. I’m sending you something. At least I’m going to try but the Internet is spotty.”

With the video shut off, she quickly sent it to Mack. **Watch this immediately.**

She waited a few minutes, wondering if anything else could be happening at the house and hoping not, when her phone rang again.

"Where are you?" he asked, and this time his tone was serious and brisk. "And don't lie to me."

"I'm beside the house," she said, "but, once again, I don't know exactly where I am."

He swore into the phone, making her back stiffen.

"No need for that kind of language," she snapped.

"Don't even start with me," he said. "You are in danger. They've already killed somebody, and here you are with the proof in your hand that can put them away, and you don't even know where you are?"

"No," she said sadly. "I really don't. I can't get my GPS to work out here with all the orchards."

"You could have checked a map, before you entered this area. Did you ever think of that? You don't ever seem to realize just how much danger you're in," he raged. "What happens the next time, if I'm not available, if I can't answer my phone?"

"I'm hidden in the trees," she said. Just then she heard the snap of a branch behind her, and she froze, then spun around, thought she caught sight of somebody stepping behind a tree. She whispered into the phone, "Mack, someone's behind me, I think. Or hopefully it's just a deer."

"Dammit," he raged. "Hunker down very quietly and try to stay hidden."

"That won't work so well," she said, as she studied her little space. "If somebody comes up to this hillock, I'm pretty well exposed."

"So why did you choose that particular spot?" he asked.

'Because it allowed me to see what was going on below."

"Did you ever think, in all that time, that maybe you weren't alone?"

She thought about it, shook her head, and said, "No, but I guess it's possible I was followed."

"You need to hunker down and stay down," he said. "I'm on the way. Just stay alive. You have no idea how dangerous this can get." And he hung up.

The trouble was, she did know exactly how dangerous it could get. And, once again, she was right in the middle of it.

Chapter 24

KEEPING AN EYE on the tree, where Doreen thought she'd seen somebody slip behind it, she moved her way up the hill in the opposite direction. With the animals keeping close to her, she wasn't even sure how they knew they had a problem, unless it was an awareness of her actions. Goliath never strayed more than one foot away from her; he didn't race off like he often did. And Mugs, instead of growling or jumping around in the leaves, walked quietly at her side, his ears twitching constantly, as he looked around. Moving ten feet, then twenty, and thirty, and so on, by the time she made it just up to a rise again, where she could go over the edge, she hunkered down at the top and studied the area below her.

The trees where she thought she'd seen somebody were a little off to the side, and it was hard to see whether somebody could still be hiding there or not. Perhaps they'd taken the opportunity to disappear as well. As she looked around, she realized that she was in an orchard. These dratted things seemed to go on forever now. But, with no other option to get away from the house and whoever might have followed her, she kept walking farther and farther up the hill.

She didn't know if Mack could track her, based on her cell phone, and whether that was even something she wanted him to do because seriously? It was kind of an intrusive thought. At the same time, if it would get her safely home again, in this case she would be all for it.

Up on the top and moving through the trees, she kept walking, zigzagging her way along, trying to confuse anybody who might have followed her. As she moved farther and farther up the tree-lined acres, she tried to reason it out in her mind. "Surely the owners have access to these orchards. Some roads must be up here somewhere."

She couldn't guarantee that the roads wouldn't lead back to that house that she was trying to avoid though. Mack was right in that, if anybody knew that she'd heard the conversation or had a copy of that recording, Doreen would be in trouble. But that was the least of her problems, considering she had so much else going on right now. And not the least of which was the fact that she was well and truly lost.

But she was still in civilization, so an answer had to be here somewhere for her. She just had to find her way out. And, if that didn't happen soon, she may scream in frustration.

But rather than giving in to that kind of stressful thought process—or giving away her location to somebody following her—she just kept going, focusing on putting one foot in front of the other. That had to be the better answer, given the chaos right now. Still it was hard not to get a little bit on the squirrely side, when she realized just how bad it seemed, when everything was completely out of control.

As she continued on, she talked to the animals, trying to stay happy and positive, hoping to recognize something soon. One good thing about her current situation was the view. It also made her realize that she was climbing higher and higher. Gorgeous, yes, but a little disconcerting at the same time. She also knew Mack was on his way, but how was he supposed to find her, if she kept going away from the house? She stopped and frowned, then looked around. She was surrounded by just trees, apple trees upon apple trees upon apple trees. She reached up, scrubbed her face, and said, "Hey, guys, any idea where we go from here?"

Mugs just woofed and laid down at her side. Goliath had stayed nearby, nothing beyond his presence that he could contribute. He was just a little farther up, staring at her, as if asking what was next on the agenda. Honestly she didn't have a clue what to say to him. She groaned and said, "I don't know what to say, boys." And that wasn't very helpful either. But it's what she had to work with. "So let's go. We'll keep on walking." And so she did.

The animals willingly got up and came with her. She wasn't even sure at this point if they thought this was a fun outing or had recognized that she was somewhat in trouble. She said *somewhat* because it appeared she had no immediate problem. Yet, at the same time, she didn't know exactly where she was, and people were nearby who could potentially do her harm, especially if they knew what she had witnessed. She understood that aimlessly wandering was confusing and made zero sense. But she would go with it.

As she continued walking, she started to sing softly, just enough to keep herself company. It was an old trick she'd learned when alone at her ex-husband's house. She was alone there a lot, and she'd found all sorts of little ways to make life not seem quite so harsh and ugly. Only as Mugs raced ahead a little bit and started growling did Doreen fall silent and stopped. She crept up behind him, her gaze searching beneath all the trees, looking to see what was upsetting Mugs. When Doreen heard a crack off to the left behind her, she immediately spun and hid by a tree. She muttered down at Mugs, "What do you see?"

She couldn't see anything, and the fact that he could was enough to drive her crazy. Then she watched as a beautiful doe stepped out among the trees, glanced around delicately, then leaned forward to sniff at an apple on a tree. The doe moved on, and Doreen noticed another little one. It looked like the doe had a fawn with her. Stunned and delighted, Doreen watched in joy as the animals moved slowly ahead of her. "I guess life for you is the same, isn't it?" she muttered. "Always about keeping yourself safe."

She wondered at the life they had, always on the lookout for predators. "I'm sorry," she whispered. "It must be tough." At the same time the doe didn't appear to care about Doreen at all. And that reminded her about their instincts and what they considered predators versus not. Maybe they were better off than she was.

Doreen didn't seem to know the difference between friend and foe, at least that's what Mack would say. She wasn't sure he was necessarily correct, but she could understand his frustration when she got into a scenario, like she was in right now, and of course had no idea where she was. Even from the vantage point she had at present, she was caught in the trees. Realizing that the doe was content where she was in her own space, Doreen moved forward and just kept walking ahead, but she was a little more lighthearted now. Something about seeing Mother Nature at her best brought out happiness.

It could also mean that Mother Nature at her worst was somewhere close by as well, but, hey, Doreen was willing to work with whatever she had right now. And that was a little odd because so much was going on. It sounded like somebody had done time for the uncle, and maybe that was the uncle who was here. But, it had been the uncle's brother who'd done time for him, how was it that he was now free?

Unless he was the gardener, who had been the one kidnapped, or the kidnapping had been more a case of him just needing to disappear for a while, but why would that be? Because nobody could know that there were the two of them? That kind of made sense, but what would cause the one brother, the first one, the criminal, to need to step forward? Unless … then she shrugged. "It's probably what it usually is," she muttered. "Greed."

Somewhere, somehow money was involved, and they needed this guy to make an appearance. And why would that be? And why the kidnapping? Except to make one brother disappear and to allow for the other brother to show up. As if each brother were interchangeable. But wouldn't the cops know then? Or would it just remain an open case? Had they been at this for so long that it didn't seem to matter to anybody anymore? She pondered the vagaries of twisted minds, trying to pull something over on somebody else, and she realized she still needed more information.

Of course the weak link here was Denise. Although Doreen wasn't exactly sure about that because it appeared that nobody knew who had killed whom.

That just blew Doreen away because how many times did somebody get killed in some family issue, like this, when you didn't really have any idea who was at fault? It was very strange to listen to them argue because Doreen had only little bits of information, and none of it was enough. She came around the side of a great big apple tree, and all of a sudden, the land dipped down, and she found herself at a road. She looked at it with relief and grinned.

"Now look at that," she crowed to the animals. "I know we're tired, but here is a road."

They looked up at her, turned toward the road, and seemed completely unimpressed.

"I get it," she said. "You're not as happy about a road as I am. But a road means that Mack can find us, and I'm not lost in the middle of that orchard."

Chapter 25

OF COURSE FINDING a road wasn't all that great of a help if Doreen couldn't tell Mack what road she was on. Still she would take this as a good sign. As were the symbols saying she had internet again. She sent Mack a picture of the road and said, "I made it somewhere." Her answer was a phone call.

"It would help if you knew where the road was," he muttered.

"I know," she said apologetically. "I was sitting here, patting myself on the back. I'm somewhere now that isn't in the middle of an orchard."

He laughed. "You always were somewhere," he said. "It's just nowhere that we could identify."

"I know," she said, "and I'm sorry. It seems like this is an awful lot of trouble."

"Not so unusual for you," he muttered. "I was just hoping that we were getting to a place where you weren't in so much trouble all the time."

"I was thinking," she said, "what would make the uncle want to disappear?"

"It could be all kinds of things," he said. "Somebody

after him most likely. Given his criminal record."

"I was wondering if he needed to disappear so that the other brother could show up again."

"So you're assuming again, based on what you heard, that we have two brothers involved, and the one did time for the other one, who was the criminal?"

"Yeah," she said, "that's what I was thinking. And then I was trying to figure out what would bring up the need for the one guy to come forward, like why kidnap the brother that's been here for seven years?"

"But that means you're thinking that they were involved in the kidnapping."

"The one guy said the other guy just needed to disappear, and that it was simple and that he shouldn't have made it complicated."

"Right, so, if he disappeared for a while, but then what?" Mack asked. "Show up again and say it was all just a mistake?"

"I'm sure you've seen things like that happen before."

"Yes, but then why? You know that if he had been manhandled into a vehicle, it would make sense if he managed to get away from them and didn't want to press charges. We would end up just dropping the case. But the ransom note makes it different. And the niece delivered it, but I'm not sure she knew about it."

"Meaning, somebody else is involved?"

"Really, Doreen? What have I told you about suppositions?"

Such doubt was in his voice that she groaned and said, "I know. My theory is really complicated, isn't it?"

"It is, indeed. But you have to remember that almost everything in life is simple. As in very simple."

"I know. I know. I know," she said. "It's just frustrating me."

"Yeah, I get it," he said, "but that doesn't mean that there's not an easier explanation."

"I don't know. This was starting to sound pretty complicated."

"But it's not a cold case," he said smoothly. "It's a live case. Remember? And you're not supposed to be involved in that."

"I know. I wasn't trying to be involved. Denise got me involved."

"Yeah," he said, "and how does that happen?"

"I don't know, and what was all that about the Bob Small stuff?"

"I'm thinking that may have been a red herring on her part," he said thoughtfully. "Especially if you mentioned that name to her first."

"Are we thinking she's involved in this?"

"Isn't that what you were already saying?" he asked curiously.

"I just don't want her to be," she muttered.

"Just because we don't want somebody to be involved doesn't mean they aren't. You knew right off the bat that something was odd about her."

"Yes, but she wasn't involved in the fighting on the ground here."

"But she didn't stop it either, did she?"

"That's the thing about being in the middle of a fight like that," Doreen said. "There's a good chance that they would have turned on her."

"True, and a judge would certainly consider that, depending on what her defense is, but there's an awful lot going on here that we still don't understand. So, at this point, we can't really assume anything."

"No, we can't presume," she said. "I would agree with that. It's just kind of odd."

"Maybe not so odd," he said. "Anyway I have a good idea where you are now, so sit tight, and, with any luck, I can be there in a few minutes."

She hung up the phone and started down the road. No matter which way he came, he would be on the road and would pick her up, but she felt the need to keep moving. She hadn't mentioned the feeling like somebody was behind her, watching her. It felt silly since she had no evidence. And, as long as she and her animals got picked up and taken out of here soon, hopefully they'd all be safe. And, sure enough, she heard a large truck coming toward her. She looked up, smiled, and waved.

Mack pulled off to the side of the road, hopped out, and immediately wrapped her up in a hug and held her close. She burrowed in, smiling, more relieved than she may have cared to admit. When he finally released her, he shook his head. "You do get yourself into a spot of trouble every week."

She nodded. "I didn't mean to," she said, looking up at him. She reached out, patted his cheek, and said, "But, once again, you came to my rescue."

"And that's getting to be a really bad habit," he said, shaking his head.

She laughed. "I know. I know. It's not exactly what I was planning on either. But at least I'm safe now." She walked over to the big truck, opened the door, and waited while Mack spent a few minutes cuddling Mugs.

He looked over at her and asked, "How's Thaddeus?"

Thaddeus poked his head out from behind her hair and

crowed, "Thaddeus is here. Thaddeus is here."

"He's been really quiet the whole time," she said. "Not sure if that's just because he doesn't like the scenario or if he's just really tired."

"If he's smart," Mack muttered, "which I know that he is, then I'll say that he just doesn't like the scenario."

"Maybe," she muttered. "They're all wary."

"Did you see anybody else following you?"

She shook her head. "Not that I could tell. I think, as soon as I left the area, they left me alone. I felt kind of watched, but it might have just been in my head."

"Hard to say. We also don't know if other players are involved here."

"I was wondering about that," she said. "If you think about it, somebody else could have dropped off that ransom note."

"But why?" he asked.

"It takes me back to the original question. Why did the wrong brother end up in jail in the first place?" she asked. "All of it seems suspicious."

"It is," he said. "But that still doesn't give us any answers."

"Are you going to talk to Denise?"

"Yes," he said. "*Alone*, as in, without you."

"Ah," she said, shaking her head. "Any way to keep me out of that discussion, like how you got that video?"

"Maybe. At least I hope so. I'll take a look at that video again and see if it identifies you at all."

"I hope not," she said, frowning at that thought.

"It depends on if the animals are in the frames," he said, looking at her. "Those are the kinds of things that you have to watch out for when you take photos like that."

"And I didn't even think of it," she said in horror, staring at him. She looked at the animals. "You guys are okay, right?"

Mugs just woofed at her and laid his head back down. "I think that was a long walk for them," she muttered. "Everybody is tired."

He laughed. "Why wouldn't they be?" he said, smiling at her. "You went quite a few miles."

She nodded. "It wasn't planned though." Before long, he pulled up in front of her house, and she smiled when she saw it. "It's so good to be home," she muttered. The animals made absolutely no argument about getting out and heading inside. If anything, it looked like relief flashed on their faces. She smiled as she walked in and said, "Coffee would be lovely."

"Will you stay home now?" he asked, standing at the doorway.

She nodded. "I will," she said. "I'm really tired. My legs are sore, and I might even have blisters."

"Walking uphill like that can play havoc on your ankles too."

She nodded. "Go off and do your thing," she said. "I don't know if what I ended up with helps or hinders you."

"At this point in time what you did was find more pieces to a very confusing puzzle," he said, "but we will get to the bottom of it."

"Good," she said, smiling. "Go for it."

He repeated, "And you'll stay out of trouble?"

"I'll absolutely stay out of trouble," she said. "I'll go back to the Bob Small stuff. I kind of like cold cases. Everybody is dead and gone, and they can't come after me."

"That's not true. What about family members, friends,

partners?" he asked, shaking his head at her. "You need to remember how people did come after you an awful lot of the time. So stay safe, please."

She watched as he left, feeling a sense of relief to be home and also a warmth in her heart that Mack had once again come to her rescue. It shouldn't have happened, but it had, and she was grateful. As soon as he was gone, she looked at the animals and said, "We need food."

She gave them all a few extra treats and filled up their food and water dishes, and, while everybody tucked into their food, she made herself an omelet. She wanted something even heartier but was too tired to make more. With everybody sitting down outside, she happily sat in her little corner of her new deck, until her phone rang. She looked at it and responded, "Hi, Nan. How are you?"

"I'm okay," she said. "How are you?"

"I'm fine. Why?"

"I just—" Nan stopped and said, "I'm not sure. I've just had a terrible feeling today."

"I was in a little bit of a rough spot this morning, but Mack bailed me out again," she said, "so I'm fine now."

"Details," her grandmother demanded immediately. "I want details."

She laughed. "You can have a few of them," she said, "but I don't really have a ton of them." Then she explained what had happened.

"Oh my," Nan said. "I know those houses up there. Let me think about it. Maybe I don't know the exact house. An awful lot of big orchards are out there now, and they've changed hands over the years. Of course it used to be that the orchards weren't making very much money, but they sure are now," Nan said.

Doreen kept eating, while Nan mulled it all over. Finally Doreen said, "Anyway, I'm quite tired. I'll just chill here for the afternoon."

"Please stay home and out of trouble."

"I promised Mack that I would," she said. "He wasn't very happy with me."

"Of course not," she said. "You really don't understand how much he cares, do you?"

"I'm not going there right now," she said.

"You don't have to. You just need to realize that what he does comes from caring."

"And I get that," she said. "Oh, and my ex called while I was walking too."

Nan groaned. "You need to ditch him."

"Wouldn't that be nice?" she said. "I need to touch base with Nick."

"And you need to stop answering phone calls from that horrid man you married," Nan said. "He'll be nothing but trouble."

"That could be. I'm not exactly sure how to get out of any of this right now. I wish none of it had happened."

"That won't help," Nan said, and she hung up not long afterward.

With a cup of coffee and sitting in the safety of her garden area, Doreen looked at the work that needed to be done and said, "I need to get back to Millicent's." Ever since she'd fallen out of the habit of going every Friday, it seemed like it was hard to get back into that same routine. Sometimes it was a Thursday. Sometimes it was a Saturday. Last time was probably two Saturdays ago since Doreen had been there, and she didn't like that the random days made things much more awkward for her.

But also she could only fit so much into a day, and she'd been so tired lately. She knew that was a bit of a cop-out, but it was kind of hard to not find excuses. But she also needed something to take her mind off of all that had happened today. So she contacted Millicent and said, "Millicent, I'm so sorry. I should have been by again last week, before now for sure. Do you want me to come by today and work on your gardening?"

"If you wouldn't mind, that would be good," she said. "Some weeds in the front yard are bothering me."

"Sure. We'll walk over in a few minutes then."

She felt better knowing she would do something helpful for somebody, while giving herself something to work on. Even though she was tired, it wasn't the exhaustive kind of tired, so she headed over to Millicent's place. Her animals were in tow, all seemingly restored in spirit. Once there, Doreen smiled to see Millicent had a teapot out and waved her over.

"I figured we might have a cup of tea before you started."

Doreen laughed. "You know I'm always up for a cup of tea."

"And it's nice of you to spend time with an old woman," she said. "I admit that I do get lonely."

"I think that's pretty normal for everybody sometimes," she said.

"Maybe. My life used to be so full, and then it just becomes so much less," she said, with a half smile.

"I'm not sure that's a problem either," Doreen said. "Sometimes my life is too busy."

Millicent asked her, "Are you helping out my son on any cases?"

"Honestly, right now, I'm sure he thinks I'm more of a bother than anything." Then she launched into a little bit of an explanation about Denise and the gardener who was kidnapped.

"Oh my," Millicent said, "I don't think Mack wants you to get into any trouble."

"I don't want to get into any trouble either, but somehow I got asked to go."

"And did you think about that?" she asked. "Like maybe why that would even happen?"

"She said it was because she'd heard about my cases."

"And you know what? That could very well be it. It's just an interesting thing, particularly if she turns out to be guilty of something."

"But I don't know that she is at this point," Doreen protested.

"I just don't want people to use you to get to Mack or to plant seeds of things that have gone wrong or that they want you to believe because of it."

"I certainly hadn't considered that," Doreen said, looking at her.

"You probably need to now, just because you are getting famous."

She winced. "I don't feel famous," she muttered. She tossed back the rest of her tea and said, "Okay, show me where those weeds are."

And, with that, they got down to the business of cleaning up Millicent's flower garden again. It didn't take much. By the time Doreen had it weeded, she got out the edger and worked on trimming up the edges a bit. Millicent had a beautiful garden, and she'd spent a lot of time over the years keeping it perfect, so this was just little bits and pieces that

Doreen needed to do to keep it that way.

As Doreen was leaving, Millicent asked, "It wasn't that house with the weird gables, was it?"

Doreen thought about it and said, "I don't know what you mean by *weird*."

"Kind of like there should be an extra gable, like one was missing."

"Kind of," she said, "in a blue trim, I think. I don't really have much of a memory of it."

Millicent nodded. "You know what? I think one of your grandmother's friends did the siding on that house."

"I wouldn't be at all surprised," she said. "If anybody in Nan's group does siding, it's not that huge of a town. I mean, I know it's a city, and I keep calling it a small town because it feels so much more that way."

Millicent laughed. "And for those of us who have been here forever, it's gotten too big for our comfort."

"I'm sure that's true too," Doreen said, with a smile. "It's way smaller than the city that I come from. I get that too. Anyway I'm sure the size of Kelowna doesn't make a bit of difference in this murder case."

"I think the siding repairs were fairly recent."

"I still don't understand. What difference does it make?" Doreen asked.

Millicent shrugged. "I'm not sure, but just something was off about it."

"This whole thing is off," she said, with a laugh.

"Some things are like that, aren't they?"

"They definitely are," Doreen said, smiling. "I feel like I'm running around in circles on this case, and nothing concrete has been sorted out. I have no files to look up. There's nothing."

"I guess it depends on if you're looking up the uncle. But what if you should be looking up, you know, the guy who was hitting him? I wonder who that would have been."

"I don't know," she said. "That whole family up there is a bit weird."

"They've got an awful lot of family history online now, though. So, if you could get a family tree lined up, you might recognize somebody."

On that note Doreen looked at her in surprise and said, "You know what? That's a good idea. I haven't done that yet," she said. "I've been tired and off-balance a little bit because of all these other Bob Small cases. I never really had a chance to get focused on this one."

"That can happen all the time in life," Millicent said, with a giggle, "but it might be time to go find some family history."

Doreen nodded and waved a hand at the garden and asked, "What else am I doing here?"

But Millicent just waved her hand. "We're good," she said. "It's gorgeous as usual. Go off and do your stuff."

And, with that, she laughed. "In that case, if you don't mind, I will."

And Doreen headed back home again.

Chapter 26

THE MINUTE DOREEN walked into the house, she sat down at her laptop. Mugs curled up at her feet, obviously tired and worn out. Thaddeus headed straight to his roost in the living room and slept. Of Goliath, there was no sign. He'd disappeared. She looked around and said, "I'm sorry, guys. Our walk today was a bit much, I know."

Thaddeus opened an eye and shut it immediately.

"Ouch," she said, "I'll take that as a yes."

She kept working away on her laptop, figuring out just what she needed to do here. Because apparently something was going on, and she hadn't done all her basic research stuff. With a pen and paper at the ready, she looked up the guy who was supposedly missing. She found the missing uncle had a brother in the archives and stopped because of a mention of his brother being *simple*. Not retarded, which is something that they would have said in the olden days, but he was on the autistic scale, yet was highly functioning. That was interesting, and, if so, she wondered how the jails had let him into the system. But, as she continued to read, she saw that he'd passed whatever tests he'd taken in school, so there was some doubt on that *simple* diagnosis as well. It was later mentioned that he was also dyslexic. She frowned at that too.

"That's hardly a jail-sentence diagnosis." She also found a sister to the two brothers, but one of the brothers is dead in the morgue, and she confirmed that the parents were long gone. So now she had three older siblings accounted for, and she wondered about that because she hadn't seen any sign of a sister in that age group at the house by the orchard. Of course she might not live here or even still be alive, for that matter. Further research pointed out that the sister had moved back east and had passed away back there some time ago.

"Doesn't mean she didn't have kids though," Doreen murmured. By the time she worked her way through the family tree, she found the dead sister had had two children, one son and a daughter—Denise. "Now we're getting somewhere," she said. "So Denise's mother is dead, and she has a brother, which Mack tried to tell me about earlier." Obviously their family kept fairly close, otherwise there would be no connection between the uncle and Denise. But who was the other stranger? That's the one Doreen wanted to identify, and she had no other way to figure it out without Mack's help. She texted Mack and asked if he would share what happened to Denise's mother and father.

He sent back a question mark.

Just following the family history. Two brothers—Dicky and his dead brother in the morgue—and a sister. Sister is dead, but she had a son and a daughter, Denise, who is here. So the two brothers are her uncles. That's the relationship to the guy who was kidnapped, but I wonder whether the mother and/or parents died of natural causes. Plus you never told me more about Denise's brother.

She got no answer for a long moment, and she finally

put down her phone and went back to her research. Only in one small article did Doreen read something about Denise's uncle Dicky having been charged with theft. And that brought Doreen back to the question of what was it that Dicky had stolen? Like the blackmail note had mentioned $100,000? What if that note was from somebody completely different? What if this started out as a way for this Dicky to disappear, and whoever was looking for Dicky found the "simple" brother instead and killed him?

She sat back, as slowly some of the pieces began to make more sense. She started writing it down. Two brothers, one goes to jail for the other. The supposedly simple guy goes to jail for Dicky, the brother who stole something. Whoever it is that Dicky stole from finds out he's free from jail and living in Kelowna, but the simpler of the brothers is living at the family's country home, while the other brother, Dicky, supports himself by being a gardener for the city on a contract basis and lives elsewhere in town.

The contract gardener finds out that the guy he cheated is in town, so Dicky fakes his own kidnapping to disappear, but this guy who's after him finds his simple brother and kills him instead. Now they have the cops looking for the one brother, and they have this victim of the theft looking for the same brother—Dicky. And the guy who did all the time and was innocent of everything is now dead.

She nodded, spoke out loud. "So who's the stranger at the house though? Who's the guy beating up Dicky? How does Denise play into this, and who is after them?"

With that written down, she sent Mack an email with her thoughts. Then she sat down and sent him a text. **I need to know who Dicky supposedly stole from way back when.**

He replied right away. **A huge data company.**

So he was their accountant? she asked.

He was part of an inventory audit that was done, but he was a computer geek.

So did he steal funds or information?

We don't know exactly.

I need more information on it, she replied.

She hoped he would get it and share that with her but had no guarantee that he was too interested in helping her out at this point. Although sharing this info with her should be helping him out too. She smiled when he texted back.

He sold data, email addresses, banking information, security information.

She nodded and, speaking to nobody in particular, said, "White-collar crime, nobody physically hurt, loss of data, no responsibility. Yada, yada, yada." So he wouldn't feel bad about what he was doing but obviously some of that information went into the wrong hands. And who knows what was stolen? Maybe he found something else when he was in there too.

"I'm thinking of the blackmailing," she said out loud, "and what could have been stolen from somebody that was worth one hundred thousand dollars."

If he sold the credit card information or the privacy information, it could be somebody whose identity was subsequently stolen, and maybe it cost him one hundred thousand dollars to get his life back on track. *Hmm*, she kind of liked that idea. Not too much in the way of choices here, but the fact of the matter included one dead person and the guy who never did the time he was supposed to do for his own crimes. Whether it was guilt or not that bothered him, the fact remains that his brother, who did the jail time for him, is now dead. That *should* bother him, but what would Dicky do about it? He had promised his niece that he was no longer doing these kinds of crimes, but who would listen to him now?

Doreen frowned, as she thought about it, because so many things were wrong with this scenario that it was still hard to work her way forward. And, like Millicent had mentioned before, what did it have to do with Doreen anyway? Why did Denise seek out Doreen? Was it a setup, as Millicent had suggested, or was something else going on here? Doreen thought about the fear on Denise's face as she watched the two men fight, her uncle ending up on the ground. The fear had looked real.

Doreen sat here for a long moment, sipping her coffee, her fingers thrumming on the phone, when a knock came on the door. Mugs immediately barked, and, even as tired and as fatigued as he was, he raced to the door in an aggressive manner. Goliath disappeared once again, and Thaddeus, now woken up from his nap, looked more than a little upset. She walked over to the front of the house, and, when she opened the door, she was surprised to see Denise here. "Hi," she said.

Denise looked at her and kind of shrugged. "Hi," she said, "I didn't really know where to go."

"What do you mean?" Doreen asked.

"I don't know," she said. "I was just really upset, and I was thinking that maybe I could come for a visit."

The last time today that Doreen had seen Denise, the woman had been definitely upset, though she didn't know that Doreen had seen that. She opened the door wider. "Come on in," she said. "I don't have much to offer, I'm afraid."

"No, I shouldn't even be here." Raising both hands, she didn't move from the front porch. "I don't know why I am. It's just that you seem like such a kind lady."

"I am," she said, "at least I would like to think I am. Are you sure you don't want to come in? We can have a cup of tea out back."

Denise looked nervously around and then stepped inside quickly and closed the door.

Doreen immediately backed up slightly, wondering why Denise had just done that. "Are you okay?" she asked. "You're acting nervous, like somebody is following you or something."

"I feel that way too," she said, "but, hey, if you're offering a cup of tea, that would be awesome."

"Sure. So I can make tea, or would you prefer coffee?" she asked. She led the way into the kitchen, half turning to look behind her to make sure the woman was following her and not acting even more suspicious.

"*Um …*"

Denise didn't seem to know how to answer that. Then Doreen just shrugged and said, "Pick one."

"Okay," she said quietly. "Tea then, thanks."

"You're acting a little strange, Denise. You know that, right?"

She laughed. "Everything has been strange in my life for a long time," she said.

"I'm sorry. Do you want to tell me about it?"

"No, I can't do that," she said. "I can't tell anybody about it."

"I'm sorry for that because it makes life even more difficult, doesn't it?"

"It sure does," Denise said, with a shrug. "But it doesn't

seem to matter. I can do only so much at any given time."

"That sounds pretty defeated," Doreen said.

"I don't think *defeated* is quite the right term. *Depressed* maybe," she said.

"I'm sorry. If there is anything I can do to help, please let me know." She didn't even know why she said that because, of course, she couldn't do much to help anyone else, but it seemed like this woman needed some encouragement. In the kitchen, Doreen motioned to the deck outside and said, "If you want to take a seat outside," she said, "I'll put on the teakettle."

As soon as the woman stepped through the kitchen door and out to the deck, she quickly texted Mack that Denise was here. Doreen knew he would be livid, but she wasn't sure what else she was supposed to do about it. Sure enough, Mack responded immediately.

What the hell?

She winced at the language. But she couldn't say a whole lot to him right now. This was too important. Something was happening. She didn't know what it was, but she needed to figure it out fast. And that was a little harder to do right now. She kept up a conversation with the young woman, trying to see what was bothering her, when Denise abruptly turned to her.

"Did you see what you needed to see?"

Doreen stopped and stared at her. "I'm sorry?"

"You were at the house today," she said. "Did you see what you needed to see?"

"I'm not sure what I was supposed to see," Doreen said, making no attempt to lie.

"I sure hope you saw enough to make a difference," she said, "because things will get really ugly soon if you didn't."

"What is it you wanted me to see?" she asked in a low tone, as she leaned against the kitchen door.

"You were there long enough," she said. "You should have seen the fighting."

"I definitely saw some fighting. That's true," she said.

Denise nodded with satisfaction. "I knew it must have been you. I was hoping it wasn't because that would put you in a difficult spot, but, of course, it was you," she said, shaking her head.

"Who else did you think it would be?" And she knew now that she was committed to this and that she would be making deep trouble for Mack too.

"I was really hoping it wasn't you," she said, "because now they'll be after you."

"Isn't that why you brought me in on this in the first place?" she said, with a sudden guess.

"Yes, and no. I wasn't thinking that you would get into trouble or that you would take as many chances as you have."

"I'm not very good at *not* taking chances," she murmured.

"Maybe, but some of these things that you're doing are dangerous."

"Only some," she said, with a note of humor.

The woman looked at her, and her lips quirked. "Right. But then my own life has become that way lately, and I don't even know how to get out of it."

"Maybe you should explain more about how you got into it."

"Love, betrayal, greed," she said, "all the usuals."

"A little more of an explanation would help," Doreen said.

"I can't," Denise said. "I'm just not exactly sure what you did and what you'll do with it."

"Do with what?"

"With whatever evidence you garnered."

"I didn't get any," she said.

Denise looked right at Doreen. "They sent me here. You know that, right?"

Chapter 27

"I HOPE NOT because that would mean a couple things. One, they saw me. Two, they think that I'm that easy of a pawn. And, three, that you are working for them."

"I'm not working for them," she said emphatically.

"No, but maybe you're off on your own agenda," Doreen said, quietly staring at her. "Because, whatever is going on, the repercussions are pretty huge now that a body is in the morgue."

"And I don't know anything about that."

Doreen didn't say anything because she knew more than what she had said. She knew an awful lot about it; she just wasn't ready to say so. As she leaned against the doorjamb, she considered something. "Are you in danger, Denise? Is this a call for help?"

"A call for help?" She gave a bit of laugh. "For me? Things are so messed up, there is no help."

"That's not true," Doreen said softly. "You can always improve your situation."

The woman shook her head. "No, that's not true," she said.

"What happened to your mother?"

Denise seemed stunned. "You know about my mother?"

"I know your parents are dead."

She snorted. "My dad died a long time ago," she said, "and my mother remarried."

"And where is she now?"

Denise looked at her, shook her head, and said, "You don't know, do you?"

"I know that she's supposedly dead, but dead doesn't mean *dead* any more than the right person going to jail means the right person went."

Then Denise's eyes opened wide. And she whistled. "Oh, wow," she said, "you know just enough to be dangerous."

Doreen stiffened. "Not enough to solve the problem apparently."

"I understood you were good at cold cases," she said. "I was hoping that maybe you could help out with a couple of them in my life. But I don't expect that you'll be much help at all." And, at that, she seemed almost distracted by something.

Doreen shook her head. "I'm not sure what you're trying to say."

"No, of course not," she said, with a wave of her hand. "That would be too simple. And I can't tell you, so it is what it is." She hopped to her feet and said, "Skip the tea. I'll just go."

"Interesting choice. You come here, try to talk to me, but don't make it clear what you want or why you're even here to begin with," she said, while looking at Denise closely to see if the woman was on some kind of medication or drugs that she hadn't detected earlier. "And the minute I mention your mother, you get irate."

"It's not that I'm irate," she said, "but I was—" Then she stopped, shrugged, and said, "It doesn't matter. Nobody can help."

"That's not true. But, if it's a cold case, I might help, if I have information. If I don't have any information, I'm not sure what you think I can do."

"You probably can't do anything. I was dreaming."

"This thing you wanted help with, it has nothing to do with your uncle, does it?"

Denise looked at Doreen and shook her head. "No," she said, "my uncle is already a mess. I was looking for help for my mother."

"Your mother who is dead?"

She shrugged and said, "I don't know that she is or she isn't. My stepdad says she ran away, then other times he says she just disappeared."

"And do you believe him?"

She immediately shook her head. "No, but then I want to believe that she's alive."

"How long ago did she run away?"

"Fifteen years," she said softly.

"And is your stepdad the man who beat up your uncle?" It was stab in the dark but a good one.

Denise looked at Doreen in shock and then slowly nodded. "You saw that, did you?" She took a slow deep breath. "You know you can't tell anybody what you saw."

"I know," Doreen said, "and you're also petrified of him, your stepdad, which is why you wanted to come here to see if I could help find your mother," she said. "But you had to come up with a reason for coming to see me because your stepfather would have a heyday with it. And he doesn't know that you would be looking into your mother's case because you think he killed her."

"I know he did," she cried out passionately. "But then that other side rears its head, where I want to believe him and to not think that he would do something like this. So I keep wanting to believe that she's alive."

"But you don't really believe it, and that's where the problem lies."

"That's just one of the problems," she said. "I'm a bit of a mess."

"A bit?" Doreen asked, with a smile.

"Yeah, just a bit," she groaned. "I know you shouldn't even be talking to me."

"Probably not," Doreen said cheerfully. "But I'm not really good at doing what I'm supposed to do."

"I know," she said. "That was another reason why I thought to come to you. Because you are so unorthodox, and you get into a lot of trouble."

Doreen winced. "Wow, so you came to me because I'm a mess?"

"I'm a mess too," Denise said, "so I figured that maybe we could help each other."

"Help you get out of this scenario? Out of the fake kidnapping?"

Denise's eyes widened yet again. "Don't let them know that you know that," she warned.

"Will you tell your stepfather?" Doreen asked curiously. Mack would be screaming at her, if he heard this conversation.

"I don't know what to tell him," Denise said.

Just enough honesty was in her tone of voice that Doreen wanted to believe Denise. But again, this woman had kept Doreen off-balance since the beginning. Definitely something was off about her now as well. Doreen didn't trust her, and that was a big part of it. "I find it hard to trust you, even now," Doreen said.

"And you shouldn't," she said. "I've spent a lifetime trying to survive, and trying to survive doesn't mean that we're always very nice people."

"It doesn't mean you have to continue to be the bad guys either," Doreen murmured.

The woman laughed. "No," she said, "but sometimes that comes more naturally."

"Again, that's a choice," she said, "and you can do something to improve yourself." Doreen hated the fact that, even in this situation, she was here and anxious to try to help this woman, yet who obviously didn't want any help. And how frustrating because this girl could still do so much with her life, if she wanted to. But Doreen was hardly a cheerleader type. "And I'm sorry to say," she said, "but I don't think your life has been all that easy."

"It hasn't been easy at all. He used to beat my mother," she said. "All the time."

"And did he ever hurt you?"

"Sometimes, but not the same. He stopped out of the blue too."

"Your stepdad probably realized he pushed the line when he killed your mother, and now he's just trying to keep the status quo," Doreen mused. "And your uncle became the punching bag, didn't he?"

Denise nodded slowly. "How'd you figure that out?"

"Because he just took the beating," she said. "He took it like he'd taken it many times before."

"My stepfather really does hate my uncle," she said. "I'm not exactly sure why, but …" Then she shrugged. "There's lots of rumors, but just suffice it to say my stepdad has no respect for my uncle."

"And that probably goes back to the relationship with your mother that the two men shared."

"Exactly, and, of course, my uncle has never said anything about my mother's death and never let me know if my stepfather had something to do with it or not. So I've never really known if that was on his mind too."

"You'd think that you would ask him about it," she murmured, staring at Denise, wondering how long it would be before Mack came.

"Maybe," she said.

"So the two of you are walking around on eggshells around this man, your stepfather, as if he did do something?"

"Of course," she said, with a half a laugh. "We don't know what to do, so we do nothing, and it's the *doing nothing* part that cripples us. But because we don't know what to do, we can't do anything."

"I get that, but, at the same time, the suspicion is killing you. Did you ever ask your stepdad flat-out if he did it?"

She nodded. "Once. I did and got belted across the face for it. He told me that I should never even think something so horrible and that he'd loved my mother."

"Loving somebody doesn't preclude murder," she said, "particularly in abusive situations."

"I don't think my mother was abused."

"You said he used to beat her up."

"Yeah, but he said she deserved it."

At that stunning comment, Doreen looked at her in shock.

And the woman sighed. "See? See what I mean? I slide back and forth."

"That is just complete garbage," she said. "Don't you ever get sucked into that kind of thinking."

"I don't want to," she cried out. "What am I supposed to do? I've got a lifetime of those thoughts going through my head."

Doreen wasn't sure exactly what was going on here, but she didn't trust anything this woman said at this point. Part of the problem was the glint of what almost seemed like laughter in her eyes, as if she were deliberately pulling Doreen's leg. "I don't know," she said, looking at her. "You don't seem to be too distraught, so I doubt that you're suffering. Is it more about curiosity now?" *Or is she truly setting me up? Using me … but for what?*

"Nope, I'm not distraught anymore over my mother," she said, "and you're right. This is probably a good time to call it quits. I'm sure you don't want anything to do with looking into my mother's death, but it would be nice."

"Yet now you say *death*, when before you said *disappeared*. I don't get it."

"It's been fifteen years," she said. "It's easier for me to think that she's dead rather than think she doesn't want anything to do with me."

That moment of bald-faced honesty—and the tears that came with it—hit Doreen as being the truth. "I might look into it," she said. "But I need whatever information you have on her in order to do that."

"I can give you what I have," she said. "I wrote it up for a private investigator at one time, but I never could come up with the money, so I didn't get anywhere with it."

She hopped up, handed over a USB key, and said, "I meant to give you this the first time I met you. Then I wondered if I should. When I heard a woman was skulking around up in the orchard, my instincts said it was you," she said, with a bright smile. "So, here. This is the information on my mother, just in case I can't give it to you later on."

"Why wouldn't you give it to me later?" Doreen asked worriedly, as she accepted the thumb drive.

Denise gave her a flat stare. "I know that I'm a mess," she said, "and I know my mom was probably a mess too. But that doesn't mean she deserved this any more than I deserve whatever the hell will be the outcome of this mess for me," she said.

"Right now the mess is the fact that a body is in the morgue," Doreen said, trying to refocus the conversation. "Your mother has been gone fifteen years, but that body in the morgue right now? That's fresh."

With that, Denise was gone.

Chapter 28

DOREEN RACED TO the front door, just in time to see Denise hop into her vehicle and drive away. She was barely gone, when Mack came flying up. Doreen held the door open for him. "She just left," she said. Relief crossed Mack's face, and she smiled. "I didn't really think I was in danger," she said, "but the whole interchange was definitely confusing. I think she was trying to play me."

"She is definitely trying to play you," he said.

"She did have a lot of interesting information to offer." She shared what Denise had said. And then added, "Plus, she handed me this information on her mother's death."

"Lord, lady," he said, shaking his head. "The last thing you need is another case."

"No, but remember? I did say cold cases suited me better."

"Of course," he said, "because you think the danger is a little more distant."

She nodded. "And yet, at the same time, it doesn't feel very distant today." She looked at him and asked, "Was any of the information from the video helpful?"

"Yes. We're running tests on the body right now. And it

looks like it is quite possible that the wrong man went to prison."

"How is that even a thing?"

"Mistakes happen. People see what they expect to see. He showed up and looked the part, so they had no reason to question it."

"And so he went to prison for his brother?"

"It's not all that odd that someone in jail repeats over and over how they are innocent. Plus, the brothers were fraternal twins and looked fairly similar, especially when they were younger, but the years have really hurt and have showed up differently on each," he said.

"And from the research, it also looked like," she murmured, "that he, uh, might not have been all there, so to speak."

"I don't know about that as much as the fact that he was probably not as manipulative as his brother. Anyway he did go to prison for the one guy, as you said. And, according to the fingerprints we have on file, the one who went to prison is the one currently in the morgue."

"But not necessarily the one accused of the crime, correct? So the gardener may end up in jail too?"

Mack nodded. "Yep, so we'll be taking care of that as well."

"Of course," she said, "but that still doesn't tell us who killed the man in the morgue."

"No," he said, "it doesn't. And I don't want you having anything more to do with this case. It's dangerous. We've had more than enough deaths involved."

"Is there another one?" she asked.

Instantly he shook his head. "One is enough. And now you're looking at what she just said about her mother."

Doreen nodded. "I do want to see what's on this key."

He nodded. "I do too because it might pertain to my case."

"Right."

With that, she went back inside, make herself a copy of all the files on the key, and handed it to him. "Do you think she expects me to hand it off to you?"

"I would assume so. I think they've been ahead of us every step of the way. I'm just not sure that they thought out the death of the one uncle."

"Which means quite probably somebody else is involved."

"Yeah," he said, "and we're working on the theory that it's whoever was involved in the original crime, Dicky's partner."

"Oh," she said, "and here I was thinking it was the victim of the crime."

"That would be a great theory, except for the fact that we've since found out that Dicky wasn't alone in this criminal venture of his, and that the other guy was never caught."

"Maybe he was never caught, but he also didn't get everything that he was expecting to get out of the robbery, I presume," she said.

"That's what I'm thinking too. And he wants one hundred thousand to stay quiet, probably about the brother who did time for Dicky."

"That would make sense, yes," Doreen agreed. "The kidnapping ruse was so that Dicky could disappear, but instead this other guy found the brother."

"But why would Dicky pay any ransom, if his partner had already killed his brother?" he asked.

"Maybe the partner never meant to kill him. Plus, we don't know which came first yet, do we?" she said.

"Right," Mack said. "So the partner probably found the wrong brother, threatened him and then realized he had the wrong guy, but ended up killing him—accidentally or not—and now he's coming after the others."

She smiled, nodded, and said, "What if—"

He waited for her to continue. "What if what?"

"What if we just leave them alone, and maybe they'll kill each other."

He burst out laughing. "That's quite possible," he said. "Though it's not exactly the level of due diligence I am required to exercise."

"Maybe not, but this whole thing's a big mess," she said.

"It is, indeed, and we still need to pick them up."

"Is that happening soon?"

"It's hopefully in progress right now," he said. "I came to make sure you stay here, while that's ongoing."

She looked at him, her jaw dropping. "Seriously? I won't go up there and cause trouble." He just gave her a flat stare. "Not intentionally."

"And yet, somehow, you *unintentionally* end up being very intentionally in the darndest places," he said.

She groaned. "And again, not intentionally," she murmured.

He smiled. "We do know that," he said. "Your heart is in the right place, but, in this instance, we just have to make sure that the rest of you stays in the right place too."

"Do you think Denise knew?" Doreen asked.

"I wouldn't be at all surprised, or at least her instincts are strong. I highly doubt she's going back there."

"No, I don't think so," she said. "I got the feeling that

she is very much a survivor."

"Exactly. In which case she won't have anything to do with them again."

"We should have tracked her," she said.

He nodded. "We are law enforcement. Remember? I put somebody on her as she left, to keep an eye on her. We also know her vehicle, so we can track that too."

She rolled her eyes at him. "You mean, *real* law enforcement, versus just an amateur, like me?"

"Exactly," he said, with a fat grin.

"So now what?" she said, as Mack's phone buzzed.

"I'm leaving. So you can go through the information she left with you, if you want. But please stay inside. Lock the doors, and, if she comes back, don't answer."

Doreen took a slow deep breath. "Okay," she said, "I'm good with that."

And, with a nod, he headed out.

Chapter 29

Wednesday Evening into Thursday Morning …

IT WAS HOURS later before Doreen finally warmed up. She didn't realize she'd gotten quite a chill, until after Mack left, and then it seemed like she couldn't get warm. With a hot cup of tea, she went to bed that night and woke up the next morning, still feeling odd and out of sorts. Deciding that she needed to change her mood, she called her grandmother and said, "Hi, Nan. Any chance of coming down for a visit?"

"Oh my, of course you can," she said.

And, with that, Doreen quickly dressed, gathered the leashes, and headed down the creek with her animals.

As soon as they saw Nan, they all broke loose, greeting her with joy, as she hugged them all. Nan sat down, looked at her granddaughter, and said, "You really needed to come for a visit, didn't you?"

Doreen shrugged and nodded. "I did," she said. "I'm sorry. It's been such a confusing couple of days. I've been so tired and still healing that I've been off my game. I think I just need to rest for a week or so."

"And I'm so sorry because it shouldn't be like that," she

said. "Your cases are normally clear-cut."

"I guess not every one can be, can they?" She laughed. "Besides, it's a little bit egotistical to think I'll solve everything."

"You've done pretty well so far," she said. "So explain this Denise thing to me."

"I'm not even sure I can," she said. "It's like everything that comes out of her mouth is a lie, and she's laughing at me on the inside."

"She probably is," Nan said. "Some people are like that."

"I know that. I mean, being around my husband in the business he was in, I certainly got used to seeing all kinds of people."

"Best not dwell on him and his ilk, dear. It will only drag you down. Let the lawyers deal with it from here on out."

She smirked. "That seems to be a theme, and I can only hope that Nick fares better than I did." Thinking about that certainly moved her mind from Denise to Doreen's own situation, and Doreen couldn't help but wonder what was going on with the divorce settlement negotiations, as well as Robin's estate. Remembering how taken in Doreen had been by Robin made Doreen all the more skeptical of Denise and her varying story.

After hearing the latest news from Rosemoor, Doreen was more than ready for another walk, and, gathering the animals, they said their goodbyes to Nan and headed back home, via the river route. Breathing in the fresh air helped Doreen immediately, and, as they walked, she began to relax, to clear her head, and to take note of the natural beauty around her. An odd sound shook her from her reverie. A check of the animals had both Mugs and Goliath happily out in front of her, beside the creek, while Thaddeus contentedly rode on her shoulder. There it was again, the sound of what could be a foot scuffing the path. She turned quickly and thought she caught a glimpse of a man—or part of one perhaps. Or maybe not.

Was she being overly paranoid? The animals hadn't picked up on anything untoward. She kept walking, picking up the pace. A few more furtive glances backward revealed nothing, but she couldn't shake the feeling that someone was behind her.

"Come on. Don't be silly. Who would it be?" she said out loud, scurrying along. "Besides, if they intended harm, they surely could have jumped me already. Why remain in hiding?" *Unless the intent was to follow her home.* "Nonsense. We just need a break from all this drama, that's all." But, when she heard what sounded like a cough, she gave up all pretense and, calling to the animals, picked up her pace to a very fast walk, just short of running. As she rounded the last corner, she caught her breath, when she saw a man hurrying down the path right in front of her.

"Mack! What are you doing here? Gosh, I'm glad to see you, but let's keep going," she said, tears threatening to spill down her cheeks, while grabbing his sleeve and pulling him along, as Mugs, overjoyed, tried to greet him. "Not now, Mugs. Let's keep moving."

"What happened?" Mack asked, recognizing she was abnormally spooked. "Have you seen anyone?"

"Yes. No. I'm not certain." She stumbled on her words. "I've heard what sounded like someone behind me, even a cough. I thought I caught a glimpse of him as he ducked behind a tree early on, but maybe it's just my imagination."

Scanning the area, looking angry, he put his arm around

her and said, "Let's just get you home, and then we'll talk."

She was a bit out of breath, so glad for the reprieve from speaking. Embarrassed to be so rattled, she was very glad to see him.

"Last one inside puts the coffee on!" he said, with a smile. Grateful for the opportunity to run, without looking like a chicken, she took off like a rocket, with him on her heels. After a brief flurry, they both were inside, and Doreen headed for the bathroom to compose herself, while Mack put on the coffee.

"I'm glad you had the alarm system on," he said.

"I do try to take precautions, you know."

"Why didn't you call me when you got spooked?" he asked.

"After that last fiasco, when I couldn't even tell you where I was, that was just too humiliating. I can't keep calling you constantly to rescue me. I am far more independent than that. At least I want to be. Plus, when I do call, I'm keeping you from your job. Speaking of which, why are you here? Aren't you supposed to be at work?"

"I am working, actually. Keeping you safe is my job too, you know? I was already on the way here anyway."

"Why were you headed this way?"

"When we started picking up our suspects last night, they scattered, and we didn't get them all," he said.

"Oh, well, you'll get them all soon enough."

"We will," he said. Yet he didn't move from her kitchen.

She groaned. "So why are you still here? Don't tell me that you're babysitting me?"

He nodded, crossing his arms over his chest, as he stared at her. "I am, indeed."

"Why?" she wailed.

"Because we have to make sure you're safe."

And that was the first inkling she had, not only of how much he cared but also of how much she was impacting the man-hours of the police to keep her safe. "You should be out there, with them."

"I should be," he said, with a nod. "But, because of our relationship, I'm elected to be the one to stay here."

She winced. "I'm sorry," she said in a small voice.

"Listen. Somebody followed you up that pathway," he said, "and that's what worries me the most."

"But I don't know even who it was," she said. "I thought it was a man, but then, when I looked again and again, I couldn't see anyone."

"That may well be," he said, "but we also got a 9-1-1 call about a woman needing a rescue on the river path, and that's how I found you. Oddly enough, they gave far better directions than you've been known to give," he said, with a sideways glance her way.

"Oh, stop," she said, shaking her head at his reminder of the orchard incident. "But, just so *you* know, someone must have known their way around to have given such good directions." she said. "And nothing happened, so it's not likely that a local just saw him and assumed he was up to no good."

He nodded. "But still we don't know who it was. And he didn't identify himself on the call. Plus, we couldn't say for sure if it was a male or a female caller. More wasted man-hours."

"A lot of those on this case, aren't there?"

"Well, there's a waste of man-hours for the fake kidnapping, if that turns out to be the case. But, more important, we're still after whoever killed our DB in the morgue."

"Did you check into Denise's location at the time of the murder?"

"We just got a time of death from the coroner," he said, "so it will definitely be one of the questions we'll ask all of them." He turned around and looked at her and asked, "Why?"

"Because she's—" And Doreen stopped and shook her head. "I don't know what to say. But something's very different about her."

"Sometimes, when you get into this element, and someone has spent a lot of years on drugs or involved in crime, even just learning to lie and to cheat and to steal," he said, "it's pretty hard to get the truth out of them. Their stories change by the second."

"I could definitely see that happening with her," she muttered. "It's frustrating."

He laughed. "Yeah, it is," he said. "But we're used to it."

"Got it," she said, and she didn't say anything more, as she waited for Mack to be updated by his team. When his phone buzzed, she watched him as he read the message.

"Okay, they got the last guy, so you're good to stay here alone. But lock the doors and stay clear of trouble. I need to run." And, with that, he turned and walked to the front door.

"Goodbye," she said, "and thanks."

He raised a hand, hopped into his vehicle, and left. She wasn't sure what to think about it all, but obviously he was off on a new lead, and one that he wanted her to stay well and truly out of. She would if she could. It just didn't seem to be all that easy to do.

Following his instructions, she turned and locked the doors. Once in the kitchen, she looked around to see just what her options were to eat and didn't really see a whole lot. But she needed to find something, so she put a sandwich together and put the TV on. It was an older model and didn't have great color, but she was just looking for a distraction.

When she heard a noise out in the backyard, she refused to get up and look, but Mugs had absolutely no such qualms. He stood and furiously barked repeatedly. Wincing, she got up and peered through the curtains. Nothing was there, as far as she saw. She immediately tried to calm him down and said, "It's okay, buddy. It's okay."

But he was having nothing to do with it. Apparently it wasn't okay. As far as he was concerned, something was out there, something he didn't want there at all. She didn't know what she was supposed to do about it, however. She had everything locked and the security system set, so nobody was getting in or shouldn't get in. As long as she stayed here, she should be good. That's when she heard a shout.

"Doreen!"

She winced when she heard Denise's voice. She didn't want to answer, but then the woman said, "Please help."

Doreen groaned because what was she supposed to do now? If the woman was involved, that would put Doreen in trouble, but, if the woman was hurt or injured or needed a place to bolt to from her stepdad, and Doreen didn't help her, how would that go? She immediately texted Mack, telling him it sounded like Denise was outside her house, saying she needed help. Mack immediately told Doreen to stay inside and to not let Denise in, no matter what. She didn't know what to do at that point in time and texted him back, saying it sounds like she's in trouble. Her phone rang immediately.

"I'm on the way," he said. "Do not open the door."

She winced and then turned to the backyard. "I don't hear her anymore."

"Don't trust her," he said. "It's not that simple."

"She asked for my help, Mack," she said in a whisper.

"Of course she did. She knows how to get to you."

Doreen stopped. "Am I that easy?"

"You're that bighearted," he said for clarity. "Not easy. It's just that those kinds of people know they can take advantage of you."

"Great," she said. "That's not exactly how I want to be seen in life."

"Prove it then and stay inside and stay safe."

He hung up the phone, and she listened again. And there it was.

"Doreen, Doreen please. I'm hurt."

She looked at Mugs. "What do we do, Mugs?" Mugs barked and barked, and, while Doreen understood how he felt, neither did she feel like he was telling her to open the door. When she tested her theory and moved toward the door, he stepped in her way, tripping her up. She fell heavily against the door and looked at him in surprise. Then he barked around, jumping up on top of her.

"Okay, well, that's as clear as day," she muttered, and then she laughed because she was unhurt, but he was obviously happy that she was where she was. "Sorry, buddy. Apparently this is a bad deal, huh?"

Just then she heard a vehicle racing up the driveway. She looked at Mugs and said, "And here's our knight in shining armor." And, with that, Mugs barked, now sounding overjoyed. She laughed as he headed toward the front door. She got up and went to the front door, then undid the alarm, and, as soon as she did so, Mack was there with his face glaring at her. Then suddenly he stiffened.

"What's the matter?" she groaned.

A woman behind him spoke. "Go in with your hands up," Denise said, "or I'll blow off both your heads."

Chapter 30

DOREEN STARED AT Mack in shock.

He looked at her and told her, "Back up."

She stared at him. "Did she come up behind you?"

He glared, and she realized that he'd come barreling up to the front door, more concerned about Doreen than anything else, and had put himself in a bad spot. She backed up slowly to see Denise standing behind Mack. She had climbed up the front steps, holding the gun on him.

"Wow. When you say you need help, you really do," Doreen said. "Have you found yourself a nice shrink somewhere? I guess we'll get one for you in prison."

"Don't laugh at me," she sneered. "Pathetic people like you make me cry with pain at how society has fallen."

"You mean because we care about people and because we don't kill off everybody?" Doreen asked curiously.

"You don't know anything about it," Denise said. "You live in your high-and-mighty little house here, looking like you've never even known what troubles are."

Mack sent a warning glare to Doreen to not engage the crazy woman.

"Troubles like yours, no," Doreen replied, "I haven't.

But I do understand that you've had some problems."

"I did time," she said, "time that I didn't have to do, that I shouldn't have had to."

Doreen stared at her. "That hasn't come up in anything."

"No," she said, "because they put me in a mental hospital instead of prison."

"I can see that," Doreen said, with a quick nod to her head. "Nothing you've said so far makes a whole lot of sense."

At that, Denise jabbed the gun barrel into Mack's back.

Aware she was the target of his glare, Doreen shrugged and said, "Okay, so you don't want me to say anything to her, but, honest to God, she's been kind of difficult to sort out this whole time," she said apologetically to Mack.

"Oh, for heaven's sake," Denise said. "They said I killed my mother, but I didn't kill her."

"Okay, so you've told me that," she said, "and you've given me information to look into the case."

"That's right, and I want you to," she said, "because I didn't kill her. Somebody else did."

"And your stepfather has been supporting you?"

"He helped me get out of the center," she said, "and, once they tested me as fully functional, then I was released into his care. That was about four years ago, and I've been with him ever since."

"Right," Doreen said, "and doing the whole crime wave thing with him?"

"No, we had jobs, and we were doing just fine. Right up until somebody who was after my uncle turned up, and my uncle called us for help."

"Right," she said, "and why bring you here?"

Mack grimaced, not liking Doreen's engagement with Denise, but he was listening intently to their exchange.

"It's where Uncle Dicky worked, and it's also where the other guy worked."

"So you know who's after him? The one who killed your other uncle?"

"We think so, yes," she said, "but we're not sure."

"Fine. I get that, but what I don't get," Doreen said, "is who this person is."

"It was my uncle's partner in crime."

"Ah, so your uncle cheated him out of his share, and now he wants his share of the money, is that it?"

"He also did time with my other uncle, but, because they were in different penitentiaries, he never realized that the one who didn't do the crime was the one who went to prison, and his partner, Uncle Dicky, the one who did do the crime, got off free and clear."

"So that means what? He feels like money and time were stolen from him, due to all the years of his life he spent in jail because his partner got free and he didn't? So he wants the $100,000 to carry on with his life, without mentioning the rest to anyone? Considering how many years he may have lost to jail, it's not a bad deal."

"It doesn't matter, but my uncle Dicky doesn't have that kind of money, and now this guy has killed his brother, Uncle Charlie. Uncle Charlie, who didn't do the crime but did pay the price, didn't have a clue what the guy was talking about, and that's when the guy realized he had the wrong brother. The two looked similar, but the years in jail were hard on the one brother."

"So why are you here right now?" Doreen asked.

She shrugged. "Because my stepfather told me to come."

"No," Doreen said. "You keep blaming other people, and you keep saying you're a victim," she said, looking back at Mack, who studied her closely. "I don't believe you. All you've done is throw out red herrings. But you're not really helping us figure this out."

"That's because you're too stupid to figure it out."

"No, I'm not," she snapped. "I'm really tired of people telling me that I'm stupid when I'm not," Doreen said, her anger rising.

"Yeah, who's telling you that you're stupid?" she said. "'Cause maybe they've been right all along."

"My ex for one," Doreen said, "and I'm not." She could feel the old ire surge over her. Mugs barked at her feet, as if understanding just how upset she was. She reached down, patted him, and said, "It's okay, boy. I know. I'm getting upset, and I promised you that I wouldn't do that anymore."

"Oh, good Lord," Denise said sarcastically. "Listen to her—talking to the dog, like he's actually somebody."

"My dog is somebody," she said, looking at the woman. "If you had an empathetic bone in your body, you would understand that."

"I don't," she said, "so it doesn't matter."

"No, what matters right now," Doreen said, "is why you're here at all. Because, if you didn't kill your uncle and if you know who did, you've got no business being here at all. You've already given me the information that you said you wanted me to have in order to solve your mother's murder, but now you're here holding a gun on a cop. Why would you do that?" she asked.

"A cop?" Denise's startled face peered around Mack's side.

"A cop," Doreen said, nodding her head. "Not smart."

"Oh no," she said, and the woman backed up ever-so-slightly. She looked over at Mack. "I didn't mean to do that."

"Yeah, you did." Doreen stepped forward. "He asked you questions about your supposedly kidnapped uncle Dicky. All you do is lie and cheat. What is really going on here?"

Mack looked at Denise and asked her, "Split personality?"

"What?" Doreen looked at him, then at Denise, immediately detecting fury in Denise's voice as it changed again.

"I do not have a split personality," she said, "but, when you bring out the temper in me, I can do some crazy things," she admitted.

"Wow," Doreen said. "I wasn't expecting that."

"Nope, nobody is," she said. "It's not a split personality. It's just that the anger allows me to do what I want to do, and right now I'm really pissed at the world."

"Why is that?" Doreen said. "Because again, you've got no reason to be here."

"Because, when I was here before," she said, "I stashed something in your house. And now I want it."

"And you could have gotten it at any time," she said, "when nobody was here. So why are you here now?"

"Because I do know he's a cop," she said, laughing with that same craziness that Doreen had come to recognize as being off. "And I want that information before it goes to wherever it is you think you'll send it."

"What information?"

"The information I gave you," she said.

A bewildered Doreen looked at Mack, who gave her a nod.

"You mean, the USB key?"

"Yes," she said.

"But you gave it to me," Doreen said. "Why would you want to take it away now?"

The woman looked at her and said, "Because it wasn't me who gave it to you."

Doreen shook her head. "Oh, brother."

"Like I said," Mack noted, his tone very soft.

And Doreen realized two personalities were here in Denise, and one had given Doreen the key for safekeeping because she really cared about her mother, and now the other one was here to get it back because she had killed her mother. "So let me get this straight. You killed your mother, but your alter ego gave me the information, so I could solve the crime, but because she doesn't know about you—"

"Oh, she knows about me all right," she interrupted, "but she doesn't know that I killed Mother."

"And you've kept that from her."

"Of course," she said. "I mean, we love each other. We're sisters."

"So how bad was the abuse from your stepdad?"

"Pretty bad," she said, "but again, what would you know about it?"

"More than you might think," she said, studying her carefully. "So all these years that you were abused by your stepdad, your mom was abused by your stepdad too, and you took the same beatings as she did. And this is your way of dealing with it, right?"

Denise shrugged.

"That is what brought you into existence, right?"

"Maybe," she said carelessly, "but what do you care?"

"I do care," she said, "and I'm so sorry that this happened to you."

"Whatever," she snapped, her voice turning hard. "Nobody gives a shit anyway."

"You'd be surprised," Doreen said. "I understand the need for self-preservation. I understand looking after ourselves and doing whatever is needed to make that happen," she said. "And the fact that the second personality was created through the abuse and that you killed your mother over it, all means that your mother was abusive."

"She was just like him, and he's the one who saved me from her. At least from the worst of it. And then, when she was gone, he's the one who helped me hide it," she said. "But now my stepdad's in trouble too, and I'm trying to save him."

Doreen considered that, computed the information, trying to determine whether it was right or wrong, then shook her head. "No, you're not," she said, hearing Mack's soft groan and sharp look. "You're here trying to save yourself. Because this guy, your uncle's partner, he didn't kill your other uncle. You did."

She looked at her in surprise. "Why would you say that?"

"Because you thought it was the other uncle. You can't tell them apart." Then she stopped, a look of understanding crossing her face. "I get it. One of you can tell them apart, but the other one can't."

"I can tell them apart just fine," she sneered. "But he laughed at me and told me that I was crazy."

"Ah, so you killed Charlie and then blamed this other guy who's after your uncle Dicky, his partner in crime. Got it," she said. "Wow, this is just so twisted."

"It's not twisted at all," she snapped. "And you don't

know anything."

"You know what? You could be right," she said. "In this instance, you could be right." She looked at Mack. "I really don't know what we're supposed to do now though."

"You're not supposed to do anything now," the woman sneered. "I'm doing it all."

"Good. What is it you're doing?" Doreen asked. Mack stiffened. But Doreen barreled on. "By the way, may I speak to the other woman?"

"No," she said, "you can't."

"Why not?" Doreen asked.

"Because I don't want you talking to her."

"Oh, that's right. You're afraid. Sorry about that. Fear is kind of ugly. By the way," she said, "have you ever seen Thaddeus?"

The woman looked at her in confusion. "What are you talking about?"

Doreen called out, "Thaddeus, are you here?"

Thaddeus poked his head around the living room wall from the kitchen. "Thaddeus is here. Thaddeus is here."

The woman looked at her, then at the bird, and said, "Jeez, you really are crazy, aren't you?"

"I don't think so," Doreen said.

"I mean, I'm holding you both at gunpoint. I've got a gun on you, and you've got a cop here, who's likely to get shot, and here you are talking about your bird."

"I am talking about my bird," Doreen said, with a bright smile. "Because these animals have been very important to me, and they're really, really good at doing one thing."

"What's that?" Denise asked suspiciously.

Doreen looked at her innocently. "Protecting me," she said.

The woman started to laugh. "Nobody around here will protect you right now," she said.

Doreen watched, as Goliath crept in the front door, still open, coming up behind the woman.

"You could be wrong about that," Doreen said. "Just when you least expect it, animals do things out of love for their owners."

"Nobody loves anybody," the woman said bitterly. "As I well know."

"And I'm sorry about that," Doreen said, "because obviously you've not had a very easy life. And this extra part of you is there to protect you." Doreen understood now that this version of Denise had a handle on what was going on, so she really did understand and was protecting the other version of Denise. It was sad, and it was heartbreaking that it had come to this in Denise's tormented life, but Doreen understood why somebody would end up having to have another part of her be strong enough to do what was needed. "I'm surprised you didn't kill your stepfather though, when ultimately he was part of the same problem."

"But then he saved me from the nuthouse," she said quietly, "so I couldn't do that to him.'

Doreen nodded. "And, of course, he knows that you killed your mother. And he knows that you killed your uncle too, doesn't he?"

"I imagine he suspects. I mean, neither Uncle Dicky nor my stepdad are killers, and I'm the only one who's killed anybody. So, if somebody ends up dying, my stepdad kind of looks to who might be responsible," she said, with a laugh. "But he doesn't know anything for sure."

"Right, and what about this guy who supposedly sent the blackmail note and is supposedly after your uncle

Dicky?"

"That was just to throw everyone off the scent. My stepdad did that."

"So nobody else is really involved in this case, is there?"

"Nope, it's just the three of us."

"You mean, the four of you," she murmured, counting Denise twice. "So your brother didn't kill anybody, but was searching for Dicky, hence why he had to hide via a fake kidnapping. But he was going to find Charlie so you killed him before your brother had a chance to talk to him. Then what about Dicky's partner in crime?"

She shrugged and said, "He's gone."

"Has anybody else *gone*?"

"You mean, did I kill anyone else? No, not yet," she said. "But I might have to change that."

"Right," Doreen said. "After all, why would you leave anybody alive who could identify you?"

"Something like that," she said. "It's not even so much about identification as much as it's about understanding."

"No," Doreen said. "See? I don't understand why you would kill your uncle."

"Because he found out that I'd killed my mother," she said. "I told you that she was his sister."

Chapter 31

"NO, YOU DIDN'T tell me that," Doreen said in confusion, although it made sense and did provide an interesting motive. She'd found it out in her own research, but the lies from Denise were hard to sort out. She looked at Mack and asked, "Did she tell us?"

Mack shook his head. "No, she kept that little bit to herself."

"And the kidnapping?" Doreen asked Denise.

"That's because my uncle Dicky is in trouble. And his victim was coming after Uncle Dicky, but he paid him off."

"Oh, this is a mess," Doreen said, shaking her head and struggling to understand the truth from the lies, which were piling up in multiple layers. "No," Doreen said, "I think there really was somebody who he did crimes with who went to jail. He got released from prison, and he found out about your uncle Dicky not going to jail, that Charlie had served time instead. But that was the first you'd heard about it, so, for some reason, you killed your uncle Charlie."

"I told you already that I had killed him," she said.

"But you didn't explain why. Were you trying to protect your stepfather? Your uncle Dicky?" When Denise didn't answer, Doreen continued, "Fine, so what's this other guy got to do with you, that you have done this for him?"

"I didn't do anything for him," Denise said.

"So who is it?" Denise stiffened, and Doreen stared at her and said, "Of course it's all in the family, isn't it?"

"I don't know what you mean," she said, but fear was in the woman's voice.

"You're trying to protect him, so he doesn't get in trouble."

"He's already suffered enough," she said. "My uncle had no business taking him into the industry in the first place."

"Wow," she said. "So who is he?"

"None of your business."

"It's your brother, isn't it?" Doreen asked.

The woman started to shake her head. "No, no, no. It's not my brother."

"Yes, it is," she said. "Your uncle Dicky got your brother into the industry. They were partners, and he threw him under the bus too, and your brother went to jail. Then he threw his own brother under the bus, who went to jail for him. Meanwhile your uncle Dicky has been living out here, free and clear, telling you that he changed his tune. But your brother gets out, finds out that, while he's been in jail, the guy who got him into trouble hasn't served a day, content to let his brother serve his sentence for him. So now your brother is furious and is after revenge, for himself and for your uncle Charlie, who served time he didn't owe. Your brother is after Uncle Dicky."

"But I can't let him kill anybody," she said. "I must protect him."

"So why didn't you protect Uncle Charlie, who had gone to jail? Why kill him? He already suffered unjustly."

"Because he would tell."

"Tell what?" Mack asked in frustration. "Everybody already knows everything."

Denise looked at him and said, "He would tell about my mother."

"Oh, so he would tell your brother about your mother," Doreen said, as finally the tumblers fell into place. "Your brother didn't know that you had murdered your mother."

"He knew that I was accused of it, but my stepdad always said that I didn't do it."

"Which is why you're staying with your stepdad, but now your brother will find out the truth—that you killed your mother—and you're afraid of him."

Denise slowly nodded. "Yes," she said, "but I love him. He's my brother, and he really loved our mother."

Even to Doreen, this was a twisted and convoluted nightmare. She looked at Mack. "It's really sad," she said. "All of these people and none of them was ever ready to tell the truth."

Mack, his voice quiet, said, "I know, and so often it's the way of it."

"But it's wrong," Doreen said. "It's so wrong."

"It doesn't matter," he said gently, "because people lie, steal, and cheat all the time."

"I get that. I've seen it even," Doreen said quietly. "I still think this is just so sad."

"Of course it is, but listen to her," Mack said. "Here we've got one of the most twisted cases ever."

Denise laughed. "You guys are just chatting away, talking like I'm not even here. Like I have nothing to do with this."

Doreen realized that the other personality was now

speaking. "Did you have anything to do with it?"

"No," she said. "I don't even know what I'm doing here." She looked at the gun in her hand. "Did you guys attack me?"

"No," Mack said, slowly turning and reaching for the gun.

But then, the other part of Denise stepped forward and said, "Oh no, you don't," brandishing the weapon at them both.

"You're losing control," Doreen said quietly.

The woman just glared at her.

Doreen continued, "And what you can't handle is the fact that this other, more innocent part of you, will find out everything you've done wrong."

"That won't happen," she said, tears welling up in her eyes. "If everybody hates me, nothing is left in my world."

"No, no, no," Mack said in alarm. "We're not going down that pathway."

The woman glared at him. "I'll just kill you both," she said, "and nobody will know anything. Nobody ever suspects. Nobody even knows how my sister and I live."

"That's because she's not your sister," Doreen said. "You're both parts of the same person. Different personalities within the same individual. One who's there to hide and to protect, and the other one who doesn't know anything."

"She's weak," the other personality said. "She's so weak."

"How do you feel about animals?" Doreen asked.

"I hate them," she said. "I'll just shoot them."

"We wouldn't take that kindly," Doreen said. She looked at Goliath, behind Denise, creeping slowly toward her, then looked back at Denise and said, "Besides, you're about to meet one very closely."

"No," she said, "animals stay away from me because they know that I don't like them."

"Maybe," Doreen said.

Thaddeus hopped up from the floor, flying a few feet, and landed on Mack's shoulder, then said, "Thaddeus loves Mack." And he rubbed his cheek against him.

The woman stared at the animal, horrified. "Oh, that's so disgusting," she said. "Gross, gross, gross! And you let that thing touch you?"

Mack looked at her quietly and said, "Yes, this animal is very close to my heart."

"Oh, my God," she said, the disgust evident in her eyes. "That's just so sick."

Then Goliath leaned forward and let out a huge yowl, right at Denise's feet.

Denise jumped, and so did Goliath, using her back to claw his way up. She cried out and screeched. "Get it off me! Get it off me!"

Mack plucked the gun from her hand and led her gently to a chair, Goliath still on her back, as she screamed and screamed. Mack held his hand over her mouth and said, "Goliath, off."

Goliath looked at him with disdain, then hopped off and curled up on the matching pot chair. The woman stopped screeching, then looked at the cat, but tears were in her eyes.

"He won't hurt you," Doreen said. "Unless you try to hurt me."

"He's disgusting."

Goliath swiftly jumped to the back of her chair, swiped a paw at her, making Denise lean backward, screeching. Meanwhile, Mack snapped the handcuffs on Denise's hands in front of her.

Doreen sighed and said, "Goliath, you don't have to torment her."

He just looked at Doreen balefully, as if to say, *Why not?* He hopped to the floor and sauntered away. Doreen looked at the woman sadly, then faced Mack and said, "I don't even know what you do in this instance."

"I do," he said, as he fished his phone from his pocket.

And the woman, instead of screaming, now just burst into sobs and sat in the chair and cried. Doreen looked over at Mack. "Is there anything you can do?"

He shook his head. "Sometimes there is nothing we can do," he said. "Sometimes there are no happy endings."

"It's all so very sad."

The woman started to laugh and laugh. "God, you're such fools," she said in a flat tone.

Both Mack and Doreen looked at her. "Was that all an act?" Doreen asked.

"Graduated top of my class in acting school," she said proudly. Doreen stared at Mack, as Denise looked at her and said, "You are such an easy mark."

"Oh, wow," Doreen said, sitting down into the other chair with a heavy *thump*. "You are quite the actress."

"I am," she said.

"How much of any of that was true?" *How many personalities resided inside Denise?*

"Most of it was true, except for all the split-personalities stuff, but I played that part to get away with my mother's murder."

"So why is it you sent me the information on that murder?" Doreen asked warmly, not at all sure she was seeing the real Denise even now.

"So it would throw suspicion off me. Because Mother

was beating me," she said flatly, "and my brother. I saved my brother, only to have my uncle send him into jail."

Doreen stared at her. "I don't know if we can believe anything out of your mouth anymore."

"Good," she said. "You should be wary of the world out there. Everybody lies, cheats, and steals."

"Was your stepdad really there for you?"

"Yes," she said. "I did kill my mother, but I had a good reason to, with all the beatings going on. My stepdad used to protect me from the worst of it, even though he lost his temper sometimes."

"Good Lord," she said, "that sounds like quite a mess of a family."

"It doesn't matter at all," she said. "You might be holding me now, but I'll get out of prison because I can play crazy so well. Even now, if you could replay this for the people who eventually will be interviewing me, you'd realize that it wouldn't hold me. Nobody will hold me."

"And then what?"

"And then," she said, "I don't know. I guess I'll move on in life and find something else."

"What about your brother?"

"He'll be free to go too," she said. "I'll serve a couple years in an institute. Then I'll get free, and we'll go off and live a better life than we've had so far."

"You've twisted my world inside out and upside downside," Doreen said.

The woman laughed. "I'm used to doing that. It's chaos theory. You confuse the facts so much that nobody knows what's up or down."

"Right," Doreen said. "And I guess that works for you because it's certainly been a crazy ride."

The woman laughed. "Yeah," she said, "that's how it works and why it works."

"Got it," Doreen said quietly. And she turned toward Mack. When he looked at her, she shrugged and said, "So what now? Go down to the station?"

"Yes," he said.

Goliath was watching and hopped back up on the chair again. Denise said, "I really don't like cats, so you better move him before I dump him."

"Oh, I'll take him," Doreen said.

As she reached down to grab the cat, the woman snaked an arm around Doreen's neck, flipped her to the floor, and then looked at Mack and said, "Give me the gun, or I'll break her neck."

Doreen struggled in her arms, but the woman was incredibly strong, and she also seemed to know some martial arts, a fact that had Mack completely frozen at the moment. Doreen looked at Thaddeus. "Thaddeus, help!"

Immediately Thaddeus dropped to the woman's head, pecking away at her. She screamed and tried to hit out at him. And, with that, Doreen broke free in time to see Mugs come barreling toward Denise, to chomp down on her arm. Mack hauled him off.

Once again the woman broke into tears. By the time Mack had everybody calmed down, Denise sat there, crying on her chair again.

Doreen just looked at her, her heart saddened by this broken woman. She looked over at Mack, and he held up a finger. "Don't," he said, "don't even say a word."

She immediately pinched her lips together and nodded. Because she didn't know what was going on with this woman, so it was better to just not say anything and let it be.

Within seconds, Arnold and Chester showed up at their front door. They looked at the woman, nodded to Mack, sighed, and came inside to lead Denise away.

Epilogue

Later Thursday …

WHEN DENISE WAS safely in the vehicle, and Arnold and Chester drove her away, Mack wrapped an arm around Doreen and said, "We'll let the shrinks sort it out."

"Is it possible to be crazy and sane at the same time?" she asked.

He laughed. "More than anything," he said, "I think she played us. But it's also possible that the person who sounded so sane and normal at the end was really yet another part of her psyche."

"I've never come across a person afflicted like this," she murmured.

"No," he said, "neither have I. Let's hope we never do again."

She nodded. "I vote that we go for much simpler cases."

"The really comical part of it is how you were supposed to be looking into the Bob Small murders." Mack lifted one eyebrow.

"I meant to ask her about that," she said, staring at the departing vehicle. "I wonder if her uncle even knew Bob Small."

"It's hard to say, but you could never believe anything she said, so there's a good chance she was grabbing at something to connect to you with. Time to park the Small cases," he said. "Now find something completely unrelated to crime to focus on for a while. Just give yourself a week off, and let's just shake this one out."

"It kind of feels dirty, like something is wrong with the world now."

"Absolutely it does," he said, "so you need to find something fun and different to make the world brighter and nicer."

"I can do that," she said. Then she smiled. "I saw a notice for an orchid show."

"Perfect," he said, "and, if you don't want to go alone, I'll take you."

She looked up at him, smiled, and said, "Really?"

"Absolutely," he said, "it might be good for me too."

"It would be," she said, grinning.

"Last time I went to an orchid show, it was because of a murder."

She looked up at him, smiled, and said, "That's not likely to happen this time, is it?"

"I hope not," he said, "but, if you're coming, who knows?" And, with that, he rolled his eyes at her.

She chuckled. "No," she said, "I have no intention of getting involved in a murder case that involves orchids."

"Yeah, well, how will you stop it?" he said, looking at her with interest.

"Hopefully it's not something I'll have to deal with."

"Maybe not," he said, and then she started to giggle.

"Did you ever solve that murder, by the way?"

He shook his head. "No, unfortunately I never did.

Why?"

"Because," she said, "we can call the case, *Offed in the Orchids.*"

He glared at her. "No," he said, shaking his head. "No, no, no."

"If it's still a cold case—"

"I didn't say that," he said.

"You did say that you didn't solve it," she said, pointing a finger at him.

He grabbed her finger and said, "Don't say that. I don't need to deal with any more murder scenes right now."

"But it's a cold case, and it's about flowers," she said, "so how hard can it be?"

He groaned. "Let's go look at the flower show and not deal with murder. How is that for an idea?"

"That works for me," she said, with a smile. This time she stepped up, wrapped her arms around his chest, and said, "Thank you for coming to the rescue yet again."

He wrapped his arms around her shoulders and held her close. "My pleasure," he whispered.

Then she popped her head back and said, "But I'm still looking into *Offed in the Orchids.*"

He burst out laughing and said, "Okay, fine. I don't think you can get into too much more trouble than you already have been."

At that, Mugs started to bark, Goliath howled, and Thaddeus flew up to her arm and walked up onto her shoulder, where he could better look at Mack, not quite at eye level, then cried out, "Thaddeus is here. Thaddeus is here."

And both of them burst into laughter.

This concludes Book 14 of Lovely Lethal Gardens:
Nabbed in the Nasturtiums.

Read about Offed in the Orchids:
Lovely Lethal Gardens, Book 15

Lovely Lethal Gardens: Offed in the Orchids (Book #15)

A new cozy mystery series from *USA Today* best-selling author Dale Mayer. Follow gardener and amateur sleuth Doreen Montgomery—and her amusing and mostly lovable cat, dog, and parrot—as they catch murderers and solve crimes in lovely Kelowna, British Columbia.

Riches to rags … Finally it's calm … At least for the moment … If she's lucky …

Needing a break from all the murder and mayhem, Doreen and Mack plan an outing to see the local orchid show. Some of the displays are in the community center, but the more prized specimens of this genus require a visit to some of the gardeners' homes, a rare opportunity not afforded to everyone.

This trip, not quite a date, affords Doreen a chance to

enjoy not only the company of Mack but to get to know a few more of the colorful locals. But, when one of these locals ends up dead just after their visit, the dark underbelly of orchid growing is exposed and, with it, an old murder, … not to mention another new one.

Doreen and Mack just can't catch a break. But can they catch a killer before he kills again?

Find Book 15 here!

To find out more visit Dale Mayer's website.

https://smarturl.it/DMSOffed

Get Your Free Book Now!

Have you met Charmin Marvin?

If you're ready for a new world to explore, and love ill-mannered cats, I have a series that might be your next binge read. It's called Broken Protocols, and it's a series that takes you through time-travel, mysteries, romance… and a talking cat named Charmin Marvin.

Go here and tell me where to send it!

http://smarturl.it/ArsenicBofB

Author's Note

Thank you for reading Nabbed in the Nasturtiums: Lovely Lethal Gardens, Book 14! If you enjoyed the book, please take a moment and leave a short review.

Dear reader,

I love to hear from readers, and you can contact me at my website: www.dalemayer.com or at my Facebook author page. To be informed of new releases and special offers, sign up for my newsletter or follow me on BookBub. And if you are interested in joining Dale Mayer's Reader Group, here is the Facebook sign up page.
https://smarturl.it/DaleMayerFBGroup

Cheers,
Dale Mayer

About the Author

Dale Mayer is a *USA Today* best-selling author, best known for her SEALs military romances, her Psychic Visions series, and her Lovely Lethal Garden cozy series. Her contemporary romances are raw and full of passion and emotion (Broken But … Mending series). Her thrillers will keep you guessing (By Death series), and her romantic comedies will keep you giggling (*It's a Dog's Life*, a stand-alone novella; and the Broken Protocols series, starring Charming Marvin, the cat).

Dale honors the stories that come to her—and some of them are crazy and break all the rules and cross multiple genres!

To go with her fiction, she also writes nonfiction in many different fields, with books available on résumé writing, companion gardening, and the US mortgage system. She has recently published her Career Essentials series. All her books are available in print and ebook format.

Connect with Dale Mayer Online

Dale's Website – www.dalemayer.com

Twitter – @DaleMayer

Facebook – facebook.com/DaleMayer.author

BookBub – bookbub.com/authors/dale-mayer

Also by Dale Mayer

Published Adult Books:

Bullard's Battle

Ryland's Reach, Book 1
Cain's Cross, Book 2
Eton's Escape, Book 3
Garret's Gambit, Book 4
Kano's Keep, Book 5
Fallon's Flaw, Book 6
Quinn's Quest, Book 7
Bullard's Beauty, Book 8
Bullard's Best, Book 9

Terkel's Team

Damon's Deal, Book 1

Kate Morgan

Simon Says… Hide, Book 1

Hathaway House

Aaron, Book 1
Brock, Book 2
Cole, Book 3
Denton, Book 4
Elliot, Book 5
Finn, Book 6

Gregory, Book 7
Heath, Book 8
Iain, Book 9
Jaden, Book 10
Keith, Book 11
Lance, Book 12
Melissa, Book 13
Nash, Book 14
Owen, Book 15
Hathaway House, Books 1–3
Hathaway House, Books 4–6
Hathaway House, Books 7–9

The K9 Files

Ethan, Book 1
Pierce, Book 2
Zane, Book 3
Blaze, Book 4
Lucas, Book 5
Parker, Book 6
Carter, Book 7
Weston, Book 8
Greyson, Book 9
Rowan, Book 10
Caleb, Book 11
Kurt, Book 12
Tucker, Book 13
Harley, Book 14
The K9 Files, Books 1–2
The K9 Files, Books 3–4
The K9 Files, Books 5–6
The K9 Files, Books 7–8

The K9 Files, Books 9–10
The K9 Files, Books 11–12

Lovely Lethal Gardens

Arsenic in the Azaleas, Book 1
Bones in the Begonias, Book 2
Corpse in the Carnations, Book 3
Daggers in the Dahlias, Book 4
Evidence in the Echinacea, Book 5
Footprints in the Ferns, Book 6
Gun in the Gardenias, Book 7
Handcuffs in the Heather, Book 8
Ice Pick in the Ivy, Book 9
Jewels in the Juniper, Book 10
Killer in the Kiwis, Book 11
Lifeless in the Lilies, Book 12
Murder in the Marigolds, Book 13
Nabbed in the Nasturtiums, Book 14
Offed in the Orchids, Book 15
Lovely Lethal Gardens, Books 1–2
Lovely Lethal Gardens, Books 3–4
Lovely Lethal Gardens, Books 5–6
Lovely Lethal Gardens, Books 7–8
Lovely Lethal Gardens, Books 9–10

Psychic Vision Series

Tuesday's Child
Hide 'n Go Seek
Maddy's Floor
Garden of Sorrow
Knock Knock...
Rare Find

Eyes to the Soul
Now You See Her
Shattered
Into the Abyss
Seeds of Malice
Eye of the Falcon
Itsy-Bitsy Spider
Unmasked
Deep Beneath
From the Ashes
Stroke of Death
Ice Maiden
Snap, Crackle…
Psychic Visions Books 1–3
Psychic Visions Books 4–6
Psychic Visions Books 7–9

By Death Series

Touched by Death
Haunted by Death
Chilled by Death
By Death Books 1–3

Broken Protocols – Romantic Comedy Series

Cat's Meow
Cat's Pajamas
Cat's Cradle
Cat's Claus
Broken Protocols 1-4

Broken and… Mending

Skin

Scars
Scales (of Justice)
Broken but… Mending 1-3

Glory

Genesis
Tori
Celeste
Glory Trilogy

Biker Blues

Morgan: Biker Blues, Volume 1
Cash: Biker Blues, Volume 2

SEALs of Honor

Mason: SEALs of Honor, Book 1
Hawk: SEALs of Honor, Book 2
Dane: SEALs of Honor, Book 3
Swede: SEALs of Honor, Book 4
Shadow: SEALs of Honor, Book 5
Cooper: SEALs of Honor, Book 6
Markus: SEALs of Honor, Book 7
Evan: SEALs of Honor, Book 8
Mason's Wish: SEALs of Honor, Book 9
Chase: SEALs of Honor, Book 10
Brett: SEALs of Honor, Book 11
Devlin: SEALs of Honor, Book 12
Easton: SEALs of Honor, Book 13
Ryder: SEALs of Honor, Book 14
Macklin: SEALs of Honor, Book 15
Corey: SEALs of Honor, Book 16
Warrick: SEALs of Honor, Book 17

Tanner: SEALs of Honor, Book 18
Jackson: SEALs of Honor, Book 19
Kanen: SEALs of Honor, Book 20
Nelson: SEALs of Honor, Book 21
Taylor: SEALs of Honor, Book 22
Colton: SEALs of Honor, Book 23
Troy: SEALs of Honor, Book 24
Axel: SEALs of Honor, Book 25
Baylor: SEALs of Honor, Book 26
Hudson: SEALs of Honor, Book 27
SEALs of Honor, Books 1–3
SEALs of Honor, Books 4–6
SEALs of Honor, Books 7–10
SEALs of Honor, Books 11–13
SEALs of Honor, Books 14–16
SEALs of Honor, Books 17–19
SEALs of Honor, Books 20–22
SEALs of Honor, Books 23–25

Heroes for Hire

Levi's Legend: Heroes for Hire, Book 1
Stone's Surrender: Heroes for Hire, Book 2
Merk's Mistake: Heroes for Hire, Book 3
Rhodes's Reward: Heroes for Hire, Book 4
Flynn's Firecracker: Heroes for Hire, Book 5
Logan's Light: Heroes for Hire, Book 6
Harrison's Heart: Heroes for Hire, Book 7
Saul's Sweetheart: Heroes for Hire, Book 8
Dakota's Delight: Heroes for Hire, Book 9
Tyson's Treasure: Heroes for Hire, Book 10
Jace's Jewel: Heroes for Hire, Book 11
Rory's Rose: Heroes for Hire, Book 12

Brandon's Bliss: Heroes for Hire, Book 13
Liam's Lily: Heroes for Hire, Book 14
North's Nikki: Heroes for Hire, Book 15
Anders's Angel: Heroes for Hire, Book 16
Reyes's Raina: Heroes for Hire, Book 17
Dezi's Diamond: Heroes for Hire, Book 18
Vince's Vixen: Heroes for Hire, Book 19
Ice's Icing: Heroes for Hire, Book 20
Johan's Joy: Heroes for Hire, Book 21
Galen's Gemma: Heroes for Hire, Book 22
Zack's Zest: Heroes for Hire, Book 23
Bonaparte's Belle: Heroes for Hire, Book 24
Noah's Nemesis: Heroes for Hire, Book 25
Heroes for Hire, Books 1–3
Heroes for Hire, Books 4–6
Heroes for Hire, Books 7–9
Heroes for Hire, Books 10–12
Heroes for Hire, Books 13–15

SEALs of Steel

Badger: SEALs of Steel, Book 1
Erick: SEALs of Steel, Book 2
Cade: SEALs of Steel, Book 3
Talon: SEALs of Steel, Book 4
Laszlo: SEALs of Steel, Book 5
Geir: SEALs of Steel, Book 6
Jager: SEALs of Steel, Book 7
The Final Reveal: SEALs of Steel, Book 8
SEALs of Steel, Books 1–4
SEALs of Steel, Books 5–8
SEALs of Steel, Books 1–8

The Mavericks

Kerrick, Book 1

Griffin, Book 2

Jax, Book 3

Beau, Book 4

Asher, Book 5

Ryker, Book 6

Miles, Book 7

Nico, Book 8

Keane, Book 9

Lennox, Book 10

Gavin, Book 11

Shane, Book 12

Diesel, Book 13

Jerricho, Book 14

Killian, Book 15

The Mavericks, Books 1–2

The Mavericks, Books 3–4

The Mavericks, Books 5–6

The Mavericks, Books 7–8

The Mavericks, Books 9–10

The Mavericks, Books 11–12

Collections

Dare to Be You…

Dare to Love…

Dare to be Strong…

RomanceX3

Standalone Novellas

It's a Dog's Life

Riana's Revenge

Second Chances

Published Young Adult Books:

Family Blood Ties Series

Vampire in Denial
Vampire in Distress
Vampire in Design
Vampire in Deceit
Vampire in Defiance
Vampire in Conflict
Vampire in Chaos
Vampire in Crisis
Vampire in Control
Vampire in Charge
Family Blood Ties Set 1–3
Family Blood Ties Set 1–5
Family Blood Ties Set 4–6
Family Blood Ties Set 7–9
Sian's Solution, A Family Blood Ties Series Prequel Novelette

Design series

Dangerous Designs
Deadly Designs
Darkest Designs
Design Series Trilogy

Standalone

In Cassie's Corner
Gem Stone (a Gemma Stone Mystery)
Time Thieves

Published Non-Fiction Books:

Career Essentials

Career Essentials: The Résumé

Career Essentials: The Cover Letter

Career Essentials: The Interview

Career Essentials: 3 in 1

Made in the USA
Middletown, DE
01 August 2021

45145173R00176